Cirque du Slay

Also available by Rob Osler

Hayden & Friends Mysteries

Devil's Chew Toy

Cirque du Slay

A Hayden & Friends Mystery

ROB OSLER

CROOKED
LANE

NEW YORK

Copyright © 2024 by Rob Osler

Published in the United States by Crooked Lane Books, an imprint of The Quick Brown Fox & Company LLC.

Crooked Lane Books and its logo are trademarks of The Quick Brown Fox & Company LLC.

Library of Congress Catalog-in-Publication data available upon request.

ISBN (hardcover): 978-1-63910-647-9
ISBN (ebook): 978-1-63910-648-6

Cover design by Nicole Lecht

Printed in the United States.

www.crookedlanebooks.com

Crooked Lane Books
34 West 27th St., 10th Floor
New York, NY 10001

First Edition: March 2024

10 9 8 7 6 5 4 3 2 1

"I'm not sure I even need a lover, male or female. Sometimes I think I'd settle for five good friends."

—Armistead Maupin, *28 Barbary Lane*

Chapter One
Then Came the Fire

A single spotlight flashed on, revealing a woman in white tux and pink top hat standing in the center of the ring. With the fading of the cymbal's crash, she asked for a volunteer from the audience. I glanced around the massive tent's interior to see who would be brave enough to join Mysterium's famed magician, Kennedy Osaka, on stage. The next instant, I was blinded by light. Despite us sitting in the rafters in the farthest row, a spotlight, as if magnetically drawn to big personalities, managed to find my best friend's raised hand.

"Wonderful!" the magician announced, lifting a tapered white sleeve toward Hollister. "Please, come down, madam, and join me in Mysterium's ring."

Like a kid rushing downstairs on Christmas morning, Hollister nearly tripped as she raced down the aisle while an assistant wheeled a large cabinet onto the otherwise empty stage. After a bit of repartee and fanfare, Hollister was ushered into the cabinet, her Mohawk brushing against its ceiling. With a grand flourish, the magician slid the door shut. Intense music throbbed as she spun the large box around. The rotation completed, she paused dramatically before throwing open the door.

Oohs and *aahs* from the three hundred people in attendance filled the tent.

Hollister had vanished.

I knew it was a trick, but it still freaked me out.

Another volunteer was recruited to the stage to examine the cabinet inside and out. Seemingly satisfied that there was no Serena Williams–size woman hiding inside, he hurried back to his front-row seat, to the audience's clapping.

The magician closed the door again and wheeled the box in another three sixty. The music crescendoed so loud that I almost covered my ears. The tiny blond hairs on the back of my neck and arms shivered in anticipation. I leaned forward in my seat. Kennedy Osaka paused again. I swallowed hard. The entire tent went quiet.

She flung open the door.

The audience's collectively held breath gave way to an eruption of applause and cheers of delight. My bestie had suddenly reappeared—now wearing an outfit identical to the magician's! Never mind that on her the white Spandex made her resemble one of those inflatable snowmen people set in their front yards at the holidays.

"Woot! Woot!" I howled. Not only was the trick next-level abracadabra-ing, but I had never—*ever*—seen Hollister wearing any color other than black. She was escorted backstage and within minutes hustled back to our nose-bleed seats in her own clothes; the quick change and steep ascent had her breathing hard.

"That was a blast, Hayden," she said. "I can't believe you didn't go for it. Then again, I suppose you volunteering was long odds, huh?"

"Somewhere between you in heels and me anywhere near a basketball."

After a brief musical interlude to settle the crowd, the ring mistress, a tall, slender woman in a sultry black gown, introduced the next act. Against the low rumble of a timpani, she touted the group's acrobatic awards collected from competitions around the globe, each accolade heightening the anticipation for the spectacle to come. The lights dimmed.

To a chaotic sweep of spotlights across the stage, she announced, "And now, ladies and gentlemen, please welcome to Mysterium's tent of splendors . . . from Romania, and celebrated the world over . . . *Adrenalin!*"

According to the program notes, an Estonian rock band—appropriately named Estonia!—replaced the orchestra on the raised stage. They served up a screeching metal riff as the four members of Adrenalin! entered the tent from the four different entrances used by the audience. The guys cartwheeled down the aisles, performed handstands on the arms of chairs, and somersaulted into the ring. Wearing the costumes I had seen in the program—studded black harnesses and essentially tight black boxer briefs—they took turns performing increasingly complex twisting flips as they raced across the stage. Next came a routine with chairs, which culminated in one guy doing a handstand on a wooden chair held by another, who stood on another's shoulders, who perched on the shoulders of the fourth guy.

Then came the fire.

Five flaming hoops descended from a catwalk high in the tent's pitch and hovered above the stage at heights of about three to six feet. One by one, each guy sprinted across the stage, jumping feetfirst or leaping head-on or flipping in a tight, spinning ball through each hoop. Next, upping the ante, one horizontal hoop was positioned about twenty feet above a trampoline. The guys took turns bouncing to unnerving heights and through the ring of fire as they performed complicated aerial stunts—it was like watching Olympic platform diving, just live and upside down, and with fire instead of water.

The mini-show concluded with Adrenalin! receiving a standing ovation. The evening then entered its final phase: a cake and champagne reception, with an opportunity for us VIP guests to have pictures taken with cast members. Hollister and I had scored tickets thanks to a friend of a friend, despite qualifying only as "P's" in that acronym. For its sold-out, monthlong run, Mysterium had set up its extravagant tent just south of Seattle's downtown. The mashup of cabaret, magic, and aerial arts, with a Michelin-starred dinner thrown in, had been taking America by storm.

Hollister gave me a shove. "Those Adrenalin! boys are here for a whole month. Go get a picture with them. While you're at it, get a phone number."

I replied with a groan. Hollister knew I would never do any such thing. Hanging around her, I'd lost some of my natural shyness, but never would I match her boldness. More comfortable watching from the sidelines, I occasionally gave in and followed her—feet dragging and cursing under my breath—onto the field. And yet I'd be lying if I didn't admit that Hollister's friendship hadn't been good for me. Because of her, I'd at least partially broken out of my shell and discovered courage I hadn't known I had. But there were limits. And one was hitting on a Romanian Adonis in short shorts.

We stood in line to get a picture with the magician, Kennedy Osaka, who we knew had also just been named Mysterium's new artistic director. Beyond her undeniable good looks, she seemed like she'd be fun to hang out with. Her cover photo on the program didn't do justice to her mischievous brown eyes that suggested she knew a tantalizing secret, and wouldn't we just love to know what it was? As we inched our way closer to the front, Hollister growled approvingly at her winning smile and stylish asymmetrical short bob of jet-black hair.

Kennedy greeted us with what appeared to be a rehearsed smile, perfect for a photo op, but which dropped the second the show's publicity manager—Jenna Jensen, according to her name tag—lowered the camera. We introduced ourselves as friends of Sarah Lee, her old college roommate, who had given us her two tickets.

"Shame Sarah Lee couldn't make it," Kennedy said with an exaggerated frown. "I guess something else came up."

Knowing that the reason Sarah Lee couldn't attend was because of a mountain of last-minute work due to Kennedy's on-again, off-again commitment to perform at tomorrow's fundraiser for a charitable organization Sarah Lee helped run, I aimed for both truth and ambiguity: "Yes, it's regrettable, isn't it?"

Kennedy had stopped paying attention. "Make sure you use the hashtag LGBTQ on the pic with these two," she told Jenna. "It's good PR."

Not having caught Kennedy's remark, Hollister said, "Your act is really something, Kennedy. I can't wait to see the entire show."

"Oh? I wouldn't think Mysterium would be quite your thing," Kennedy said, appraising Hollister's black boots, black jeans, black jacket, and Mohawk. "It's not at all alternative." Shifting her gaze to the room, she added, "Mysterium is elegance under the big top. It will be, anyway, once I've made all my changes."

Before Hollister could issue a reply sure to singe the magician's pencil-thin brows, Jenna stepped forward. "I think what Kennedy *means* to say is that the show won't be exactly what you'd expect. She has many improvements in store. Isn't that right, Kennedy?"

"A comprehensive reimagining is more on the mark." Kennedy sniffed. "I'll be making some long-overdue upgrades. More polish, refinement, sophistication. Essentially, stamping the show with my personal brand." She straightened her tall pink hat. "So wonderful meeting you both. Give Sarah Lee a smooch for me. I hope to see her while I'm in town. Ta-ta."

She sauntered off into the crowd, publicity manager in tow.

"What's that supposed to mean?" I said. "Kennedy will see Sarah Lee tomorrow night—she agreed to provide the entertainment at the fundraiser. Didn't she?"

"I'm sure she's just busy," Hollister frowned. "Probably spaced out about it. How does Sarah Lee even know Kennedy Osaka anyway? I don't see those two having much in common."

"Kennedy and Sarah Lee both grew up around here," I explained. "And they were roommates at some fancy-pants, women-only college back east."

"Sounds like the perfect environment for a well-rounded education," Hollister quipped.

Ignoring the remark, I went on. "That performance, though! A-plus."

Hollister clapped my back, causing me to stumble forward a step. "Always the teacher, giving everything a grade."

"Shall we?" I gestured toward the tent's exit.

Hollister gave me the type of look I saved for my students' worst behavior. "You're really not going to chat up one of those hot Adrenalin! dudes?"

I rolled my eyes. "We both know that's not happening."

"Not with that attitude, it's not."

Despite our differences—Hollister's Black, I'm white; she sports a Mohawk, I'm a ginger with unruly hair; she's fearless and physically imposing, I have all the swagger of a downtrodden middle school teacher—we were pretty much inseparable.

As we passed through the open flaps into the cool night air, Hollister grabbed my shoulder. "He winked at you," she said. "Did you see?"

"Who?" I narrowed my eyes, sensing mischief.

"The acrobat. The one with the Marine haircut. Blue eyes."

"Not funny." I wriggled out of her grip and marched toward the parking lot.

"I'm not kidding!" she shouted after me.

As sure I was that my BFF was trying to trick me into getting my game on, I couldn't help but smile. Hollister had my back. Always.

And who knows? Just maybe she was telling the truth.

Chapter Two
Who, Me?

Seattleites love their coffee and pastries. Every neighborhood from Madison Park to Magnolia, from Rainier Valley to Greenwood, has a bakery the locals swear is the best in the city. And yet, if strapped to a lie detector machine and asked to name the crème de la crème, the hands-down winner would be Slice. Lucky for Hollister and me, our good friend Burley owned the place.

It was the morning after the show, and we were meeting early before work. Hollister hadn't arrived yet when I nabbed our usual table by the window. Burley was behind the counter, spiraling chocolate onto a golden-brown mound of deliciousness. I'd made the mistake of calling it a *doughnut* when I ordered one along with my cappuccino and a double-shot espresso for Hollister.

"Oh no, Hayden." Burley appeared dismayed. "This is a pączki. It's a Polish favorite, deep-fried leavened dough. Mine are filled with Bavarian cream. I don't mind saying this batch is particularly tasty." She patted her round belly. "I was so amazed by how well they turned out that I had to eat three just to make sure the first two weren't a crazy fluke."

Hollister and I called Burley our gentle giant. For good reason. Six foot six and big-boned, she was bigger than your average baker. While her size was distinctive, her personality was what really set her apart. To say Burley was eccentric was like saying Adele could carry a tune. Besides being a virtuoso with flour, sugar, butter, and eggs, she cultivated a ganja farm in her basement, was raising a stinky family of emus in her backyard, and hosted karaoke at our favorite gay bar.

"Ready for the big night?" I said, referring to that evening's special event at the bakery.

"You should be asking Sarah Lee." She pointed her banana-size thumb over her shoulder. "She's been working her patootie off to ensure everything goes off without a hitch."

While I preferred to keep a safe distance from Burley's second-in-command (my neighbor), I didn't want to appear rude. "How's it going, Sarah Lee?" I said, my voice raised so she could hear me over the bean grinder.

Seeing me, she scrunched her nose as if smelling sour milk. "I got three hours of sleep. How do you think I am?" She concluded her morning's greeting by blowing a strand of blond bangs from her eye and wiping her hands on her jam-stained apron.

Typical. No "thanks for asking" or "and you?" I shrugged and turned my attention back to Burley. Beaming with pride, she said, "Now, don't be modest, Sarah Lee. You've been a super trouper and then some. Tell Hayden all about the shindig you got planned." She slapped an oven mitt against the counter. "It's sold out! How we're going to fit everyone in here will be a trick all in itself." Burley giggled at her joke.

I didn't need Sarah Lee to provide the details. For months I'd been hearing how she had been elected chapter president of

Bakers Without Borders, a charitable organization that provided food—and not just pastries—to communities across the country. She had put in a ton of work for their annual fundraising event, highlighted by her coup of getting Kennedy Osaka, a star of Mysterium, to provide the entertainment. We'd heard all about Sarah Lee having to deal with her friend's constant waffling, however. One week, Kennedy would gush texts bubbling with ideas for the show. The next, she would bow out entirely, making an excuse, such as *Emergency costume fitting!* followed by a string of sad-face emojis. Although Sarah Lee was my number-one frenemy, I did feel sorry for her. We'd started a low-level feud last summer when a sweet guy, Camilo, I'd met at the local dance club suddenly went missing—and left behind his dog. Anyone who knows me would know I'd take in the dog despite my building not allowing pets. Sarah Lee, also my next-door neighbor, was furious I'd violated the policy. Since then, she had further penetrated my orbit, taking a job at Slice, which was Hollister's and my main hangout.

"I just want to get the night over with," Sarah Lee said. "My reputation is riding on the event being a success. I've made a lot of promises to a lot of people."

"Sarah Lee is being humble," Burley said. "She doubled attendance from last year."

Not one to be *too* humble, Sarah Lee added, "Along with ticket prices. And that's before the silent auction or raffle. The grand prize alone should drive enough raffle ticket sales to achieve our entire annual goal."

Eager to hear just how grand a prize was on offer, I said, "Well? What is it?"

"What's what?" asked Hollister, sidling up to the counter, her Mohawk still dewy from the shower.

"Sarah Lee was about to reveal tonight's big prize," Burley said.

All eyes turned to Sarah Lee. As if hearing her name announced at an award banquet, she blushed with a "who, me?" smile. "Kennedy is providing four VIP front-row tickets with backstage passes for an exclusive meet and greet. Plus, the winner gets a framed poster signed by the entire Mysterium cast."

Okay. Color me impressed. Considering the cost and demand for Mysterium tickets, even I'd plunk down twenty bucks of my minuscule teacher's salary on a chance to win.

After carrying our coffees and my paczki to our table, Hollister and I sipped in silence while we caught up on social media. This was our twenty-minute pre-workday routine. Hollister wasn't a morning person. She was only marginally functional before downing her first of a half-dozen daily espressos. I needed just one cappuccino to fire my engine, and the sugar content of my Polish doughnut—likely three hundred percent of my daily allowance—would give me an energy boost, if only to last through my first class.

With a thirty-minute commute to my middle school ahead of me, I pocketed my phone. "See you later. Have a good one." Hollister replied with a single-finger salute, her French tip nails a glittery gold. On my way out, I waved goodbye to Burley and Sarah Lee.

As I swung open the door, Burley hollered across the bakery, "Don't be late, Hayden. I got a feeling it's going to be one heck of a night!"

Chapter Three
Cancelitoed

Colorful lights skittered across the night sky. I nudged Hollister on her shoulder and pointed my chin toward the light show ahead. We picked up our pace, excited to get to the fun awaiting us.

Hollister gave me a gentle hip bump, "Remember, Hayden, you got crushed, so two-drink limit." Hollister referred to our pre-event ritual of rock-paper-scissors to determine the night's designated driver. I didn't mind having lost. I was a lightweight when it came to drinking, anyway. Hollister, however, could throw back shots of Gentleman Jack as if it were seltzer.

Not only was it a Friday night and not pouring rain—a minor miracle for February in Seattle—but Hollister and I both had mini-vacations ahead. As the owner of her own furniture design business, she'd finally cleared her schedule to allow for some much-needed R&R. For the next two weeks, she had promised she was going to do only three things: kick off her boots, turn off her phone, and crack open a case of primo wine.

In keeping with her good spirits, she had zhuzhed up her look by weaving a strand of fuchsia-dyed hair into the blade of her

Mohawk. As for me, the past five days had been the last week before spring break. The hundred and fifty middle schoolers to whom I taught social studies, from the first to the final bell, had set a new bar for unruliness and inappropriate remarks.

Exhibit A: *"Mr. McSmall, do you get up early to get your hair to look like a troll doll's?"* Despite a somewhat accurate description of my hair's tendency to look as if it were trying to flee my scalp at all cost, it wasn't polite. And no, Mr. McSmall was not funny. Mr. *McCall*, their psychologically abused teacher, was desperate for the time away. The Bakers Without Borders fundraiser at Slice promised to be the perfect kick-start to my staycation.

The rubber soles of my new Converse sneakers met the sidewalk's cement with a percussive squeak played out in double time to the heavy *thwap, thwap, thwap* of Hollister's heavy boot heels. As we rounded the corner to the bakery, Hollister stopped abruptly and raised a finger. "Hayden, you hearing what I'm *not* hearing?"

That's odd. There should have been music and sounds of a large gathering. Curious, we picked up our pace. As the bakery came into view, it was apparent Burley and Sarah Lee had indeed outdone themselves. But not in the way we'd expected.

"Uh-oh." I grimaced, my eyes falling on a pair of female police officers.

"Mmm. That can't be good," Hollister agreed. "Those ladies in blue do not look happy."

"I don't suppose they're friends of yours or Burley's? Maybe they're on the guest list?"

She shot me hard look. "Do they look like they're there for any reason other than business?"

Burley stood on the bakery's steps, a dozen people huddled behind her, no doubt drawn outside by the presence of Seattle's

Finest. A patrol car parked at an odd angle suggested its arrival hadn't involved gentle braking. Beams of red and blue light swept across the crowd from the cruiser's roof. The effect was similar to the dance floor at our favorite club, Hunter's, but rather than having fun, everyone in the crowd looked angry or concerned—or, in Burley's case, worried.

"Big Miss looks wound up," Hollister said, aiming a finger pistol at our host.

Burley's gesticulations gave the appearance of a human windmill. Her long, dark pigtails swung like pendulums across her flannel shirt and her chunky turquoise jewelry. To complete her outfit, she was decked out, as usual, in jean cutoffs, bright orange Crocs, and a worn buckskin jacket with fringe dangling from the arms.

Hollister and I reached the edge of the property as the two cops turned to leave.

"Event's cancelitoed!" Burley shouted to the cluster of people huddled behind her. Then seeing us trudging across the soggy lawn, she said, "Hey, Hollister. Hey, Hayden. This is serious, compadres. We have ourselves a situation."

I shot Hollister a glance as Sarah Lee stomped out of the bakery and joined us on the steps. "This is so humiliating," she hissed. "I ask Kennedy for one favor. One favor! I've put up with this since we were kids. Then all through college. It's always been about her. *Her. Her. Her.* She promised she'd be here. We've sold all the raffle tickets. Everyone is asking when the show will start. This is mort-i-fy-ing!"

"Kennedy is a no-show." Burley frowned.

"Just this once, *I* ask for help. And this is how she repays me. I've got sixty people crammed inside, all of whom paid a hundred bucks a ticket, along with reporters from *The Times* and *Emerald*

City Insider. Kennedy should have been here an hour ago. She won't pick up her phone and hasn't returned my texts. I could kill her."

"Hold up," Hollister said. "You mean to tell us the police were here because Kennedy didn't show up to the fundraiser?"

With a low growl, Sarah Lee threw her hands in the air, spun her zippered brown boots around, and stomped back inside. I couldn't imagine how mad Sarah Lee must be. And rightly so. No one deserved such treatment. I made a mental note to try and be kinder to her—at least until she called me "Midge" again.

Burley gestured toward the Dodge Chargers pulling away from the curb. "That had nothing to do with *or without* Kennedy."

"I'm totally confused," I muttered.

Hollister pinched the bridge of her nose, then sighed. We both loved Burley like a sister, but conversations with her often took circuitous routes, demanding patient perseverance—and that was when Burley wasn't stoned.

In an attempt to move things along, Hollister tried, "So why *were* the cops here?"

"Freakin' Louise," Burley answered.

I leaned forward, anticipating more, but she seemed satisfied with her explanation.

"Who the eff is Louise?" Hollister said, using a sanitized version of the exact words I was thinking.

"Louise. You know, Louise," Burley insisted.

I shook my head. I knew a Louise Fellerstein, a cafeteria worker at the junior high school where I taught. But she was married to a Pentecostal pastor, had eight children, and prayed over each student as she spooned instant mashed potatoes onto their tray. I doubted she'd be in attendance.

"No, Burley," Hollister said. "We don't know Louise. So perhaps you'll tell us who the blazes—"

"Louise Berman. Bottle-rocket Berman!" Burley thrust a finger skyward. "The woman has issues. *Serious* issues. How does a city councilwoman wind up with a bottle-rocket fetish?"

Hollister turned back to Burley. "Let me get this straight. This Louise Berman chick set off bottle rockets at your fundraiser?"

Burley didn't just nod; she rocked back and forth, her Crocs squeaking at the arches. "I was inside when the explosions began. It was like *Apocalypse Now*."

I nodded. "Incredible movie."

"Movie?" Burley scoffed. "No, no, no. It was like for real. The neighbors freaked. Cops showed up with their panties all in a twist. They gave me a choice. A citation, along with a hefty fine, or shut down festivities for the night. There ain't no way I'm paying the city one thin dime for throwing a private shindig at my own business, so . . ."

"You'd rather close it down?" I groaned. Burley was the sweetest human I knew, but we'd make different decisions nine out of ten times. My tendency, which wasn't always ideal—something I was working on—was to view things in black and white. Burley saw only blurs of color, often through a thick haze of pot smoke.

The door swung open, and Sarah Lee clomped past us down the steps. "I'll be back later to help clean up," she said over her shoulder. "I'm too embarrassed to face anyone."

Hollister and I exchanged glances. I was no mind reader, but I still had a pretty good idea of what she was thinking. Her furrowed brow and narrowed stare provided all the clues I needed.

"You're leaving your own event?" I said.

Burley added, "Sarah Lee, honey, are you sure?"

Sarah Lee spun around on the sidewalk. "Kennedy can't just blow me off like this. This was supposed to be *my* night. My success. Kennedy just turned it into the worst of my life."

"Where are you going?" Burley asked.

"Her hotel! Where else?" Sarah Lee shouted before marching toward her car.

Burley closed her eyes tightly. *"Peril awaits those whose emotions overflow. Find comfort at home. If you must be adventurous, try a new recipe or hairstyle.'"*

This routine I knew. Burley didn't hoist herself out of bed before reading the day's horoscope for herself and her closest friends.

She lifted her long arms toward the heavens. "Stars never lie. Something hinky is afoot." She routinely dismissed anything that conflicted with her superstitions faster than she would a pair of missionaries from her front porch.

As Hollister and I followed Burley into the bakery to help deal with the crowd, Sarah Lee climbed into her lemon-yellow VW Beetle. Usually a cautious driver, she punched the accelerator. I winced as the tires squealed and the red tail lights disappeared down the street.

Three hours later, I sat wedged between my two gal pals in front of Burley's ginormous television with every streaming service—all of them "borrowed"—as the credits rolled for *Apocalypse Now*. There'd still been no word from Sarah Lee. Burley had phoned and texted, but no response. I berated myself for not getting the name of Kennedy's hotel. As we debated what to do next, Burley's phone buzzed. Over the next minute, I watched her expression slide from bewildered to frightened. Nodding into the phone, she said, "Yes, I understand. Listen, thanks for calling. I owe you big-time."

I swallowed hard. Worry tensed every muscle in my body. "Well? What was that all about?"

Burley dabbed the corner of her eye with a trembling finger. "That was Judy, a friend of mine and Sarah Lee's. She's a regular at the bakery."

Hollister said, "And?"

"Judy was having drinks in the bar at the Park Olympic Hotel when all of a sudden there were cops everywhere and paramedics running through the lobby. About a half hour later, she saw the cops lead Sarah Lee outside. Before she could find out what was happening, the cops had put Sarah Lee in the back of a squad car and driven away."

"Oh my God. Why?" I said. "Did Judy say what happened?"

"She doesn't know. She asked the bartender, but he didn't know anything either. The front desk wouldn't say. They just said it was police business."

"The Park Olympic," I said. "That must be where Kennedy is staying."

Hollister and I sprang into action. Burley lumbered to her feet but seemed confused about our intention. I fumbled in my pocket; Hollister scrambled for her bag. We pulled out our phones simultaneously, but voice command beats long-nailed fingers every time. Within seconds, I had someone at the hotel on speakerphone. "I'm trying to reach a guest. Her name is Kennedy Osaka."

On the other end of the line, awkward silence followed muffled whispers. Finally, the woman on the other end said, "I'm sorry, sir, but I am unable to connect you to that room. May I be of any other assistance?"

I flinched. Something was wrong. Hollister whispered, "Ask her if Kennedy checked out?"

I nodded. "Can you tell me if Ms. Osaka has checked out?"

Another round of silence and muffled words. "I'm sorry, sir. I am unable to share that guest information."

"What the—" Hollister shook her head, which made her Mohawk waggle like a shark's fin, signaling danger. "Is Kennedy staying there or not?"

Burley leaned in close to my phone. "Listen, ma'am. I know you're just trying to do your job. But a friend of ours—"

"Kennedy," Hollister said. "Kennedy Osaka. She's a close friend. We're worried about her. So we can either come down there, and you can answer us in person, or you can save us all a lot of trouble by telling us what's going on."

Burley leaned in again. "Please, ma'am."

I squeezed the phone and stared at the screen as if the slightest inattention might dissuade the voice on the other end from leveling with us. Burley leaned closer still, each breath heavy with anxiety.

"You might want to check the news," the woman said, her tone softer. "I'm sorry."

Hollister snatched up the remote for the television while I scrolled on my phone. It took only seconds. I gasped.

Hollister spun around. "What?"

Unable to speak, I handed her my phone with a shaking hand.

She read aloud from a news report posted five minutes earlier. *"Mysterium star found dead in Seattle hotel. Earlier this evening, police discovered the body of thirty-two-year-old Kennedy Osaka in her sixth-floor guest suite at the Park Olympic Hotel. Police have yet to issue further information."*

Hollister skimmed the following few paragraphs. "The rest is just boilerplate bio info on Kennedy and Mysterium. Nothing about what just happened."

The muscles in my jaw clenched. I croaked out, "Did Sarah Lee . . . ?"

Burley stood in the middle of the living room. She closed her eyes and dropped her head, expelling a soft whimper as she started to cry. Instinctively, Hollister and I moved to comfort her. Hugging her shaking body was like clinging to a mattress in an earthquake.

After a long moment, Hollister stepped back. "I need to make a call. Hayden, catch the lights. Burley, you lock up. We're going downtown to find out what the blazes is going on."

I scrambled for my sneakers and raced around the house, flipping switches. Burley pulled on her buckskin jacket. In the kitchen, Hollister spoke calmly with someone on the phone. Minutes later, with a cringeworthy squeak, I closed the ripped screen door behind us.

"Who did you call?" I asked Hollister.

She was already ten paces ahead of Burley and me, crossing the front lawn. She didn't slow, didn't turn back. She—*we* were on a mission.

"Someone who doesn't leave justice to chance."

Chapter Four
The Transitive Property

Despite the flickering fluorescent light and peeling decals (and Hollister's snide "You got a death wish?"), I plunged my coins into the coffee machine—I'd exchanged a dollar bill with an elderly lady, who fortunately carried a change purse. Under any other circumstance, I'd have kept a safe distance from the machine's menacing buzz and sticky buttons, but it was one AM. Despite the armless plastic chairs in the lobby, which must have been designed by a sadistic school principal, I was fighting to stay awake.

"I can't believe you're drinking that." Hollister winced, shaking her head.

"You're not the only one." I gestured toward the elderly woman. She watched with an expression of disgust—or possibly fear for my life—as I sipped tentatively from the white paper cup.

When Hollister, Burley, and I had entered police headquarters an hour earlier, we strode up to the front desk, anxiety-fueled and bursting with questions. Now, slumped in a corner, shoulder to shoulder, we continued to wait for any news. Every quarter-hour or so, a door leading into other parts of the building opened, and we jerked to attention, hoping it would be Sarah Lee. We'd been so far disappointed.

To stay up late waiting in a police station was what a friend would do. But Sarah Lee and I weren't exactly friends. I wasn't entirely unsympathetic to whatever mess she'd gotten herself into, but I was grumpy and stressed knowing I'd not get enough sleep.

Finally, at 1:40 AM, out came Sarah Lee, escorted by a man I assumed was a cop, despite his ordinary clothes. He said something to her before leaving her in the lobby. Although we were three of only four people sitting in the waiting area, Sarah Lee somehow didn't see us. We jumped to our feet as she bolted through the exit.

"Sarah Lee!" we all shouted in unison, hurrying to catch up with her.

Sarah Lee didn't stop. She kept bustling down the sidewalk. We broke into a run.

"Where does she think she's going?" Hollister said.

"Away from the police station," I replied. "I think that's the entirety of her plan."

As we caught up to her, she glanced up at Burley on her right, Hollister on her left, then at me one step behind. "Where'd you come from?" she asked.

"We were waiting in the police station," Burley said between breaths. "We've been waiting for over an hour. You motored right past us."

Sarah Lee nodded but continued her pace. Hollister and Burley could stay with her by taking long, quick strides, but with my shorter legs, I had to keep jogging or fall behind.

"Sarah Lee, do you mind? Will you slow down, please?" Burley said.

"We know you're upset," I tried. "But, please, stop. We'll sort this out."

Sarah Lee glanced over her shoulder.

"No one is following you," Burley said gently. "You've got to stop."

Then Hollister did what I didn't dare: she grabbed Sarah Lee by the arm. Like a tugboat gaining control of a ship, she clung to Sarah Lee's sleeve and coaxed her to a stop.

Burley, her eyes wet with tears of worry, wrapped her arms around Sarah Lee. "Let's get you home, honey."

Sarah Lee nodded, and her emotional dam broke.

The four of us climbed into Burley's ancient Bronco—we'd figure out how to reclaim the Beetle later. During the thirty-minute drive to Orca Arms, the West Seattle apartment complex where she and I rented studios, Sarah Lee kept her eyes closed and didn't speak. Once inside her unit, we settled her on the sofa with a cup of Chamomile. Burley sat beside her. I might have considered lacing the tea with a shot of something, but there was nothing handy. Sarah Lee only drank rosé—with a single ice cube.

Hollister and I sat at the table, exhausted and uncomfortable. After a long pause, Sarah Lee spoke. "When I got to Kennedy's hotel, I took the elevator up to the sixth floor. I wasn't exactly sure which room was hers, but Kennedy said she was staying in a suite, and the front desk said they were all on six. I got to Kennedy's room. The door looked closed, but when I knocked, I discovered it wasn't shut all the way.

"I called out, not wanting her to think I was an intruder. I didn't hear anything, so I went inside. I kept on calling her name. 'Kennedy? Kennedy? It's me, Sarah Lee.' I got as far as the sitting room, when I thought I heard the shower running. I tiptoed toward the bedroom. I didn't want to spook her, you know, create a *Psycho* shower moment. But she didn't reply."

Sarah Lee said she'd crossed the threshold into the bedroom. From that moment on, reality had blurred. The next minute or so was like static on the television—on and operational, yet unintelligible. It wasn't until hotel security burst into the room, shouting for her to step away from the body and threatening her with pepper spray, that she regained her senses. Worse, so much worse, was their command for her to drop the large scissors in her hand.

With the hardest part of the story told—at least what she could remember—Sarah Lee told us what had transpired at the police station. "I'd been there for what seemed like hours when a lawyer arrived. I was so worked up that I didn't catch his name. His card is in my purse. He argued that Kennedy and I had been friends, that I had no motive, and that I'd been trying to save her. That's why I had hold of the scissors, I'd removed them. There was nothing to suggest events hadn't happened as I described them. All that and a bunch of legal mumbo jumbo I don't pretend to understand. What seemed to make the biggest impression on the cops was his claim that I must be experiencing a condition called 'dissociative amnesia.' I'd never heard of it before, but apparently it's a real thing, caused by a super stressful situation like a traumatic event, and you can't remember important information."

Hollister and I traded looks that said, *"What the—?"*

Burley said tenderly, "So you don't remember . . ."

"I know it sounds crazy!" Sarah Lee blurted. "But it's the God's honest truth. Between entering the bedroom and hearing the men shouting at me, not a blessed thing." Appearing exhausted, Sarah Lee plopped back onto the sofa.

"So what next?" Hollister said. "What did Mr. Gemalto tell you to expect?"

"Who is Mr. Gemalto?" Burley and I asked in unison.

"The lawyer. I made the call from Burley's kitchen before we left the house to go downtown." Hollister said. "Gemalto runs ads for his legal services in the *Rainbow Gazette*."

Registering my blank look, she explained, "You know, the *Rainbow Gazette*. It's like the queer phone book—listings and ads for LGBTQ-owned businesses and services. "Gemalto specializes in criminal defense. His slogan is 'Don't leave justice to chance.' I thought it was catchy. Though I never imagined having a reason to call."

"Thank you, Hollister," Sarah Lee said. "I appreciate it. Truly I do. But Mr. Gemalto doesn't work for free. I'm pretty sure I can't afford him. His suit must cost what I make in a month." A look of alarm washed over her face; she turned to face Burley. "I'm not complaining about my salary. I'm just saying—"

"Now, don't you worry about the money, Sarah Lee," Burley scolded gently. "If Hollister says this Gemalto fella is the best in the business, then you need him on your side."

"To be clear"—Hollister raised a hand—"I've never met the man. I've only seen his ads."

Sarah Lee rubbed the back of her neck, clearly stressed and exhausted. "He said he'd be in touch. I'm to stick around town, and I'm supposed to call him immediately if the police want to talk to me again, which he said they would. He also emphasized the importance of saying nothing to the cops without him being present."

"That's good news!" I said, hoping the positivity would direct the night toward a close. "They don't have enough to charge you."

Burley added, "Sounds like you've got a terrific lawyer on your side."

Hollister sat up straighter. "I'm glad he came through for you."

I sat impatiently, watching the rolling eyes and long switching tail of the Kit-Cat Klock on the kitchen wall. Minutes later, Sarah Lee nodded off.

Burley looked at her friend and workmate with concern. "I just keep imagining this poor, sweet girl in the pokey. Being put behind bars is my worst nightmare. But at least my magnitude would give the ladies pause before messing me about."

The comment triggered thoughts impossible to ignore. What would happen when a new inmate required a size twice that of the largest available in ready-to-wear prison attire? Did the Department of Corrections employ a seamstress to make alterations? And what about accommodations? When an inmate is a foot longer than her assigned bunk, what then?

So as not to wake Sarah Lee, Burley gently laid a blanket over her, and we stepped outside. Like Hollister and me, Burley was obviously out of gas. After promising to check in with one another later that day, she headed home in her Bronco. Hollister followed me next door to my place. Once inside, she gave a loud sigh, the length of which caused me to marvel at her lung capacity.

"So that was an epic cluster," I said. "Listen, I hate to kick you out, but I really need to get what sleep I still can."

"I'm going to ask you a question, little dude. And like always, I expect you to be honest."

I glanced over, served an annoyed look. "Okay, but just this once."

"You think Sarah Lee could have done it?"

"Seriously?"

"It was a serious question. It deserves a serious answer."

Relieved that Hollister shared my doubts about Sarah Lee's innocence, I made my case. "She's asking us to believe she blanked out the most crucial moments of being in the hotel room. And let's not forget that Kennedy royally screwed her by not showing up tonight. We both saw how angry she was when she left. Remember what she said before storming off? *I could kill her.*'"

Hollister raised a hand. "Okay, okay. You know I'm not the woman's biggest fan either, but however angry she was or whatever she said and does or does not remember, she's no murderer."

"Then why ask me what I think?"

"Because we should know where the other stands if we're going to take this on."

"Um. Take what on?" I already knew the answer. Last summer, our search for Camilo had somewhat accidentally brought down an insidious criminal enterprise. Since then, Hollister had had it in her head that we were a proven crime-fighting duo. I chalked up our previous success to forty-nine percent belief in our cause and forty-nine percent pure luck. The remaining percentage—you do the math—only qualified as skill if setting the lowest of low bars.

"There's no way we're going to sit on our butts and hope for the best. No way. Not happening. I worry Burley can't handle losing Sarah Lee, her number two at the bakery and good friend. They work side by side, six days a week. Sarah Lee is fiercely loyal to Big Miss, and reliable. Ever since she started working at Slice, Burley has been happier, less stressed. You know how she is. She takes worrying and sensitivity to another level. I mean, remember Poppin' Fresh?"

I nodded. Poppin' Fresh had been the name Burley had given to a gopher that had set up camp on her property last Fall. Refusing to take any action that might harm the rodent, she had allowed it to ravage her yard. It wasn't until Poppin' Fresh moved next door to the lawn of the far less hospitable neighbors that his reign of destruction ended.

"So yeah, Hayden, whatever our opinion of Sarah Lee, she is found family, like it or not. Besides, Burley *is* our girl. And Burley has always—*always*—been there for us."

"It's two thirty in the morning and you're arguing the transitive property?"

Hollister replied with a baffled look that bordered on irritation.

"You don't remember your basic algebra?"

This earned me a searing stare. "Are you seriously choosing now of all times to geek out on me?"

"I'm just saying that if Sarah Lee has Burley's back, and if Burley has our back, then we've got to have Sarah Lee's."

We.

And with that, the chill staycation I had planned was going to be anything but.

Chapter Five
No Shame

I kept standard hours with few exceptions, such as New Year's Eve or an epically good weekend party, meaning I was pretty much awake during daylight hours and slept at night. So waking up on Sunday at one in the afternoon was discombobulating. I felt groggy and anxious about missing a large chunk of the day. Propped up on an elbow, I reached for the phone, which started ringing the moment I picked it up.

"Top o' the afternoon," I croaked.

"First, you owe me a thank-you."

Typical Hollister. A telephone call or text exchange often started midstream. She seemed to assume I could telepathically read her thoughts, so she needn't bother establishing any context. As a result, I often spent the first several minutes of a conversation figuring out what she was talking about.

"Is that so?"

"Despite some of us having been up for hours, I waited to call. I know how it is with you. If you don't get your beauty sleep, you're impossible to be around for the rest of the day."

"You needn't have waited. I've already manscaped, run five miles, and made an egg-white omelet." I grinned into the receiver.

"Then why didn't you call me?" A short pause. "Oh. Ha ha. You're still in bed, aren't you?"

I threw my legs over the edge of the mattress, jumped to my feet. "Nope. I'm up."

"Good. Then you won't mind."

"Won't mind what?" I asked cautiously.

"Letting me in. I'm standing outside your door."

After promising Hollister I wouldn't take forever in the shower, I left her in my studio apartment's great room—all one hundred and eighty square feet of it—and closed the bathroom door, excited to try a new shampoo I hoped might tame the red-orange hair that sprang from my head with the chaotic frenzy of children racing onto a playground. I enjoyed few things more than a long, hot shower—but I'd promised Hollister I'd keep it snappy. I toweled off, shaved the Ed Sheeran scruff from my chin, and gave my pearly whites a brisk brushing.

"Avert your eyes," I said, stepping from the steamy bathroom; a towel hitched around my thirty-inch waist.

Hollister glanced up from her phone. "I may be a lesbian, little dude, but I have seen a penis before."

"Yes, but you have not seen my equipment. I prefer to keep it that way."

"Suit yourself. But were this my house and our roles reversed, I'd have no issue being buck naked in front of you."

"I appreciate the warning. Thanks."

"I got nothing to be ashamed of."

I pulled open a drawer, snatched a pair of white briefs, and pulled them on under my towel. "I'm not ashamed. I'm just not comfortable going full frontal with friends."

She raised her hands in mock surrender. "Okay, okay. We all got our hang-ups."

"Not a hang-up."

"Whatever you say." She added an eye roll.

I stepped into a pair of jeans and pulled on my prized Wimbledon T-shirt. "So what's the plan, anyway?"

Neither of us had heard from Burley since we'd left her place at the crack of dawn. She hadn't replied to Hollister's multiple texts, and we didn't want to call and risk waking her.

"The plan is simple," Hollister explained. "We find the sick and twisted psycho who murdered Kennedy Osaka. Do we really need to go over that again?"

I turned from the mirror, where I was working my hair into a suggestion of a part. "That's the *objective*. I'm talking about the *plan*."

"See what I mean. You didn't get enough shut-eye. Now you're all Mister Cranky Pants."

Ignoring the taunt, I grabbed my laptop and plopped down next to her on the small sofa, the only seating for two other than the foot of my queen bed. I'd once made the mistake of referring to my bed as such in front of Hollister; she'd mercilessly riffed off that for a month.

"Kennedy had quite a social media following," I said, tapping the keyboard. "There's bound to be a ton of online content about her."

"Lucky us," Hollister said. "We need to know everything. Somewhere along the way, she made an enemy of the wrong person."

I grimaced and threw in a grumble for good measure.

"What? You disagree?"

"At this point, we have to assume anything is possible. There's no shortage of crazies on the internet. Perhaps someone Kennedy didn't even know formed an infatuation. There is no denying she was pretty, rich, and famous."

Hollister flopped back. "Oh, great. So you think she had some creepy secret stalker? If that's the case, it could be anybody."

I opened Kennedy Osaka's website. Much of the homepage was dedicated to her rise up the performance ladder, from touring, opening-act magician to Las Vegas headliner, to the top creative role under Mysterium's big tent—artistic director. The most recent article discussed her plan to "bring a new artistic vision to the show" and noted her intention to "reinvigorate the acts by upleveling the experience with an elegant panache."

"What did she have in mind? Trapeze made from gold bars?" Hollister quipped.

As interesting as that was, what most caught my attention was her precedent-setting contract rumored to pay her a sweet ten thousand dollars per show, with an initial guarantee of one hundred performances. I did the quick math in my head. "That kind of salary could make a parent think twice about their kid running off to join the circus."

Hollister pointed at the screen and let out a whistle. "Four hundred bucks a ticket? To start! I knew it was expensive. But still."

Reading from the blurb on the screen, I said, "'A four-course dinner conceived by a Michelin-starred chef, followed by ten dazzling, breathtaking circus acts.' Sounds like a bargain, if you ask me."

Hollister scoffed. "Still. At that price, the wine had better be included. And it had better be amazing."

"So, I take it you wouldn't have plunked down your credit card for a front-row table? You must admit the preview was pretty freakin' awesome."

"No doubt. But I draw the line at a hundred bucks. Would you pay that much?"

"Spend three months of fun money on one night?" I tapped an image on the screen. "If that guy came with the ticket, I might." The shirtless photo was of one of the four Adrenalin! guys. Named "Vlad," he had the ripped body of an Olympic gymnast. As if genetics hadn't already been kind enough to him, he looked like he could be Timothée Chalamet's better-looking brother.

I opened another window on my laptop and searched for *Kennedy Osaka* and *Mysterium*. As I'd expected, results populated several pages. By scanning through her socials, I could see that Kennedy—or the publicity manager, Jenna Jensen—had been relentless in retweeting, commenting, reposting, and replying to Kennedy's messages, whether from fans or haters. Kennedy's ability to strike the perfect pose, capture the right light, and accentuate her envious beauty was no less impressive than her making a two-hundred-pound woman vanish on stage.

My head was swimming. Millions of people had ready access to a mountain of information about Kennedy Osaka. Her professional success had been predicated on letting her fans in, giving them an intimate view of her life, and making them feel like they were true friends. In Agatha Christie's novels, a victim's friends and acquaintances often warranted suspicion. But could Kennedy's killer be a social media "friend" who was also a complete stranger?

I navigated back to Kennedy's website, clicked on the "About" page, and found an extensive biography.

Hollister's phone buzzed, alerting her to a text.

"It's Burley," Hollister said, reading from the screen. "Damn that woman."

"What's she done now?"

"She went to work. That's what she's done. She should be rattling the windows with her snoring, but she's at Slice, glazing pastries and steaming milk."

"Speaking of which, I just got up. I need my morning coffee."

"It's nearly two in the afternoon."

"Your point?"

"I'm due a double shot myself."

Chapter Six
Find a Killer, Easy-Peasy

Standing inside the door at Slice, Hollister and I wondered where to sit, when a mom and her teenage daughter got up to bus their table. The mother appeared to have borrowed her daughter's skin-tight jeans and midriff T-shirt, while the daughter might have been wearing her older brother's oversized gray sweatpants and hoodie. Before they'd stepped two feet from the table, I swooped in while Hollister grabbed a place in line.

Burley stood stooped behind the counter, pouring beans from a bag into a coffee grinder. She had opted for her usual hair-style of twin braids, each tied with a strand of rawhide. In what I assumed was an attempt at keeping with the health code, she'd pinned a pink bandana to her head, the ends of which fell just short of her ears. Much to my surprise, Sarah Lee was taking orders and working the pay station. Hollister's wave caught my attention. From the front of the line, she raised a finger, then two. I replied with a single digit. She returned a thumbs-up and turned back to Sarah Lee.

Several minutes later, Hollister slid a cappuccino in front of me and plunked down a maple bar. Registering my surprise, she said, "Burley insisted. She said she might have overdone the vanilla and wants to know if they taste funky."

Clearly, Burley was in a bad headspace. Never before had she lacked confidence in anything concocted in her kitchen. And for good reason. Everything I'd ever tasted—from cherry-chocolate croissants to apricot pound cake, to buttermilk waffles with marmalade, to a cheddar and hazelnut scone—had been, crumb for crumb, *dee-e-licious*.

"Perhaps people are intimidated," I said, appraising the glistening treat the size of a baguette. "That, or they don't want to appear gluttonous."

"Can you OD on sugar?"

"We're about to find out." I cut the maple bar in half, tipped my head toward the kitchen. "How's she holding up, anyway?"

"Depends on who you mean. Burley says she's too freaked to sleep. Being here helps take her mind off last night. Oddly, Sarah Lee's acting pretty normal. She got a call this morning from the lawyer, Gemalto. Despite some pretty damning evidence, he said it's still too early in the investigation to know just how bad it is." Hollister looked back at the counter. "You'd think Sarah Lee would be the one distraught, but she's actually trying to keep Big Miss's spirits up. Gotta give the girl some credit."

"Hmm." As much as I didn't want to agree with Hollister, she had a point. But the possibility that Sarah Lee could be growing on me was too uncomfortable to think about.

"Now don't you start. We agreed. Innocent until proven guilty."

"I don't recall having that specific conversation."

"We both thought it."

"Is that so? Can you read what I'm thinking right now?"

"That you don't want to come at me before I've had my coffee?"

Dispute paused, we got down to business. Earlier, I'd found floor plans of the Park Olympic Hotel online and sent them to Hollister, who had a large printer in her work studio. One question that bothered us was how the killer could have fled Kennedy's room without being seen by Sarah Lee in either the hallway or elevator. Hollister spread the printouts on the table.

"So?" Hollister asked, examining the sixth-floor layout. "Any thoughts on how the killer escaped?"

I stood, leaning over the schematic. There were four suites at the south end of the sixth floor. To reach them from the elevators, one would walk down a long hallway, passing the floor's other guest rooms, and take a right. From there, a foyer on either side led to two suites. Pushing my empty mug to the side, I tapped my finger on the spot where the stairs were indicated. "The killer must have escaped by taking the stairs."

"Not necessarily," Hollister replied, drawing out both words.

Answering my shrug, she pointed to each of the adjacent suites. "Here, here, or here."

"I got it!" Like an excited game-show contestant knowing the correct response, I blurted, "The killer could have ducked into one of the other nearby suites or any other room on that floor."

"Bingo. Or taken the stairs to another floor, not necessarily the lobby." Hollister plunked down her mug. "There must be cameras. That should clear everything up. The video should show anyone coming or going from Kennedy's room." She brushed her hands as if flicking off crumbs. "Watch the video, find the killer. Easy-peasy."

Remembering that Hollister's high-end furniture business, Holl&Wood, had been commissioned to design barstools for the hotel several years ago, I asked, "Are you still in touch with people at the hotel? Someone who could show us what camera recordings there are?"

"Good idea, little dude. I met the security manager, Gwyneth Lang, at the grand opening reception. She should have access to the video recordings. I'll make a call."

Chapter Seven
Mates on Dates, Post No. 22

Before leaving the bakery, Hollister and I agreed to meet up at Burley's place that night for dinner with Sarah Lee. Having a few hours on my own, I opened my laptop. A topic for a blog post had been rattling around in my brain, and I was ready to put it into words.

MATES ON DATES: Carlos Encounters
Several months back, a guy—I'll call him Carlos—returned safely home to Seattle. Before Carlos's mysterious disappearance—solved by my friend Hollister and me—he and I had spent one night together, just cuddling. Cards on the tables, guys. I like Carlos. A lot. But how does he feel about me? We're definitely friends, but he sends infuriatingly ambiguous signals whenever we are together. In response, I have established a resoundingly ineffective approach-avoidance strategy for what I call my "Carlos Encounters." While I intentionally visit where he works on the nights I know he'll be dancing (that's all the hint you get), I try for aloofness when he bounces my way during a break. He'll drape a muscled arm over my shoulder, pull me close, and say

exasperating things like, "Hey, buddy, why don't you ever call me?" To which I want to scream, "Why don't *you* ever call *me*!" Or he'll say—and this one really makes me crazy—"Why don't we hang out?" *Perhaps we would, Carlos, if you ever made good on your promises to follow up!*

I've never been in one of those twelve-step programs, but I'm pretty sure the first step is to admit you have a problem. So here goes. I am the diabolical mastermind of my own torment.

I am a crazy person when it comes to dealing with Carlos. Here's all the proof you need: I hope he finds a serious boyfriend because that might drive a stake through the heart of my infatuation. Of course, the healthy wish is for a boyfriend of my own, but then I'd be unavailable for Carlos. See what I mean? It's beyond embarrassing.

I'm not sure about the right second step, but I'm pretty sure it's not continuing to put myself in a situation that makes me feel like crap.

I offer this unflattering story about myself for two reasons. First, if you've ever been similarly stuck, know you're not alone. And second, by coming out as a victim of unrequited love, I hope to start building the strength to stand up for my self-worth. Before I can find love, I must refuse to compromise my own need to be loved in return. You, my friends, should join me in demanding nothing less for yourselves too.

So the next time you're getting ready for a date, along with checking for nose hairs, making sure you smell good (deodorant, yes; body sprays marketed to straight teenaged boys, *no*!), and pulling on a shirt to complement your eye color, don't forget your self-worth—it's the one thing that, for any date, you should never leave home without.

Till next time, I'm Hayden.
And remember, if you can't be good, be safe!

I was ready to hit "Publish," when I had a sudden thought of recent legislation out of Florida. The bizarre and maddening "Don't say gay" law. True, I was on the opposite corner of the country, but if a parent got wind of my blog, what then? Because I was a teacher, might someone decide that, just by talking honestly about personal issues, I was "grooming" my students? . . . It gave me pause. I'd better have a think before posting. It was getting a little scary to be a schoolteacher.

Chapter Eight
This Is Weird

Lincoln Park's expansive lawns and dense pockets of ferns sprawled above a long sliver of Elliott Bay beach in West Seattle. It was a place I knew well. Not far from my apartment at Orca Arms, the park's paths had witnessed all my moods, from giddy highs to "I-can't-imagine-ever-feeling-okay-again" lows. At the positive end of the spectrum: rescuing Hollister last summer, foiling an international crime ring, and making possible the return of Camilo. As for my darkest moments, nothing came close to losing my mom to cancer eight years ago.

My current funk was due to Kennedy's murder and my code-red worry about plunging into another crazy investigation with Hollister. And so I went to the park to "interrogate" (a cringy word for introspection that many of my fellow teachers were throwing around these days) my sadness. Apparently, Sarah Lee had literally stumbled into a murder scene. When she'd been led away in handcuffs, I was grateful that Hollister had had the presence of mind to call a criminal defense attorney. And I was impressed by Burley's generosity in footing the bill for him to continue representing Sarah Lee. I still had my doubts about my neighbor, but even Sarah Lee deserved justice. I just hoped any need for the lawyer's services—and our investigation—would be short-lived.

Puget Sound's salty, fishy smell mingled with the scent of pine, creating the fragrance of home. My long stroll through the park hadn't made me feel better, but I didn't feel any worse, which I would have had I stayed cooped up in my apartment. At least I'd stretched my legs, and the view of the Olympic Mountains had once again proved a reliable comfort.

I glanced at my Spider-Man watch—a gift from Hollister last summer to celebrate our crime-fighting partnership. We jokingly referred to ourselves as Batwoman and Spider-Man. She was surprised I wore it, as she'd meant it as more of a gesture than a legit timepiece. Nevertheless, the watch lifted my spirits. It was a persistent reminder that I had terrific friends.

I picked up Thai takeout on the way to Burley's place. Hollister was on wine and dessert detail. Burley's sole job was "to chillax with the emus" and hang out with Sarah Lee until we arrived. I found the gigantic birds ornery and stinky, but if they could mellow Burley's anxiety about Sarah Lee's plight, I would cut them some slack.

Hollister had parked her Porsche—named Mo after her favorite author, Toni Morrison—behind Sarah Lee's Beetle, which sat beside Burley's Bronco in the driveway. An electric car of some kind occupied my usual spot in front of the house.

Weighed down by three paper bags of food, I went around the side of the house and entered the kitchen through the back door. Hollister was setting the table, a round, pale yellow Formica throwback that was one item in Burley's house I wouldn't mind having for myself. I could hear Burley and Sarah Lee talking to someone in the living room. Whoever it was, I didn't recognize the voice. Hollister saw me look in that direction.

"That's Jess Gemalto," she explained. "Sarah Lee's lawyer."

"What's he doing here?"

"Burley invited me." The voice I hadn't recognized was now in the room. I spun around. A man stood in the kitchen doorway, looking back at me with an expression that teeter-tottered between curiosity and delight. I felt the room tilt as if reality had shifted, causing the house to slide from its foundation. Was I being pranked? Was "Jess Gemalto" an elaborate hoax ginned up by Hollister and Burley? He must be. *But how? Why?*

"I'm Jess. I hope you don't mind my crashing your dinner. Burley insisted I join you all. She said if I was going to be Sarah Lee's 'lawman,' I needed to 'pass mustard.'" Then, grinning, he added, "I knew what she meant." He stepped farther into the room and extended a hand. I couldn't help but notice the silver cuff link on his perfectly ironed, perfectly white dress shirt. Also notable were the paisley bow tie, dark trousers, and polished black lace-ups.

"You must be Hayden."

What the—? I examined my own hand as I reached for his, stupefied by how much they matched, right down to the faint trace of blue veins beneath our pale skin. "Uh, I'm . . ."

"He's Hayden." Hollister gave my arm a soft punch.

Sarah Lee entered the room, followed by Burley, who stood between Jess and me. As if watching a game of ping-pong, she swiveled her head to look at Jess, then at me, then back to Jess. "Holy Connick Junior! Didn't Sarah Lee and I tell you?" she said to Jess. "You and Hayden look exactly alike."

Jess was practically my double, with few differences: bigger eyes, a more rounded chin and nose, and slightly wider hips.

44

While he looked like a man—or as much of a man as I did—there were just enough visual cues to suggest he might be transgender.

"Okay," I managed to say. "This is weird."

Jess zeroed in on our most pronounced physical difference. "Dude, your hair is off the hook."

Although we both had a similar shade of red-orange hair, mine refused to be subdued, no matter what I tried, whereas Jess's was a marvel of current barber styling. Super short sides and back, a meticulous fade, laser-straight part, and—what I most achingly envied—longer hair on top, combed back and *lying flat*.

Finally, Hollister weighed in on our separated-at-birth similarities: "Appears you have a secret twin, little dude."

There was no way Hollister could have met Jess Gemalto and not been astounded by our nearly identical appearance. "Really? You're just now seeing the resemblance?"

Hollister scowled, clearly not appreciating my clipped tone. "He was already in the living room when I arrived! Like you, I'm just meeting him now for the first time."

"But you're the one who called him."

This won a "what-is-wrong-with-you?" glare from Hollister. "I knew of him from his ads—and they don't have a picture. We've only talked on the phone."

"It was a good thing you made that call, Hollister," Jess said, removing his jacket and draping it over the back of a chair. "You'd be amazed how many people take no action. Not out of laziness, mind you. Rather, they innocently—pun intended—assume everything will work out. They think whatever they've got themselves mixed up in is all just a terrible misunderstanding and that a bit of honest explaining will clear everything right up. Well, it doesn't always work out that way. And thanks to Burley, I'm now representing Sarah Lee"—he nodded assuredly at his client—"who, I'm sorry to say, very much needs a good criminal lawyer."

Hollister nodded in enthusiastic agreement. "Justice is expensive in this country."

"I hope this isn't the civics lesson you plan for my classroom," I said, referring to my invitation to Hollister to speak to my class one day during Boss Women Week—one of my curriculum inventions.

She shot me a look. "Of course not. They're eighth-graders. Practically adults. For them, I won't sugarcoat it."

Burley stepped forward. Like a child pressing her face closer to the cage of a zoo animal, she leaned down to scrutinize first me and then Jess. Her examination lasted so long that I began to wonder if she might have become confused about which one of us was which. "I've been poking around the internet lately, looking into cloning the emus. But *this*—this is next level."

I traded glances with Jess. The double whammy of being compared to a barnyard animal and learning that our host was researching biological replication explained his look of bewilderment.

Sarah Lee had taken a turn for the worse since seeing her that morning at the bakery. She now looked like she hadn't slept for days. I guessed she'd been running on adrenaline that had run dry. And the absence of any makeup added to her sullen appearance. She was polite but reserved and soft-spoken, not at all her normal blunt and unapologetic self. Having never been witness to a murder—then arrested and questioned about it—I could imagine the experience would take its toll. But I'd gone out of my way to be nice, and took her lack of reciprocation as evidence of her just feeling too dreadful to muster any pleasantries.

The dinner conversation should have focused solely on Sarah Lee's case, but she seemed subdued, and I sensed we all tacitly agreed to give her space. Besides, Jess and I couldn't avoid the doppelgänger in the room. We spent the first hour discussing our parentage and other heredity highlights. We couldn't find a single shared relative between us. Jess had been born in Helena, Montana, had graduated high school there, and then gone to undergrad and law school at Berkeley. After passing the Washington State bar exam, he'd moved to Seattle four years ago, where he'd transitioned. I did the easy math in my head. Jess was three years older than me.

"Well, that's a puzzling puzzler," Burley said.

"I'd put my money on a secret adoption," Hollister said, topping off Jess's and my glasses with the pinot noir she'd brought along to the meeting. Burley sipped from a large Mason jar of apricot nectar. Sarah Lee had yet to touch the tap water she'd asked for.

"So, Jess," Burley said, "we owe you a big thanks for getting Sarah Lee released from the pokey." She placed a dinner-plate-sized hand on top of Sarah Lee's. "But what's your thinking? What happens next?"

Jess told us what had occurred the night before at police headquarters. The homicide detectives had focused on the precise timing of Sarah Lee's actions that night. Security cameras showed her entering the hotel's main entrance at a few minutes past seven o'clock. She walked straight through the lobby and waited briefly for an elevator to arrive. Minutes later, a guest in a nearby room phoned the front desk to report hearing a woman's scream. Soon after that, two security men entered Kennedy's suite. They found Sarah Lee standing in the room, near the body. She was holding the murder weapon—a pair of tailoring shears.

I liked this Jess Gemalto. He was matter-of-fact, but not arrogant. And he didn't, as my good friend and mentor Jerry would say, throw around twelve-dollar words just to impress, like most lawyers he'd come across. Jess's conversation style was similar to Jerry's down-to-earth, on-screen legal hero Matlock's.

"So? Where are we at?" Burley said. "On a scale of one to ten? How bad is it?"

Jess scrunched his face, an expression I often made. Seeing how it looked to others on a face almost exactly like mine, I told myself never to do it while on a date.

"Well . . ." Jess said, "to tell you the truth—which you should know is the only way I roll—the situation isn't great, but it could be worse. At this point, there isn't much to be done until the police get further along in their investigation. Sarah Lee's prints are certain to be found on the scissors and perhaps elsewhere in the room, at least on the door. But hopefully they'll find someone else's too." Jess glanced over at Sarah Lee's hand, encircling her water glass. "The police will review all the security camera recordings and interview guests and staff, and they'll determine who was where, when, and so on. They'll do what they do, which is a lot. We hope those efforts turn up something that points their inquiries in a different direction."

"Hoping for the best doesn't strike me as a particularly proactive approach," Hollister huffed.

I winced at the remark, which seemed harsh. But if Jess had been offended, he didn't let on. Poker face? Rehearsed courtroom cool? Or was he just empathetic to worried clients and their families and friends? I hardly knew him, but I landed hard on option number three.

Jess spread his hands wide. "Let's get something straight from the get-go," he said. "I offer one and only one guarantee throughout whatever is to come: I will do my very best for Sarah Lee. Beyond that . . . but I can tell you this. The circumstances suggest Ms. Osaka knew her killer. That person had a reason to want her dead. This was personal, nothing random about it.

"You're saying if we find the motive, we find the killer," Hollister clarified.

"That's usually how it unfolds." Jess nodded. "But here's the strangest thing—"

"The scissors." Hearing Sarah Lee's voice startled us. We all turned to face her. She had said only a few words all night. "You'll understand, I hope, that I don't want to discuss what I *can* remember. It's too painful. But I will tell you this. The scissors . . . it's so just strange. Why scissors?" She shook her head and again fell silent.

"The scissors were large and heavy," Jess explained to us. "Not an average household pair one keeps in a drawer. We will argue that, in a state of shock, Sarah Lee reacted impulsively to save her friend. She was holding the scissors because she had removed them." He went on to posit that there were only two ways those scissors could have gotten into Kennedy's room: "First, they were there beforehand, which begs the question: Why would Kennedy have such an unusual pair of scissors lying around her hotel room? Or to my mind, the second and more likely method is that the killer brought them with him."

"Could be a she," Hollister pointed out.

Thinking of Jess, I added, "Or *they*." Jess hadn't corrected our use of *he, him, his*, so I assumed we were referring to him as he preferred to be addressed. He did dress—very nicely—as a man. But was it cool to just hope we had it right? Like doing a cannonball into a cold pool, I took the leap.

"Jess, speaking of pronouns . . ."

"You're good, Hayden. You and I share the same set. But I appreciate you asking. Most people seem to be afraid to bring it up. But I appreciate the question. It acknowledges that how I identify may be different from what you assume and that I have a preference."

Jess's frankness was as sensible as it was refreshing. In my life, I occasionally got the vibe that someone scrutinized my voice, gestures, and shyness to determine whether I was gay. As if that would . . . what? Influence the perception of me? Limit the idea of me? Define me? I wondered in how many of those past situations I had been too sensitive. Perhaps some people are just curious, and that's really all there is to it.

Jess took a sip of wine before saying, "At the moment, we know next to nothing about the perpetrator. But nine out of ten times, criminals screw up. It's often a boneheaded mistake." He shook his head woefully. "You'd be amazed. You'd also be astounded by how often the guilty party is a family member. Or a friend, a colleague, a neighbor, an ex . . . It's almost always a person the victim knew. And usually a male when the victim is female. In Ms. Osaka's case, that could be someone associated with Mysterium, a former lover, or a friend she had a falling out with."

All eyes turned to Sarah Lee, and I suspected Hollister and I were again replaying what she'd said before leaving the event to find Kennedy: *I could just kill her.*

"Sounds like the list of suspects is endless," I said.

"Yeah, but we got this." Hollister reached over and gave me an encouraging smack on the back.

"Ouch!"

"Got what?" Jess said, suddenly alarmed.

"Not to worry, Counselor. Hayden and I have proven that we have undeniable skills when it comes to investigating."

I winced. "You might be overstating things just a bit."

"Always glass half empty." She shook her head in disappointment.

"I think it's more that my cup does not runneth over with unwarranted optimism."

"Wait." Jess's gaze bounced from Hollister to me and back again. "You two are detectives?"

I started to correct the record, but Hollister was too quick.

"On a whole other level," she said.

Appreciating the ambiguity of the remark, I figured that sounded about right.

Chapter Nine

Freeze It

At 8:10 AM on a Monday, I would usually be flipping on the lights in my classroom, but it was spring break, and I had the entire week off. I'd toyed with the idea of taking a short, easy trip somewhere but decided to save the money for something grander over the summer. Although "grand" on my budget only went as far as economy fare, hostel stays, and savvy use of travel points.

Usually a champion sleeper, I had tossed and turned all night. Only twice before in my life had I been so worked up. Once was when my mom first told me about her cancer. The second time had been last summer when Camilo went missing. Now, a sort of friend of my frenemy had been murdered, and Hollister had it in her head that it was up to us to solve it.

Last night at dinner, Sarah Lee had nibbled on an appetizer but otherwise ate nothing. I was no nutritionist, but a woman of any size cannot function on a half bite of spring roll and a few sips of water. Her appetite, usually healthy, clearly had been overwhelmed by an impossible-to-stop replay of the grim scene at the hotel. Jess had managed to win her release, but given the gravity of the crime and the evidence (being caught next to the body while holding the murder weapon), there was a feeling among us that she could be rearrested at any moment.

As beat as I was, I needed to rally. Hollister had made good on her promise to connect with Gwyneth Lang, the security manager at the Park Olympic. We were to meet her in the hotel's lobby in an hour. I was eager to see what, if anything, the cameras had recorded the night of Kennedy's death.

The Park Olympic was one of Seattle's few five-star hotels. The lobby's sleek Scandinavian aesthetic extended to the smartly clad staff, all of whom looked to be the offspring of Norwegian supermodels. A pleasing fragrance of woodsy sweetness permeated the air. I inhaled deeply, savoring the whole sensorial experience of refined luxury, knowing it was the only part of the hotel I could afford. Swanky environs didn't match up well with my schoolteacher's salary. The hotel catered to techie urbanites who spent fortunes to achieve their bed-head, thrift-store looks. So, despite the hotel having an average nightly rate that surpassed my monthly rent, I looked like I fit right in.

I arrived early, so I wasn't surprised that Hollister wasn't there yet. I lowered myself onto an austere tan leather chair. A guy, early sixties and stuffed into iron-creased jeans and purple suede slip-ons, strolled into the lobby. He was followed by a twenty-something woman teetering on heels, who in turn was followed by a bellman pushing a trolley laden with matching Louis Vuitton luggage.

My students once asked me the meaning of the word *cliché*. I recalled stitching together a reasonable definition, but a photograph of the hotel's newest guests would have been a more impactful answer—certainly more memorable. Then again, what did I know? Maybe what appeared on the surface to be a union of convenience was, in fact, a true love match. Who's to say they didn't giggle at each other's humor, create handmade gifts at birthdays, and take turns reading passages of *Tales of the City* aloud while lying in bed? As the caravan marched into the elevator, I decided to believe they did do all those things.

"It's not polite to stare." Surprised by what was clearly a child's voice, I turned. About ten, the boy looked like he'd give even the most intrepid babysitter a run for their money.

"Observing is not staring," I replied.

"What's the difference?"

"Staring lacks empathy. Observing seeks understanding."

Rolling his eyes dramatically, he called out, "Freak," before running off.

"No Gwyneth yet?" Hollister said, suddenly appearing from behind me.

"Now that we're both here, I suspect she'll be right out."

"Oh, right. She can see us." Hollister turned a slow pirouette and waved to the corners of the room.

Not five minutes later, a woman who looked the same age as my aunt approached. Seemingly comfortably into her fifties, there was nothing old-fashioned about her. Tall, lanky, and of Asian descent, she wore a tailored navy men's three-piece suit punctuated by a brilliant yellow tie that seemed to signal a sunny disposition. She had pinned a small medal of some sort, complete with two cascading crimson silk ribbons, to her jacket's breast pocket. Her short-cropped gray hair, heavily gelled and neatly parted to the side, looked as hard-shelled as a custom-made bicycle helmet.

Gwyneth Lang greeted us with an unmistakable Canadian accent. "Sorry to keep you waiting," she said, pronouncing sorry as *sore-y*. "Please, follow me."

I fancied myself a good judge of character, and this woman immediately enamored me. She exuded a casual charm, worn soft with age rather than polished for effect.

Gwyneth Lang led the way down a series of corridors. Her head bobbed along with her loping giraffe-like gait. At the end of a hallway, we crowded inside a small room marked "Security Center"—although "Video Closet," would have been more apt for the tight space. Gwyneth's sleek modern style appeared worthy of a starship-like command station, but she sat in a simple roller chair before a built-in countertop on which sat a keyboard and large monitor. Hollister and I took a half step forward to stand close behind her.

"What I'm a-boot to show you, I've already shown the police," Gwyneth said, punching keys. "That's one of the reasons I agreed to do this."

"One of the reasons?" Hollister repeated. "And the others?"

My head snapped toward Hollister; I gave her a stern look. She needed to lose the attitude. The woman was doing us a huge favor.

Gwyneth shrugged. "I think you'll find it hardly matters."

Hollister appeared taken aback. "I disagree. The reason does matter," she said. "It matters a lot."

Gwyneth turned, wearing an easy smile. "I think you misunderstand me. I mean to say nothing you will see matters much to clearing *or* implicating your friend. When I show you, you'll understand." She tapped the right side of the monitor's split screen. "I'll display here."

A moment later, Sarah Lee appeared in the video. She stepped through the hotel's double doors, glanced to her right and left, then walked across the lobby. When she reached the elevators,

Gwyneth froze the screen. The time stamp in the lower corner of the monitor read 7:04:13 PM. Gwyneth turned in her chair. "So we know precisely the time your friend Sandra Lee went up to the sixth floor."

"Sarah Lee," Hollister corrected.

Gwyneth nodded. "I beg your pardon. Sarah Lee." Turning back to the keyboard, she continued, "After your friend steps into the elevator, we don't see her again until—" More taps on the keyboard, and Sarah Lee stepped out of the elevator and into the lobby, a uniformed police officer on either side of her. Bystanders gawked as she was escorted toward the exit. Gwyneth froze the screen a second time when they left the lobby. The time stamp read 7:32:58 PM.

"Hold up!" Hollister said. "That's it? That's everything you've got?"

"I'm afraid so," Gwyneth answered. "That's all the footage of your friend."

"But that doesn't help at all!" Hollister said, too loudly for the tiny space. She leaned over Gwyneth's shoulder and tapped the screen. "You must have more cameras, more angles. Something useful."

"I'm sorry, miss. Really I am." Gwyneth said. "The security cameras cover only spaces accessible to the general public—not elevators and guest floor hallways. It's for privacy reasons."

Hollister rolled her head and muttered something I didn't catch.

Gwyneth turned off the monitor and spun the chair around. "Again, I truly am sorey a-boot your friend. I'm sure this will all sort itself owt." Adding to *sorey*, my brain worked to convert *a-boot* to *about*, and *owt* to *out*.

Hollister, clearly distressed, said, "You've seen everything there is to see. So at least tell us this: Were you able to show the police anything that might point to someone else?"

Gwyneth shifted uncomfortably in her chair and glanced back at the monitor, as if seeking its approval to share a secret. The silence allowed me to hear the low electronic humming of the room's computer equipment for the first time. We waited. I sensed Hollister was also holding her breath.

"Very well," Gwyneth sighed, "I trust I can count on your discretion."

Hollister and I nodded, like kids agreeing to behave before being let loose at a carnival.

Gwyneth continued, "Staring at these screens for as long as I do, you notice things that don't seem right. Afterward, when the tragedy came to light, the timing of what I'm about to show you . . . well, it didn't seem like it could be a coincidence."

With that teaser, we huddled even closer to the screen.

"The time is 7:01:02." Gwyneth hit "Play."

A woman with messy blond hair and a large, dark-colored bag slung over a shoulder entered through the hotel's main entrance. Judging by the camera's angle, she appeared to be nearly six feet tall, but the unknown height of her heels made it difficult to tell. Her weight, cloaked in a bulky, full-length furry coat, also proved hard to estimate. She crossed the lobby and disappeared into an elevator. After fast-forwarding the video, Gwyneth said. "Now, it's six minutes later. 7:07:17."

The same woman, tugging at her unruly hair, ran-walked across the lobby and left through the hotel's double doors.

"Well, *that's* not suspicious," Hollister said.

Gwyneth said, "Before you ask, I don't know which floor the woman visited."

"You really have no idea who she is?" I asked.

Gwyneth shook her shiny head, reflected in the greenish glow of the monitor. "But you should take comfort in knowing that the police are extremely interested in her. You'll understand that I'm in no position to say whether she had anything to do with the crime that happened here or if she had even visited the sixth floor, but you wanted to know if there might not be something else. So, there is your something else."

"Thank you, Gwyneth," I said before turning to Hollister. "Time to go. We've taken up enough of Gwyneth's time."

Hollister nodded. "Yes, of course. Thanks."

"I'll see you both out."

Gwyneth led us down the hallway. As we neared the lobby, Hollister stopped abruptly.

"Shoot. I left my phone back there on your desk."

Before Gwyneth or I could react, Hollister was jogging back toward the Security Center.

"Oh, but you can't . . ." Gwyneth's words were futile. Hollister had already rounded the corner and disappeared.

"She'll be back in two shakes," I said breezily, though sure my crime-solving partner was up to something. I just hoped it would be quick. When a minute became two, Gwyneth let loose a Canadian grumble (a grumble that somehow sounded polite) and started marching back to her office. Hollister appeared from around the corner, waving her phone in the air.

"Sorry, sorry! I dropped it and then must have inadvertently kicked it beneath the chair. It took me a minute to find it."

Gwyneth's expression teetered between skepticism and relief. Gratefully, she seemed to settle on the latter.

Outside the hotel, I said, "What was that all about?"

Hollister gave me a blank "whatever-do-you-mean?" look.

"C'mon, woman. Out with it."

Her stoic expression cracked to reveal the hint of a smile. She reached into the pocket of her tight jeans and pulled out a flash drive.

Chapter Ten
The Show Must Go On

Hollister was discouraged that Gwyneth Lang had shown us nothing that proved Sarah Lee's innocence. When Hollister felt down, I'd learned the best strategy was to give her time alone to rebound. Besides, I wasn't much company—I was hardly brimming with optimism. I still wasn't entirely convinced that Sarah Lee was innocent, but as time went on, I had switched from the "she-probably-did-it" camp to the "can't-really-see-her-committing-a-violent-felony" camp.

I had my car headed toward Jerry's place before consciously deciding to go see him. Jerry was ninety-one and lived in the townhome next door to my Aunt Sally. I'd first met him when my aunt asked me to look in on him when she was away. Over the past year, Jerry and I had become friends, and I found myself visiting not because he needed a lift to the pharmacy or his rain gutters cleaned, but because I enjoyed talking to him. He was wise and grandfatherly, but I mostly appreciated that he provided a safe space while never coddling me. Jerry tolerated whining and self-pity as well as he accepted what had become of his

Republican party, billing statements from his doctor, or the intrusion of reverse-mortgage commercials during *Matlock* episodes.

As I raised my hand to ring the buzzer, the door opened.

"Hello, Hayden." Dressed in his "uniform," as he liked to call it, Jerry greeted me wearing khaki pants bunched high at the waist with a thick brown belt, a solid light blue dress shirt, and brown boat shoes. Oh, and white socks, which made me crazy. Jerry had refused to even open the three-pack of tan dress socks I'd bought him at Target. "We'd better just save these," he'd said after pulling them from the bag. When I'd asked, "For what exactly?" he'd replied, "Your inheritance."

I followed Jerry up the short flight of stairs. Slowly. We took our usual spots at his round kitchen table. As my butt hit the seat, he said, "If you're feeling adventurous, there's a new brand of Earl Grey in the cupboard. A gift from your aunt. The box isn't homemade, so I have modest hopes."

"Ha. Just modest?"

"Well, you know your aunt as well as I do. I don't see her spending more than five dollars on something like tea. Or a pound of coffee. Or one of those figurines she can't get enough of."

Jerry was referring to my Aunt Sally's army of porcelain angel figurines. Collected from flea markets and online shopping sites, or traded like baseball cards among friends at her evangelical church, Aunt Sally's collection lacked craftsmanship but made up for it in number—she had hundreds of them.

I heated the kettle and snatched a carton of biscuits from the cupboard.

"Did you read the label?" I asked as I examined the unfamiliar box of Earl Grey.

Jerry picked up the giant magnifying glass he kept on the table for reading magazines and his nonfiction books on warfare, science, and American history. "Even with this," he said, "I couldn't possibly read that tiny type. Why? What don't I want to know?"

"Let's just say I'm having our usual." I reached for the familiar white tin with red and gold lettering. Jerry had introduced me to Harney & Sons English Breakfast Tea, and I'd never looked back. Like choosing my favorite dish at a restaurant, ordering anything else risked grave disappointment.

"If that's the case, I'll have the same."

After making a pot, I returned to the table with two cups.

"So, what's new in Hayden's world?"

Jerry must have noticed my changed expression. He matched my grimace. "That bad?"

As we sipped tea, I regaled him with an accounting of recent events—from the Mysterium preview to arriving at the fundraiser that wasn't, to collecting Sarah Lee from the police station, to the review of hotel security videos. Jerry had a knack for breaking down a problem and understandably framing the particulars, if not always finding an answer.

After splitting the crinkled cellophane wrapping, he pulled a biscuit from the tray and waggled it in the air. "I imagine the best hope for Burley's friend . . . name, again?"

"Sarah Lee."

"And she works at a bakery?"

I lifted a hand. "I know."

"This Sarah Lee better hope the police find a better suspect. As you describe it, the timing suggests that the Osaka woman's killer was either a hotel guest or a visitor. If a guest, the police investigation should determine whether that person knew . . ."

"Kennedy."

Jerry went on. "If the killer wasn't staying in the hotel, it would be tricky for them to escape the building without being captured on one of the cameras. I would think the police would try to identify all non-guests and determine whether they had any association with Kennedy. At least, they would discover if anyone coming or going looked suspicious."

I told him about Gwyneth Lang showing Hollister and me the recording of the disheveled blond woman dashing through the lobby. "It's maddening," I grumbled. "There must be something we could be doing. I'm not as distrustful of the police as Hollister, but not knowing whether they're making any progress in finding the real killer is frustrating. I don't suppose you have any ideas?" I raised my brow in classic Bond-like fashion.

"This Kennedy did what for a living?"

"Magician mostly. From my online research and what Hollister and I learned firsthand from Kennedy at the preview, when she joined Mysterium, she added the artistic director role, becoming the performers' boss and deciding which acts got a place in the show's lineup, along with the order in which they went on stage. She seemed very much into the idea of making the show more sophisticated. Or as much as possible for what's essentially a circus."

His eyes widened. "So it's a circus? But fancy? Should I be thinking—what? Elephants with tiaras? Clowns in tuxedos?"

"Very funny." I shared what I had seen and read about Mysterium. "It's a high-end, live-performance event. No animal acts, however. It all happens under a large, lavish tent. There are singers, dancers, aerialists, magicians, and high-wire acts—that sort of thing. Oh, and you get a gourmet dinner. Kennedy was new to the show. Her contract reportedly committed her to one hundred performances for a million dollars."

"A million dollars?" he marveled. "That Kennedy woman didn't need to worry about the electric bill or paying for a cupboard full of prescription drugs."

"You okay? Something bothering you?"

"Money issues. Nothing to waste our time talking about, Hayden." He waved a bony hand. "I shouldn't have brought it up."

"You insist I talk about things that are bothering me. So— what? You get to play by different rules? I don't think so. Spill it, old man."

Jerry had just taken a bite of biscuit and nearly choked on it. "If you must know, the doctor prescribed me another medication. Don't ask me what it's called or what it's supposed to do. It doesn't matter because I can't afford it. Or even pronounce it. The entire stinking medical system in this country is a racket, is what it is. How can a pill cost more than an entire bag of groceries? Which, by the way, lasts a whole week. I'm supposed to take the damn pill once a day!"

"But if you need it?"

"I need all of them. You've seen the cabinet, Hayden. My own little Walgreens. Unless I can muster the humility and energy to become a burger flipper or Walmart greeter or rent out a room, I'll be letting nature take its course. I'm ancient, if you haven't noticed. And I refuse to skimp on tea or biscuits or cable television just so I can pop another pill. So there. Now you know what's on my mind. But please, let's not talk about it. It's too depressing. Your job is to distract me with more fascinating topics. And last I checked, a murdered magician-slash-artistic director figures high on that list." He pushed his cup in my direction. "Fill 'er up, please. Your hands are steadier."

I silently agreed to table the issue of Jerry's unaffordable prescription, but there was no way I could ignore his financial or health worries. I had no extra money lying around, but I'd find a way to help. I had to.

"Who do you think murdered this Kennedy woman, anyway?" he said.

"Could be anyone. That's the problem. There were hundreds of hotel guests at the time, along with dozens of non-guests."

"Anyone? No. I don't think so. *Someone*, yes. Don't roll your eyes. Think about it. Just anyone doesn't creep into another person's room and plunge scissors into their chest. Whoever killed that woman wanted her dead for a reason."

"That's what Sarah Lee's lawyer said. He thinks it was someone Kennedy knew."

"And who is this lawyer? Does he know what he's doing?"

I explained that Jess Gemalto was a lawyer whose ads Hollister had seen and that he had an outstanding education and track record. He nodded, absorbing the information. I then added that he resembled me to a freakish degree and that he was a transgender man. Was that last bit necessary to add? I decided it was. Jerry might have an occasion to meet Jess, and despite Jess's male appearance, I didn't want Jerry to blurt out an inappropriate remark. Jerry's initially furrowed brow slowly relaxed.

"Name's Jess, you say?"

"Yes, Jess Gemalto."

"Well, good for him. A person's got to be who they are. Live your truth. If anyone else has a problem with it, screw 'em."

I blurted a laugh. Whether because of Jerry's age or his white-ness or straightness, or his baffling reverence for Ronald Reagan, I had once again underestimated him.

"So. Back to who might want the magician dead?" he said. "Let's run through the standard-issue reasons why people decide they hate one another." He pointed a biscuit in my direction. "Go."

"Family dispute."

"An oldie but a goodie. Keep going."

"Emotional torment."

"A variation of the theme, but point taken."

"Physical abuse. Trash talking, telling lies. Racism. Religion. Getting screwed in a business deal. Greed. Infidelity. Jealousy."

I stopped, noting his changed expression.

He snapped his fingers. I cringed at the sound, fearing for his fragile bones. "The way you tell it, Kennedy was a highly paid performer, living a glamorous life. Few people can afford to stay at a five-star hotel, let alone in a suite."

I gasped. "It was a fan frustrated with their own crappy life. They were jealous of Kennedy's luxurious lifestyle." Jerry's gri-mace deflated my enthusiasm. "Either your tea is cold, or I just said something stupid. Since the pot is still hot . . ."

"I think you got that last bit right. But you need to rethink the first."

Rewinding my words, I slowly muttered, "Kennedy's good life . . . a fan wanted that good life . . . couldn't have it for themselves . . . got frustrated and angry." I shrugged. "I don't get it."

"Try again. What's the motive we're playing with?"

"Jealousy."

"So? What's to be jealous of?"

I threw my hands up in exasperation. "We've been through that already. Kennedy's lifestyle."

"Follow the money."

Suddenly it hit me. "Her job! Kennedy's new artistic director gig would pay her a million-dollar salary."

Jerry grinned as he reached for another biscuit. "City after city booked. Pricey tickets. Sold-out shows." He took a slow sip and lowered his cup. "Surely you've heard the expression 'the show must go on.'"

"That's it!" I raised a biscuit triumphantly in the air. "The show must go on! So who gets the artistic director job now?"

Jerry smiled broadly, showing off his large white dentures. "Now that's a question worth answering."

Chapter Eleven
Knock, Knock

Rain. Most days the rain didn't get me down, but today for some reason I found it irritating. The *thwap, thwap, thwap* of the windshield wipers, the chill in the air, and my soaked Converse sneakers conspired to darken my mood. I raced from the carport and up the stairs to my second-floor studio. At the door, I slipped off my shoes and padded in damp socks across the floor to the bathroom. I hung my jacket over the shower faucet for drip-drying—one of the countless practical pointers that my mom had taught me, and because of that, it never failed to make me a bit sad. After exchanging my socks for slippers, I got comfy on the loveseat and fired up my laptop.

Jerry was right: I should focus on those who would benefit from Kennedy's death. Two hours and dozens of online news articles later, I learned there had been three finalists to fill the role of artistic director. The two runners-up were both veteran performers with Mysterium.

The first was Kit Durango. Raised by a struggling single mother in a small Colorado ranching town, Kit had achieved initial fame as a rodeo cowgirl. She had since defied her humble beginnings and grown a ginormous fan base with a comedy act involving audience members, precision shooting, and rope tricks.

The other woman rumored to have been considered for the top job was Yazminka Smilova. Were Yazminka's beauty a book, it would be shelved between Taylor Swift and Jennifer Lawrence. Yaz, as her celebrity friends called her, was all about style. While swaddled in an animal-print leotard, she would attach her hair bun to a cable suspended from high in the big tent's rafters and to the accompaniment of a violin-rock track, spin by the bun fifty feet above a crowd's gaping mouths.

In researching Yazminka, I found another fascinating fact: her father, Boris Smilov, was Mysterium's owner. According to several investigative reports, he had moved from Russia to Romania and become extravagantly rich thanks to a web of criminal enterprises and associations with former Eastern Bloc government officials. At first I thought it odd that someone of such wealth would bother with a relatively small business. But my further digging unearthed that Mysterium was among dozens of shows operated by a holding company called Smilov Entertainment Group. Yazminka's brother, Sasha, traveled with Mysterium as the head of operations.

Considering the three finalists for the lucrative lead role, I was somewhat impressed that Boris Smilov had not rewarded his daughter with the job. Pretty and privileged people had enough going for them as it was. As for Kit, from everything I'd read, she was a decent person and a fan favorite.

A few clicks later, I confirmed that Kit and Yazminka remained Mysterium headliners. I guessed that the odds favored them staying at the Park Olympic Hotel. I phoned Hollister, told her what I'd learned from my online search, and posed my theory. After a long silence, she said, "Okay. Nice work. Now we need to confirm whether Kit and . . . what's her name again?"

"Yazminka."

"Sounds like a supermodel. Don't tell me, size-two dress?"

"Why you'd think I'd know her dress size is beyond me, but judging by the online photos and videos, yes, she's a twig."

Hollister harumphed. "As I was saying, we need to find out whether those other performers are guests at the Park Olympic. While you're at it, find out which rooms they're in. Get the room numbers. Remember what we discovered about the sixth-floor layout?"

Skipping past the insinuation that the task was mine alone to do, I went with the easy answer: "Yep. The suites are all clustered together at the south end. Two off each foyer."

"Exactly."

I understood what Hollister was getting at. The proximity of the rooms made for a convenient crime. Is that what bothered me? I couldn't envision the killer relaxed in bed, casually flipping channels or perusing the mini-fridge to the sounds of the police commotion in the room next door. How could anyone stay composed throughout that? Wouldn't a killer want to put maximum distance between themself and the crime? I know I would. But mine was not the mind of a killer. Maybe to solve this mystery, I needed to try and adopt such a mindset.

"Hayden?"

"Sorry, I'm here. I was just thinking."

"We on the same page? We agreed that the next step is to find out if those two other Mysterium chicks are staying in the other suites?"

I sighed, realizing the topic of job assignments couldn't be put off any longer. "About that . . . First, why is that my job? And second, how do you suggest—"

"Sorry, little dude. I have a client emergency. And yes, this *is* supposed to be a vacation week. But I'm the boss. Crap rolls uphill. I just need the morning, then I can refocus on the case. In the meantime, it shouldn't be too hard for you to find out where Yazminka and Kit are staying. Why not knock on each hotel room door and see who answers?"

After letting the notion settle for a moment, I warmed to the idea. Sarah Lee's ease in accessing the sixth floor confirmed that the elevator didn't require a keycard. And going solo had an advantage. One stranger—especially yours truly—at the door would be more disarming than two. And let's be frank. My size, red hair, and freckled complexion exuded all the danger of a Muppet, whereas Hollister's Mohawk, muscular stature, and leather jacket could easily make a guest wary.

An hour later, I stepped onto the plush hallway carpeting of the Park Olympic Hotel's sixth floor. I checked my hair in the mirror above the sitting area opposite the elevator. Recalling the floor plan, I walked to the east end of the corridor, toward the suites.

Any question about which room had belonged to Kennedy would have been answered by the yellow barricade tape strung across the doorway of number 611. The reminder of the crime scene must be unnerving for whoever occupied the room opposite. Or had management moved that guest to another room? However, these two rooms and the two in the adjacent foyer were the hotel's only suites. From what I had gleaned from websites and social media, I could imagine Kit accepting a downgrade, but not Yazminka.

I turned to the broad black lacquered door opposite 611. I took a deep breath, knocked on suite 610, and smiled up at the peephole. My second knock stirred movement within. The sliding of a dead bolt preceded the door's opening.

"Oh, hello." The person standing inside the doorway was not whom I'd expected. He couldn't have been much older than me and was at most four inches taller, or around five feet eight inches. He wore only a pair of body-hugging black boxer briefs and spoke with what I guessed was an Eastern European accent, though, with only three syllables to go on, I wasn't entirely sure.

"Oh, sorry," I sputtered. "I must have the wrong room."

He narrowed his slightly crossed ice-blue eyes. "Did you bring the extra towels?" This time he said enough to confirm that he was indeed who I thought: one of the Adrenalin! Romanian acrobats. At some point on his journey to adulthood, he'd developed the body of a god. That I had no towels, nor was I dressed as hotel staff (nor did I look like a Scandinavian male model) explained the guy's expression.

"Sorry," I managed. "I made a mistake."

His eyes, or one of them, anyway, fixed on mine. He grinned. "You sure about that?"

Time stretched. I felt my ears getting hot. I couldn't think of anything to say. I stared at the wisps of black hair on his sculpted chest.

He took a step back into the room and opened the door wider. "Come in?"

"I . . . I'm afraid I don't have your towels."

"Yeah, I noticed."

Stepping inside room 610 was like stepping into a movie set where I'd been mistaken for the actor who was *supposed* to be in the scene. My sneakers sank into carpet so plush I envied the guy's bare feet—curiously, he'd painted his toenails to match his underwear. A dozen or so large trunks and several wheeled clothes racks occupied the spacious suite of soft blues and beige. Each rolling rack was crammed with clothing hidden within bright red garment bags. I imagined it would have taken a large SUV to cart all the luggage from the airport, and then required the bell staff to make more than one trip up in the elevator to transport the entire wardrobe to the room.

"Close that, would you?" the guy said. "My friend's pain-in-the-arse brother is staying in a nearby suite, and he'll get all up in my business if he catches me using her room."

I spun around, shut the door. When I turned back, he was gone. I assumed he'd hurried into the next room to pull on some clothes. While waiting—for what I couldn't guess—I marveled at the room's unobstructed view of the Puget Sound and the Olympic Mountains. I often took for granted the beauty of the place I called home. As I turned away from the window, I noticed several women's wigs—one brown, one black, one blond, all big hair—resting on stands.

"Those are for me if you can believe it."

I spun around. The guy returned to the room, still wearing only briefs and carrying a heap of towels. Noticing the look on my face, he added, "My friend borrowed them for me from work. I didn't want to ask. Not that I care what anyone thinks about my doing drag, but the woman who manages our costumes is a bit terrifying." He grinned.

I chose a nod as the safest reply.

"I only wear one at a time, though." He laughed at his joke and dropped the pile of damp towels into my awaiting arms.

"The bath in my hotel doesn't even have a decent shower. There's a steam and sauna in there." He tilted his head toward the bathroom. "My friend said I could use it while she's out. But she'll have my balls if I leave a mess."

My porno fantasy had lasted for less than a minute. I spun around to leave, but his hand caught my shoulder.

"I didn't catch your name," he said, his mouth close to my ear.

"Hayden," I answered before thinking. Was it wise to give him my real name? He could check with the hotel, and I'd be found out as a fraud. I was posing as someone I wasn't and had entered a private room under those false pretenses. Was that a crime? I suddenly felt queasy.

He squeezed my shoulder, "Pleasure, Hayden. I'm Vlad. So you're sure you need to hurry off?"

Buzz . . . buzz . . . buzz

"Just a sec." He jogged to the coffee table and scooped up his phone. "Crap. It's my friend. She's back early. Sorry, man, you gotta go." Alarmed, he hurried past me and opened the door. Matching his urgency, I stepped out. When I was two steps down the hallway, he called my name. I looked back at his head poking out from around the doorframe.

"Room 310, Queen Anne Inn," he said with a sly grin before shutting the door.

Lugging the heap of wet towels, I headed toward the elevator. When I passed a doorway to the stairwell, I dumped the towels inside—*my apologies, housekeeping*.

As the elevator doors opened, a woman I recognized from pictures as Yazminka Smilova stepped out in absurdly tall black riding boots. Her long, blond, French-braided hair was draped over a shoulder and down the front of her ripped denim overalls. And she wore a lemon-yellow silk fez hat and an opulent pearl necklace. The fragrance of fresh-cut grass filled my nose as she brushed past me. If our eyes had met, I couldn't tell; hers were hidden behind black designer shades the size of ski goggles.

Once in the lobby, I took stock of what I'd learned. First, room 610 belonged to Yazminka Smilova but was being used by an insanely sexy and slightly cross-eyed acrobat named Vlad. He'd said he and Yazminka were friends, but that didn't explain his presence in her hotel suite. While he was good-looking enough to be seen on Yazminka's arm, why would her boyfriend stay in a different hotel? Were they on the down-low? Speaking of which, he'd just invited me to his hotel room. Jerry had taught me to methodically rule out the possibilities en route to the most probable, which Vlad's chiseled physique answered. He must be bi and involved with Yazminka. As for his staying elsewhere, his role in the show must not qualify him for five-star accommodations of his own.

I decided to wait an hour before returning to the sixth floor to discover who, if anyone, answered the doors to the other two suites. That would also give me time to make another decision: whether to swing by the Queen Anne Inn afterward.

Chapter Twelve
Mates on Dates, Post No. 23

Although I felt disloyal for ducking into a coffee shop other than Slice, Grounds Zero was just around the corner from the hotel, alongside the steps leading from Pike Place Market to the waterfront. On the way there, I grabbed my laptop from the trunk of my car. With an hour to kill, I could write a new post. After doing some research, I had decided to move Mates on Dates to a private subreddit group, where I could control who could view my content (read: keep it away from parents' and students' eyeballs) by approving community members after I'd confirmed their identity (read: verified applicants were my friends). I archived past posts, wiped the blog, and invited my current followers to join me over at Reddit.

MATES ON DATES: More Than Our Parts
We've all been there. A bit of innocent, playful texting on a dating app leads to this: *Send pics?* This request is rarely satisfied with a photo of you and your high school girlfriend—even with her face blurred, which I have to say, has always struck me as rude—or of you enjoying ice cream sundaes on a summer holiday with

your parents. What the guy on the other end of the exchange wants to see is you. Naked. I'm no prude, but could there be anything less romantic? Mind you, if your purpose is to get busy with maximum speed and efficiency, then sure, why not cut to the money shots and progress straightaway to assessing fit? However, if you're looking for a date that might lead to a second and, should the gay stars magically align, yet another, then I ask you: Is it wise to bare it all so soon?

You might wonder what set my mind on this topic. I just met a guy (I'll call him Trevor). Skipping the hard-to-explain circumstances, I saw Trevor in his underwear within the first few minutes of us in the same room. As best as I can recall, the following thoughts shot through my brain in lightning-fast succession: *Wow! Don't stare. Seriously? How can I not? This is so exciting! You should be embarrassed for being so easily aroused. Stop staring. Oh c'mon, when will something like this ever happen again?*

That's pretty much how it went before I was hurried out the door (another one of my long stories for another day, if ever). The entire event, by the way, lasted no longer than five minutes. Tops.

A part of me wants very much to see Trevor again. But I am conflicted. Now that I've seen him in only his undies, all my thoughts of him gravitate to the physical. Honestly, it's all I can think about. But is it helpful that my primary interest is his body? And here's the kicker, guys! It goes both ways. How would I feel about his only interest in me being about *my* body? Are we not more than our parts?

Many of you might be saying, "Don't be such a prude, Hayden. That doesn't mean you can't go on to have a long-lasting relationship." Fair point. It can happen, sure. But when you go there right off the bat, you race past the fun of flirtation and the tummy-twisting anticipation that distinguishes dating from hooking up.

So the next time you're about to share a carefully filtered pic of you flexing in front of a bathroom mirror wearing nothing but a smoldering look, ask yourself: What do I want out of this encounter? If it's a steamy, no-strings romp, by all means, hit "Send." However, if you're like me and desire something longer lasting, I urge you to proceed more slowly. Skip the romantic buildup, and you'll miss discovering those things about each other that are more than just your parts.

Till next time, I'm Hayden
And remember, if you can't be good, be safe!

Chapter Thirteen

She *Really* Likes You

Back at the Park Olympic Hotel, my knocks on doors 612 and 613 off the other foyer went unanswered.

Time for plan B. I retrieved the blank greeting card I had just purchased at a nearby stationery shop, wrote *Kit Durango* and *Room 613* on the envelope, and stepped up to the front desk. The pleasant-looking woman behind the counter wore a brass name tag telling me her name was Penny and that she hailed from Alaska.

"I'm not sure whether I have the right room number," I said. "I'm pretty sure Kit said 613 on the phone, but in her text, she wrote 612." I smiled amiably as Penny tapped a few keys. "Ms. Durango is in suite 613. Would you like me to have that sent up?"

"That would be swell, thanks."

Swell? I'd been hanging out too much with Jerry.

I recapped what I'd learned about which room was whose: Kennedy had been staying in suite 611; Yazminka had set up camp across from her in 610; and Kit Durango's suite, 613, was off the adjacent foyer and directly across from 612, which, by process of elimination, must belong to Yaz's brother, Sasha.

On my way out to the street, I tipped my invisible hat to the doorman. As tempting as it was, I couldn't follow up on Vlad's invitation to visit him at his hotel. However casual the encounter might be, Vlad was close—oddly close—with Yazminka. I couldn't risk stirring up anything that might compromise our investigation. Each day Burley's worries about Sarah Lee were growing stronger, as were mine. She was sure the police considered Sarah Lee the prime suspect and that they were working feverishly, not to find the real killer, but to put together enough evidence to charge her friend with the crime. Until we heard from Jess Gemalto (and he heard something from the police), Hollister and I could do nothing for Burley besides offering reassurances, which even I had started to doubt. There was another reason I skipped a visit to the Queen Anne Inn and room 310.

Vlad wasn't Camilo.

Camilo, Camilo, Camilo. The Venezuelan dancer-slash-computer science student-slash-dog dad's effect on me was overwhelming—and he didn't even know it. I liked to think I was a reasonably sane human being. But whenever Camilo was nearby or merely in my head, I turned into a crazy person. My longing for him was unhealthy, but I hadn't the willpower to pull free of his orbit. That he didn't return my feelings had been pretty well established. He had never clearly indicated that he liked me as anything more than a friend. I say "clear" because he only ever sent confusing signals. Never did Camilo not greet me with a hug, but the same went for all his friends, none of whom could escape being wrapped in his muscular arms and squeezed tightly for a beat longer than one might expect. And how many times had Camilo ignited my excitement with a suggestive remark whispered in my ear, only to turn and say the exact same thing to another guy? Being in

Camilo's presence never failed to tie my stomach in knots and make me feel like the gay village idiot for holding out hope. *It had to stop.* I needed to take the advice I dished out in Mates on Dates and become a champion of my self-worth. I needed to quit—once and for all—wishing and waiting for Camilo Rodriquez.

Reading the text that lit up my phone, I couldn't help but feel that someone upstairs thought it would be a laugh to test the strength of my seconds-old conviction.

Camilo:

Hey, buddy. It's been way too long since we had some 1 on 1 time. Game?

One-on-one time? What did he mean by that? And didn't "way too long" suggest an activity we'd done before? Camilo and I had never had sex, just a night spent cuddling (which I'd replayed in memory a bajillion times over). The only other occasions that might qualify as one-on-one time were a few minutes here and there at Slice or Burley's house when we'd been left alone. He couldn't mean those random moments, could he? As usual, Camilo's communication was maddeningly ambiguous. While my thoughts played bumper cars between my ears, my fingers took the wheel.

Game for what exactly?

I stared at the phone, waiting for his comeback. Would he accurately read the annoyance in my words? *Good!* I reconsidered my reply. Ugh. He could just as easily interpret my text as flirtatious. Why was I relieved by that? *Dammit!* This was precisely my problem. As minutes clicked by on my Spider-Man watch, my outrage returned. *Typical.* No sooner had I committed to a Camilo communications blackout than my phone buzzed, alerting me to another text.

Dunno—hang?

Careful to aim for the pillows on my bed, I threw my phone. *Lame, lame, lame!* As infuriated as I was, another insidious thought weaseled its way into my brain: I wondered if Vlad might be in his room.

This was no time to think. I had to act. It had been too long, and it would do me good. I reached for my running shoes. Locking the door behind me, I knotted the door key into the laces. I raced down the steps and dashed past my car. Lincoln Park was a half mile from my apartment. I needed to clear my mind. I would run it out on my usual five-mile loop.

Three miles in, I was startled by an older woman dressed in a green velvet tracksuit, curiously effective camouflage in the thickly wooded area.

"Oh, young man, thank heavens," she said with labored breath. "My dog. Her name is Alice. She's run away. She's usually well behaved off her leash, but she saw a squirrel and was gone in a flash. Would you help me look for her? I'd be ever so grateful."

After I'd learned that Alice was an extremely friendly two-year-old Dalmatian, I set off with a promise to keep an eye out for the dog. If I should see her, I'd do my best to catch her. As I emerged from the thicket of evergreens and ferns, I caught a glimpse of fast-moving spots before they disappeared behind a utility shed up ahead. As I approached, I slowed to a walk and called, "Alice!" It turns out the dog's owner hadn't overstated Alice's friendliness. She bolted around the corner of the building and, head down, four legs pumping, ran straight for me.

"Hey, Alice! Hey, girl!" I crouched and opened my arms.

The dog ran into me, and I fell back with a laugh. Her tail whipped in a happy frenzy as she set about cleaning my face with her tongue.

"Okay, okay, okay. That's enough." Shielding my head with an arm, I sat up on my knees and grabbed hold of her collar before any further squirrel sightings occurred. A minute later, the woman in the green tracksuit appeared in the distance. Seeing Alice and me, she waved and shouted as she ran-walked in our direction.

"Oh, thank heavens! You're a lifesaver." She leaned down and snapped a leash onto Alice's matching collar. "Oh, she likes you."

"Yes. She's a friendly one, all right."

"No, I mean, she *really* likes you."

I climbed to my feet and gave Alice a scratch behind the ears. The woman rummaged in her fanny pack. "Could I get your name and address? I'd like to send a little something for your trouble."

I waved away the offer. "No need. Really. Happy I could help."

"No, no, I insist," she said. "Call me old-fashioned, but I'd like to. Mind, if you expect anything monetary, you'll be disappointed."

I was intrigued to discover what she might send me as thanks. Crocheted toaster cozy? Sachet of hard candies? A jar of home-made marmalade? The prospect of receiving any of those items delighted me immeasurably. Besides, I didn't want to come across as rude. I scribbled my name and address onto her small notepad.

Back home, I fell back on my bed. I should shower, sticky as I was. But too drowsy, I closed my eyes. Seconds from sleep, my phone rang.

"Little dude, you up?"

"You asked me that the last time you called in the middle of the afternoon."

"And like last time, I'm outside your door."

Chapter Fourteen
You're a Dead Woman

With no small amount of pride, I filled Hollister in on what I'd found out at the Park Olympic, highlighting my encounter with the acrobat Vlad—his apparently close relationship with Yazminka Smilova—and confirming that Yaz, Kit Durango, and Sasha Smilov occupied the other sixth-floor suites. As I talked, she flipped the switch on the kettle, step one in making herself a pour-over coffee. Rummaging in the fridge for a bag of beans, she said behind the open door, "It's about time you put on your big-boy pants—or took them off—and made a bold move."

So surprising was her reaction to my independent sleuthing that I found myself searching for a suitable reply.

"Did you move the filters?" she asked.

"Cupboard on the left."

"I mean, Camilo is a lost cause if you ask me, which, I've noticed, you never do. This Vlad dude, however. He sounds hot. I have a cousin with a lazy eye, but I know it's not the same thing as being cross-eyed. Anyway, good to hear the acrobat is interested. I hope you two had fun." She let a beat pass before adding, "Within reason."

Suddenly Hollister's reaction made sense. The "bold move" she'd referred to was not my solo act of visiting the hotel. She had mistakenly connected the dots of my story, believing that I had hooked up with Vlad.

Before I could correct her, Hollister said, "So seriously, nice detective work, little dude. Recognizing it's too early in the investigation to know for sure, I got a hunch our bad guy is one of those two circus chicks staying next door."

I wasn't so sure. In fact, I was hunch-less. My head swirled with competing thoughts. Jess Gemalto argued that the murderer was someone known by the victim. Jerry encouraged me to follow the money: Who stood to gain by Kennedy's death? Hollister was apparently focused on who was most proximate to the crime. And still, there was the disheveled blond woman Gwyneth Lang had pointed out in the video, not to mention dozens of other Mysterium cast and crew members. Oh, and I still wasn't ready to fully exonerate Sarah Lee.

For the past few weeks, Hollister had been reliving her Mary J. Blige era, so I wasn't surprised to hear "Real Love" when her phone rang in her pocket. The half of the conversation I could hear didn't sound encouraging. But the look of increasing alarm on her face caused me to sit up straight, listening intently for clues to the caller's identity. The mystery was solved when she finally said, "Got it. We'll be there in thirty minutes. Thanks, Jess."

I pulled on my shoes as she poured her coffee into my insulated mug. Jess had called an emergency meeting. Ten minutes later, Hollister skidded Mo to a stop inches before a railroad crossing gate and smacked her palm against the steering wheel. "Dammit."

"You need to relax. We'll get there. Preferably in one complete piece, please."

She gave me a look. The look that said, *"Don't. Even. Start."*

Knowing I couldn't possibly win, I switched on the stereo. The album that spilled from the speakers was one of three I would have guessed: Ms. Blige's *Share My World*. Remarkable how the right music can immediately improve the vibe. We sat peaceably rocking to the rhythm until four songs later a blaring bell signaled the raising of the crossing gate. Hollister's boot hit the gas pedal.

Burley had reserved Slice's largest table nearest the kitchen. Jess sat facing the entrance, wearing an outfit similar to the one he'd worn when I'd first met him: a white pressed shirt and a paisley bow tie. Seeing Hollister and me arrive, he waved and smiled. Never would I get used to there being someone who looked like my far better-dressed twin—with terrific hair. Unlike sharing mannerisms, interests, or perspectives with a person, I'd discovered that wearing a freakishly similar body united you with someone in a special way. Before meeting Jess, I had no reason to consider whether the face I saw in a mirror was mine. To whom else could it belong? But now, another human being saw what I saw when eyeing their reflection. How weird was that? When I watched Jess, it was as if I were observing me as others did. Perhaps that was the nature of the bond I felt with him: when people looked at us, they saw the same thing, and based on that alone, they formed judgments. Jess and I were not only equals but equivalents—at least by outward appearance.

We sat with Jess at the makeshift conference table. Seeing that we'd arrived, Sarah Lee and Burley came out from behind the counter and joined us. To say Sarah Lee looked haggard would have been a compliment. Her face had more creases than a rumpled sheet, and she'd pulled her usually well-kept long blond hair into a slapdash ponytail bound with a white shoelace, as if in homage to Burley's style.

Surprising myself, I laid a hand gently on her shoulder. She returned a surprise of her own by not shrugging it off.

Getting right down to business, Jess said, "I'm afraid, there's been a development. As you're Sarah Lee's best friends, she asked that I fill all of you in at once."

Hollister and I traded quick glances. Was this true? We were Sarah Lee's best friends? Could that truly be what she considered us? Or had the stress of being a person of interest in a murder investigation muddled her wits?

Jess paused for a moment, consulting his notes. "Now, before we start, let's agree to keep everything said among us confidential. Having this type of conversation in a public space or with anyone other than my client and an immediate family member is highly unusual. But Sarah Lee insisted I include you in this conversation. Sarah Lee and Burley were here already, and I was nearby, so the bakery provided an expeditious location."

"Besides, law offices give me the legal jeebies," Burley added, shifting her weight on the chair, which protested with a worrisome cracking of wood.

Jess continued, "I've learned that the police have discovered some questionable communications between Sarah Lee and Ms. Osaka."

Responding to Sarah Lee's quick intake of breath, Burley enveloped her hand in her own, squeezing it reassuringly. Whether Sarah Lee's slight whimper and teary eyes were due to the unintentional force of the gesture or Jess's impending news I couldn't be sure.

"What?" Hollister sat taller. "What sort of communications?"

Jess placed his hands flat on the table in what I read as a practiced display of control, conveying steadiness to anxious clients. "Texts, I'm afraid. Texts from Sarah Lee to Kennedy Osaka. Five in number. All were sent to Ms. Osaka within ninety minutes of her murder. Tonally, the messages express an escalating pitch of aggressiveness. Moreover, the wording of one particular message is not helpful."

Hollister and I looked at Sarah Lee. Burley stared straight across the table, eyes unblinking, at Jess.

"Well?" Hollister said.

Jess read from his yellow legal pad. "First text, sent by Sarah Lee at 5:48 PM: *See you in a few. Park in back.*"

I breathed a sigh of relief. Nothing bad there. If anything, thoughtful.

"Next, sent 6:01 PM. *You nearly here?*"

A reasonable question—nothing to be concerned about.

"Third, sent 6:06 PM. *Hello? We said 6.*"

Hollister wriggled her shoulders—her tell of feeling anxious.

"Fourth, sent 6:13 PM. *Call me. You're late!*"

Factual.

"Fifth, sent 6:17 PM: *???*"

Ambiguous.

"Final text, sent 6:31 PM. *Seriously? You're a dead woman.*"

A long silence.

Sarah Lee groaned. "It's not what it looks like," she said. "I was pissed, okay? By the time I sent that last text I knew. I knew Kennedy wasn't going to show up. She's always been like that. Why I put up with it for so long . . ." Sarah Lee shook her head, loosening the shoelace and her ponytail. "In high school, I covered for her. I swore to her parents that she was staying overnight when she was actually with her boyfriend. Then in college, I can't begin to tell you how many papers I wrote for her. She promised to return the favor by helping me with calculus. I got a D. So, yeah. Big help there. Kennedy has been in my life for nearly two decades, and it's only ever been one-way traffic."

Another silence.

"But why?" Burley asked. "Why put up with her selfish nonsense for so long?"

As uncomfortable as I was with the sharing, I'd be lying if I said I wasn't curious to hear the answer.

Sarah Lee snuffled. Jess handed her a paper napkin. "I know how I can be. I'm trying to be . . . less annoying. Growing up, I didn't have any friends. Not really. Then Kennedy came along, and suddenly I didn't have to eat alone in the cafeteria. More than that, she was a knockout. Very popular. She was our high school's head cheerleader."

I threw a wry look at Hollister.

Pressing on, Sarah Lee said, "You can pretty much fast-forward the next twenty-plus years. Then I met you guys. Finally, I made a few real friends."

That I could be touched by anything Sarah Lee might say was surprising. That it involved me was nothing short of a shock. Had her previous orneriness toward me been a defense? Now wasn't the time to delve into our dysfunctional past, but once we got on the other side of this mess, I vowed I would try to be more of a friend to her, if she was willing and provided her usual crankiness didn't return.

"I promised myself I was done taking Kennedy's crap. But when I was searching for entertainment for our fundraiser and realized Mysterium and Kennedy would be in town, I decided to reach out one final time. She owed me. Plus, it was for a good cause."

The word *final* seemed to reverberate across the table.

In full defense mode, Hollister said to Jess, "Sorry, but why is this even a thing? Since when is texting someone who's late considered damning evidence? How did you even find out about the texts?"

"I can only say that the police department is like any other organization. It is an assemblage of people. And people talk. Part of my job is forming relationships with people. I think you get my meaning. As you'll understand, the messages don't come across very well without proper context. But rest assured. I will provide that context. That is part of my job."

"Okay, I get that, but what do we do about it?" Hollister said, flashing a hard look at Jess. "Knowing that the cops think Sarah Lee sent Kennedy threatening texts just before she was murdered just adds worry on top of worry."

I winced at Hollister's combative tone and hoped that Jess understood her anxiety was because of the situation.

"Listen," Jess said, "We all need to accept that this is an extremely unpleasant business. A murder investigation is bound to stir up anxiety. I won't sugarcoat or conceal anything. I'm assuming that's an approach you agree with. However, if I've gotten that wrong, I will certainly understand if you feel you need to go a different direction."

Burley jumped in, "You're not going anywhere, Jess. You are Sarah Lee's lawyer. No ifs, ands, or butter cookies."

Sarah Lee nodded, tears streaming down her pink cheeks.

I was impressed by Jess. He was in command and unapologetic about his role as leader, but low key and accommodating when dealing with clients' emotions. This approach instilled much-needed confidence in a stressful situation. I sensed that Hollister, who wasn't comfortable anywhere but in the driver's seat, was pleased to have Jess take the wheel.

"That settles it," Hollister declared. "You keep doing your lawyer thing, and Hayden and I will continue running the investigation."

"Investigation?" Jess said, suddenly alarmed. "Are you actually conducting one?"

"We've already been to the hotel, interviewed the security manager, and reviewed the video footage. We're making solid progress."

Jess's eyes saucered, his face flushed with alarm. "At this stage, I don't believe an investigation is required. But if you are determined, I know people. Professionals who—"

"No, no." Hollister waved a hand in the air. "Hayden and I got this."

Unconvinced, Jess continued, "The police are investigating as we speak. A celebrity was murdered in a swanky downtown hotel. The police are motivated to solve this. The best action for us at the moment is to take a deep breath and let them do their jobs. I know it feels wrong to do nothing, but that doesn't mean others—namely, professional homicide detectives—aren't working their tails off to find Ms. Osaka's real killer."

Hollister stared at Jess as if peering over readers, "So you're saying what? Trust the police to get it right?"

Jess dropped his head in defeat. I got where he was coming from, but he didn't know Hollister as I did. She had legit reasons for her doubts.

Slowly, Jess raised his head. "Okay, okay. I can see I won't convince you not to do whatever you intend to do. But the less I know, the better. No. Scratch that. Don't tell me anything."

"Deal, Counselor." Hollister nodded. "Unless, of course, it's something we feel you need to know."

"Oh, brother," I moaned.

Chapter Fifteen
Half Full

"You do know, hon. We can't always know God's plan. But that doesn't mean he doesn't have one and that things won't turn out all right. You just need to have faith, Hayden. That's our job. We just need to have faith."

I held the phone away from my ear and gazed up at the ceiling. My trust in protection from above extended only as far as my apartment's patched white ceiling. My Aunt Sally meant well, but I found her unwarranted optimism maddening. Still, I knew better than to enter a debate. My odds of rewiring her fundamental belief system were as low as hers in changing mine. We had long ago reached a spiritual détente—an agreement she was dangerously close to violating.

"All right, all right. I know where you stand on such matters. I won't push. I'll just have to supply enough faith for the two of us. How's that sound?"

Appreciating her good intention, I replied with a relieved yet cautious, "Fair enough."

Aunt Sally's call, like all her calls, had arrived out of the blue. Caught off guard and being one thousand percent out of sorts,

I'd filled her in on the grim details of Hollister's and my current investigation. Once she'd issued her familiar platitudes, she pivoted to the reason she'd called in the first place: Jerry.

"Something's up with him," she said. "He's usually . . . so . . . so . . ."

"Chipper?"

"Exactly, yes. Chipper. Can I borrow that?"

"Public domain."

"What's that mean?"

"It's free to use."

"Oh! Marvelous!" Aside from salvation, Aunt Sally delighted at nothing more than a free offer or a deep discount. I could never visit her townhome without a detailed review of the most recent half-off of half-off deals she'd scored on lightly used furniture, no-name dishwashing detergent, or hand-crafted angel figurines from Etsy.

"Usually it wouldn't take much to get a laugh out of him, but today . . . not a blessed chuckle. Not even the hint of a smile. At first, I thought, *Oh boy, here we go. He's not feeling well. He's starting to slip.* When I asked if he needed to see a doctor, he nearly bit my head off. 'I need to see that pill-happy quack like I need a hole in the head' were his exact words. See what I mean? Not good."

"So why didn't you just—"

"Ask him what was bothering him? I did. He just flipped on the History Channel and said I was reading too much into him having a bad day. Well," she fretted, "I didn't buy it then. I don't buy it now."

I knew the reason for Jerry's bad mood: not enough money to pay for his latest prescription. Sharing that news would assuage Aunt Sally's concern that it wasn't something worse, but would betray Jerry's confidence. That I would not do. Jerry could qualify as a surrogate grandparent.

After promising Aunt Sally that I'd swing by Jerry's place to see if I agreed with her assessment and "do my darndest" to find out the cause of his being down in the dumps, I reached for my car keys. I'd already planned on driving over to his place.

Seattleites had an expression: "It doesn't rain a lot, just often." So it was unusual to need to switch the car's wipers to their fastest setting. This out-of-the-ordinary downpour, made worse by the water thrown onto my windshield from the semitruck in front of me, slowed my roll to forty on the highway. I gripped the wheel tighter and leaned forward as if those three inches would increase visibility. Thirty minutes later, I pulled into Jerry's driveway, damp from humidity and stress sweat.

Jerry answered the door with a somber nod before turning toward the living room. He carefully lowered himself onto the sofa. That my ninety-one-year-old friend was still wearing pajamas signaled the situation was even worse than Aunt Sally had described. The television was blaring—had his hearing aid stopped working?—and most of a frozen dinner sat on the coffee table alongside a smudged glass of ice water. I surveyed the surroundings with a critical eye.

"Isn't it a bit premature to throw in the towel?"

"Now, don't you start. I got an earful from your aunt already today. I'll tell you the same thing I told her. I'm just having—"

"No, you're not. You're sulking. Or to borrow your own expression, you're 'wallowing.'"

Were it not for Andy Griffith shouting at the jury, I'd say an uncomfortable silence settled between us. When five minutes of commercials targeting older viewers—a walking cane, memory care facility, and denture adhesive—came and went, it became apparent he wasn't going to initiate conversation. The old Hayden, the pre-Hollister Hayden, would have muttered something about "another time, then" and retreated. But Jerry needed help—whether he would admit it or not. I had to step up.

I reached for the remote and shut off the TV. Jerry furrowed his bushy brows and started to bark something, but I cut him off. "Go to your room, young man, and get dressed. I'll clean up this sad excuse for dinner. You and I are going out to eat—my treat. And I won't take no for an answer. You need to get out of this house. *I* need to get out of this house. The current circumstance is too depressing for the both of us."

Again, Jerry started to say something, and once more, I spoke before he could get a word out. "I understand why you're upset, but this isn't your problem alone. It's *our* problem, and together we'll solve it. Now, get a move on. I'm getting hangry."

"Hmm," Jerry said, pulling himself up by gripping the arm of the sofa. "You just watch a PBS special on tough love or something?"

"No need." I gathered up the aluminum tray and drinking glass. "I simply channeled my inner Jerry. So you've no one but yourself to blame for missing Matlock's final argument."

He waved his hand at the now-silent television. "Spoiler alert—he wins."

* * *

"Seat belt," I said.

"Don't rush me."

"Sorry. I thought you forgot."

"Where are we going, anyway?"

"What sounds good?"

"Wouldn't say no to an enchilada." Jerry's voice carried an encouraging bounce.

I shifted into reverse. "That we can do."

The change in Jerry's mood was dramatic. My mini-intervention had, for the moment anyway, righted the Good Ship Jerry. Though I knew it was only a matter of time until the weight of his impending financial woes again threatened to push him under.

The parking lot at El Mirasol was mostly empty, reflecting the slow time long after lunch and a few hours before most customers would come in for dinner. We settled into a red Naugahyde booth. Jerry said, "Aren't you a bit young for early-bird specials?"

"Let's think of it as a pre–happy hour with entrées."

He smiled for the first time, "Now you're talking!"

Typically, I'd not have ordered a margarita at three in the afternoon, but Jerry wanted one—if only a few sips. And so our server brought the Cadillac to our table, split into two salted glasses. I glanced up from my mole poblano. The telltale gurgling sound of a straw sucking at an empty glass grabbed my attention. Jerry was a drinker only if by *drink* one meant tea. So I was more than a little surprised when he grinned and said, "Share another?"

I was driving, but another half was under the limit, so why not? Before I could agree, Jerry waved over our server.

Throughout our meal, I'd forced thoughts about the murder investigation to the corner of my mind, refusing to let them intrude on our boozy mid-afternoon supper. However, Jerry's financial troubles were front and center. I'd promised him we'd find a solution, but how? My money was tight, and what free time I had was committed to working with Hollister to clear Sarah

Lee's name. But helping one friend couldn't come at the expense of helping another.

As if I'd spoken my thoughts aloud, Jerry said, "So what's the latest scuttlebutt on your investigation?" He grinned. "I don't imagine the morale at the circus is too good. Even the clowns may be unable to turn those frowns upside down."

I rolled my eyes. "Don't quit your day job."

"Ha. My job is being a very old man, and I have tenure. Even I can't fire me."

"To answer your question, Hollister and I have only been to Mysterium once. And that was just a mini preview. Though with Hollister, she'll soon be wanting to"—I added air quotes—"'infiltrate the grounds.'"

"I recall you mentioning the murder weapon, scissors. Unusual, don't you think?"

"I do. A very odd choice. I mean, *hello!* This is America, land of a bazillion guns. I'm surprised they don't come in cereal boxes."

"Don't suggest that to the marketers."

We each took a sip of our drink.

Jerry continued, "Scissors just seem so peculiar."

"Sarah Lee made the same comment. Of the things she *does* remember, the scissors stood out most." I explained Jess's assertion that Sarah Lee was experiencing 'dissociative amnesia.'

He shrugged. "Those scissors are not incidental. Find out why the scissors were used and I think you'll find your killer. Or at least you will narrow the list of suspects down considerably."

As my brain absorbed that insight, our server returned to our table with our fresh margarita.

"Salud!" Jerry said, hoisting his half glass of margarita and looking happier than I'd seen him in a week. I'd managed to cheer him up, and now I needed to cut myself some slack. Tomorrow was a new day. Anything could happen. Camilo might pull his head out and confess his love! Jerry might win the lottery and be able to afford his new medication! Hollister and I might find a famous magician's killer!

"Cheers!" I replied, meaning it. With the back of my hand, I wiped salt from my lips.

Despite my natural default setting, I was determined to see my half-empty glass as half full, if only for the next half hour.

Chapter Sixteen
Wish Me Luck!

Eager to make progress in the case by narrowing the list of suspects, Hollister and I decided to visit Mysterium. Hollister piloted Mo into a parking space next to one of the many trailers that appeared to house dressing rooms, offices, and storage. To gain access to the grounds, we were posing as a reporter and photographer from a local newspaper. Hollister had borrowed a high-end camera from her on-again, off-again girlfriend, Mysti. My preparation consisted of donning a fedora (borrowed from our school's drama department) and tucking a wire-bound notebook under my arm. At the rear entrance, a guard reclined on a gray metal folding chair, his long skinny legs stretched out before him, blocking our path.

"Help you?" He peered up at us from beneath a sweat-stained cap embroidered with the Mysterium logo.

"We're from the *Seattle Examiner*," Hollister announced.

"Sorry, we're running a bit late," I added.

The guard made a labored show of sitting up. He reached into a box beside his chair and pulled out a clipboard. "Jenna ain't around. She didn't say anyone was coming by. She's usually pretty good about giving me a heads-up."

"I'm not surprised," I chuckled. "Jenna has been great. She's made everything easy-peasy. Usually, setting up interviews with performers of this caliber is a huge pain. But not with Jenna. She's a champ."

"Uh-huh," the guard replied, unimpressed. "You're not on the list, though. So . . ."

"Listen," Hollister said. "We don't have much time if we're going to get this promo piece into tomorrow's edition. I don't suppose management will be too stoked to find out they missed out on free publicity because—sorry, we didn't catch your name—"

"Dean."

"Dean," she repeated. Turning to me, she said, "Better write that down."

"Now, hold on," Dean said, now fully engaged.

"No, no. I get it, Dean," Hollister said. "You need to cover your ass. What sucks, though, is that this is one of those times when following the rules will come back to bite it. But, hey, we understand. Don't we, Chet?"

I nearly looked behind me before realizing Hollister was addressing me. "You know it, Bernice." Two could play this game.

Once we signed our names to the visitor sheet, Dean pointed us toward a cluster of trailers. "Dressing rooms are over there. Everyone but the solo performers share. In any case, you'll find the names on the doors. When Jenna comes back, I'll let her know you're here."

Hollister and I exchanged a concerned glance. "When do you expect her?" I asked.

"She just ran out for a bite of lunch. Should be back any minute."

"Super," I said. "Isn't that just super, Bernice?"

Hollister shot me a hard look. We hurried across the asphalt toward the dressing rooms. We rounded a corner. On impulse, I grabbed the leather arm of Hollister's jacket and pulled her to the side of the path.

"What the—"

"Shh," I scolded. "Look."

She followed my finger. Two guys, one on the other's shoulders, were pressed against the side of a distant trailer. The one on top was peering through a window. The next instant, he jumped down, and they both turned momentarily toward us before scrambling around to the back of the trailer just as a big bald man opened the door and clamored down the steps.

"Hey," Hollister said. "Wasn't that two of those Adrenaline! acrobat dudes?"

I nodded. I'd recently seen one of them up close: Vlad, the guy whom I had met unexpectedly in Yazminka Smilov's hotel suite.

We watched from the shadows as the large man swaggered past us. "Sasha Smilov," I said to Hollister once he was beyond earshot. There could be no mistaking Mysterium's director of operations from his voluminous online photo gallery. Exuding the charm of a hand grenade, he wore a faded Metallica T-shirt, tight ripped jeans, and heavy combat boots. Beneath his meticulously sculpted beard hung a Mr. T starter set of three thick gold chains, which lay nestled in a thatch of black hair.

I added, "You sure about the lesbian thing? See what you're missing."

The remark earned me a punch on the shoulder. "Ow!"

Time to resume our search for a star of the show. After passing by two trailers, each with four names indicating supporting cast members, we arrived at a door with "Kit Durango" written in red marker on a star-shaped decal. It was at that moment that I realized our plan had run its course.

"What now?"

My question was answered by Hollister's knuckles rapping on the door.

"It's open!" The voice from within the trailer sounded like expensive whisky, husky and smoothed out by warmth.

Hollister pointed her Mohawk toward the door, signaling me to enter first. I climbed the three steel steps and entered Kit Durango's trailer. In the background, new-country sensation Stanley Kellogg was purring his latest hit, "You Caught Me Good," with his telltale buttery twang. I blinked, taking in the dizzying effect of the room's interior. Cowboy hats, lariats, boots, belt buckles, chaps, vests, and even a large saddle—each of them an unexpectedly vibrant color—filled the small space. It was like viewing a tack room through a kaleidoscope.

"Hello? Ms. Durango?" I shouted over the music pouring from the speakers.

"Whoa," Hollister said, stepping into the room behind me. "Check this place out."

"Be right wich ya!" came the voice from behind a thin door.

The room was so cluttered I wondered whether anyone, even Kit herself, could find anything without rummaging about it. There was no place to sit unless I counted the simple wooden stool, but it had a white leather vest bedazzled with pink gemstones draped over it.

"Well, howdy-do!"

I spun around toward the voice.

"Sorry to keep y'all waitin'."

Looking at Kit Durango, I realized that I had only ever seen her publicity glamour shot on Mysterium's website and advertising posters. What her headshot hadn't shown was that she was on the chubby side. Her frilly skirt was tutu short, showcasing legs ending in fire-engine-red cowboy boots. Her long-sleeved denim shirt featured rhinestone buttons laddering up to a cheerful double chin, sparkling eyes, and a spotless white-on-white-on-white ten-gallon hat.

"Hello, Ms. Durango," I said. "I'm—"

"This is Chet," Hollister said.

"And may I introduce my colleague, Bernice."

"Pleasure to meet ya." Kit snatched up the vest on the stool and swung open the front door. "Y'all folla me."

For having such stubby legs, Kit moved with impressive speed. By the time Hollister and I stepped down from the trailer, Kit was already entering Mysterium's main tent through a wide opening marked "Cast and Crew Only." I traded shrugs with Hollister, and we hurried to catch up with the cowgirl performer.

The sudden transition from daylight to darkness was startling, as were the brilliant stage lights illuminating the large center ring surrounded by thirty-six rows of audience table settings rising steeply away and up toward the rafters. Kit had climbed a discreet staircase at the back of the stage and was stamping toward the center of the ring. At some point between the trailer and stage, she had acquired a rope and was swinging the loop end high above her head.

"No time to be shy, now! I need ya'll to come on up," Kit shouted at us.

"Who does she think we are?" I whispered to Hollister.

"How should I know? But I doubt we'll ever get another chance to be center stage at Mysterium. So screw it. What's the worst that can happen?"

"I'll remember you said that," I said to the back of Hollister's jacket as she headed for the stairs. How many times had my best friend put me in this type of position? Stay behind, feeling wimpy and unadventurous, or, despite my natural instincts, race after her while muttering profanities under my breath.

Watching Hollister strut onto the stage, I marveled at her fearlessness, not for the first time. Her unchecked courage had gotten us into trouble in the past. Still, it had been instrumental in us finding a missing friend, shutting down the nastiest of criminal enterprises, and in my journey of becoming less of a spectator of my own life. And so, in proper prizefighter form, I jogged boldly into the ring.

"Okay!" Kit shouted cheerily. "I only need one of you for this first trick." With her free hand, she pointed at Hollister, "You'll do fine. I'll do my darndest not to mess up that purdy hairdo of yours."

Hollister handed me the camera. "Anything happens to that, Mysti will dropkick your balls to Canada."

Two stagehands appeared and rolled into the ring a large wheel resembling the one on the *Wheel of Fortune* game show, except that instead of displaying numbers around the outside edge, it was upright and adorned with balloons matching the various colors of Kit's outfit. With help from a step stool, the stagehands strapped Hollister onto the wheel. Regardless of what Kit had in mind, what was Hollister thinking? She wasn't the type of person to take anything objectionable lying down—or upside down. She didn't have to go through with this—whatever *this* was.

Kit gazed up into the darkness toward the operations booth. "Hit it, fellers!"

Instantly, music blared from a constellation of massive black speakers suspended from cables high in the tent. The boot-stomping, fiddle-frantic track sounded ideal for a slapstick clown-car race at a rodeo. The stagehand reappeared and handed Kit a bundle of bowie knives. Looking frightened wasn't a good look for Hollister. Her eyes bugged. Her jaw clenched. Knowing she needed reassurance, I shouted, "You got this!" She glared in my direction and mouthed a spicy two-word reply.

The wheel started to spin.

Kit chuckled. "Hope this works! I can't bear seeing my mama's look of disappointment if I get her favorite trick wrong." She turned toward the empty audience seats and winked, rehearsing even her impromptu interactions with an imaginary crowd. The wheel spun faster. She did a little jig, shouted a wild *whoop!* and threw the first knife.

Pop! A balloon burst no more than twelve inches from Hollister's boot, spilling confetti onto the stage.

"Whoo-hoo!" Kit yelped. "I just might get the hang of this!"

Hollister spun faster.

Kit threw a succession of seven more blades, each of them popping a balloon encircling Hollister's body. When Kit had run out of knives, and the music's intensity dipped, I wanted to believe the dangerous part of the act had passed. But there was still one unpopped balloon—pinned to the wheel just an inch above Hollister's Mohawk.

The stagehand steered a mechanical bull into the ring. With surprising agility, Kit deftly mounted the bull and was handed an old-timey rifle as the bull was switched on and started to buck. The music sped up to a galloping pace. Kit drew the gun, readying her aim.

Playing to the empty seats, she hollered, "Never tried this before. Wish me luck!"

"No, no, no!" I sprinted into the ring between my best friend and the barrel of Kit's gun. "Stop!" I waved my arms. The music abruptly died. The wheel started to slow. Kit appeared crestfallen as the mechanical bull slowly rocked to a stop.

"Well, darn it all. That's a first. And I don't mean my shootin'. That's just something I say to the crowd to give 'em a laugh. So what gives?" Kit slid off the bull as the stagehand helped Hollister down from the wheel.

Hollister was in her mid-thirties. As far as I knew, she was fit, young, and in fine health. Never before had I had any reason to consider her mortality. But watching her spin on that wheel with knives thrown at her had nearly done me in. Then, when the rifle came out . . . well, there was no way that was happening if I could put a stop to it. Hollister meant a lot to me. Seeing her in such a life-threatening situation, I realized how much.

With the speed of an auctioneer, I explained to Kit that she had mistaken us for rehearsal stand-ins when we were, in truth, a reporter and photographer, from a small local newspaper, who'd come to conduct an interview. I raised the borrowed camera and my notebook as proof of our press credentials. Kit greeted the news with a whoop and a laugh.

"Y'all are good sports!" Kit clapped me on the back and pointed the brim of her ridiculously large cowgirl hat in Hollister's direction. "With opening night creepin' up, I can hardly think about anything but perfectin' the act. Mostly new tricks." Kit winked. "High stakes, considering I could just as easily skewer a person as not." She paused dramatically and lowered her voice as if in an aside. "Ain't nobody bought a ticket for that."

Kit pointed toward the employee entrance. "Folla me, kids. I'm parched. We can talk in the canteen."

Chapter Seventeen
Big-Top Gossip

Hollister and I sat across from Kit Durango in a double-wide trailer that served as both lounge and lunchroom for Mysterium's cast and crew. After a half-dozen softball questions about how Kit had gotten her start in comedy and roping, how long it took to develop the act, and what her fans had to look forward to next, we eased into questions about the murder of her colleague and would-have-been boss.

"Awful, awful, awful." Kit swung her head in lament. "I hear from someone on the crew that they caught some woman red-handed." She shook her head mournfully. "Same crew member said they released her the very next day, though. Don't make a lick of sense. Guilty is guilty where I come from. I'll tell you this, though, Kennedy Osaka had some funny ideas." She raised her brows.

"Funny? Funny how?" I said.

"Let's just say she didn't quite understand what our show is all about. Adults come here to escape from bosses and bills and babies. They come to be entertained. Kennedy had some half-baked notion of turning Mysterium into some no-fun affair where people didn't know when to clap, let alone have a reason to laugh or smile. She aimed to turn Mysterium into an opera when at its heart it's a hoedown."

Registering our baffled expressions, Kit explained more succinctly. "She had a mind to make some big changes to the show."

I recalled that when Hollister and I had met Kennedy after the preview, she'd spoken of her intention to reimagine the show, stamp it with her personal brand, and make it more refined and sophisticated.

"Any idea who might have wanted to harm Kennedy?"

Kit looked offended by the question. "Of course not. She may have had some goofy ideas, but those are just creative differences. People have them all the time, believe you me. Replacing light beer with prosecco at the concession stand is hardly worth killing a person over."

Hollister picked up the thread, saying, "Who else didn't agree with Kennedy's artistic direction?"

Kit smiled wryly. "Oh no, you don't." She locked her lips with a twist of her fingers. "Not on your life. The last thing we need around here is a bunch of big-top gossip."

Changing topics, I said, "Any word about when Mysterium's owner will announce a new artistic director? We understand that you were among the finalists for the job before it went to Kennedy. Might the job go to you? Has anyone with Smilov Entertainment Group said anything? Made any hints? What direction would you take the show if given the reins?"

Kit met the questions with a winning smile. "Oh golly. I'm just pleased to have a patch to do my thing. Just among us chickens, I'm not so sure I'm cut out for bossin' anybody. Prolly just a whole heap of headaches, if you ask me. Which I guess you are—asking me, that is." She let slip a giggle.

"Your modesty is commendable, Kit." I hovered my pen above a blank sheet of paper. "But our readers are dying to know. Are you going to be Mysterium's new artistic director?"

Kit cocked her head playfully and wagged a finger. "Now, now, I don't care how cute you are"—then, as she turned to Hollister—"or what a good sport you are, missy. But you won't charm me into spillin' any beans. That's a job for Mysterium's mucky-mucks. When they decide on a new director, they'll tell the press when and how it suits 'em."

"Where were you the night Kennedy was killed?" Hollister asked. "I imagine the hotel must have been a chaotic scene."

Kit leaned forward. "Off the record?"

I glanced at Hollister. My throat suddenly dry, I croaked, "Yes, if you'd like."

Kit's eyes darted right and left to ensure no one else was within earshot. "Chaos doesn't begin to describe that all-mighty ruckus," she said softly, then sat back. "First, you should know I have a heck of a time sleepin'. Oh, it's dreadful. Suffered with it for years. You've seen a sampler of my act. It's a barn burner. I get plum tuckered out. I take two pills and hit the hay. Usually, I sleep like the dead with two tablets. Not that night. No, sir."

I knew from my visit to the sixth floor that Kit's room was directly across from Sasha's. In the adjacent foyer, Kennedy's was opposite Yazminka's. "Kennedy was staying in the room just around the corner from yours. Did you see anyone come or go?"

A look of concern washed over Kit's face. "How did y'all know which room is mine?"

"Oh . . . I . . ."

"A lucky guess," Hollister said smoothly. "Everyone following the story knows which suite was Kennedy's. As another star of the show, we figured you'd be staying in one of the other nearby suites."

The explanation appeared to satisfy Kit; she smiled. "Clever of you. But the answer is still 'no.' But you haven't asked me if I heard anything."

I exchanged excited glances with Hollister.

"A scream. Woke me up like a lightning bolt."

"A scream?" I blurted.

Kit nodded. "It wasn't no rooster, I'll tell you that. I dialed the front desk as quick as you please. Hats off to hotel security. Took only a minute or two before I heard them runnin' down the hallway and enterin' a room nearby. Of course, at the time, I didn't know which room. Could have been Yazminka's or Kennedy's. Had it been Sasha's right across from mine, I'd have known. I can see his door through my peephole. Anyhoo, soon as the cavalry arrived, the yelling started." Kit sighed dramatically. "We all know the rest of the sad, sad story, I'm afraid."

Kit went on to say that detectives had visited Mysterium the next day. Like the rest of the cast and crew, she had spent an hour answering their questions.

"Now then." Kit stood. "I hope y'all got what ya need for your story. This gal's got target practice. My mama's comin' for openin' night." She reached out a hand and laid it lightly on my shoulder. "And the last thing this rodeo girl is gonna do is disappoint her mama." She added a final playful wink as she left us sitting alone in the canteen.

I gave Hollister the "I'm-not-fooling-around" look I saved for my students' most egregious behavior.

"What?" she said.

"Back there on the stage. I can't believe you went through with that! That was beyond dangerous, Hollister. You could have been killed."

"Can you believe that Kit heard the scream?" She paused a moment. "Don't tell me you saw that one coming?"

"Surely, the cops would have confirmed her story. As for motive, Kit didn't seem that interested in Kennedy's job. She seemed not to want it."

Hollister looked at me as if peering over eyeglasses. "Hate to burst your bubble, little dude. People lie."

"Yeah, well, the more a person lies, the more likely they are to get caught."

"If you say so." She thumbed a worn program that someone had left on the table. She appeared fixated on a photo of Yazminka Smilova.

"Earth to Hollister."

She glanced up from the program. "What?"

"I know Yazminka is a fox, but will you focus, please?"

"Did you just call her a fox?"

"You know, as in foxy lady."

Hollister laughed. "Thanks for the history lesson. The last time a lady was foxy was in the 1980s."

"Whatever."

"She is fine, though."

"And she's next on our list. Perhaps this time you'll do me the favor of not proving how fearless you are. For the record, my heart can't take it."

Hollister hadn't heard a word I'd said. With a long sigh, I snatched the program away from her. "C'mon, Bernice. Let's see if we can find your new crush."

Chapter Eighteen
Nice Socks

The door to Yazminka Smilova's trailer swung open, and out stepped the Russian acrobat in a flurry of silk and cinnamon. She took one look at Hollister and me, then saw the camera and barked, "Tell Jenna I don't have time. I'm late as it is." She slipped the long thin straps of a large, pricey-looking snakeskin bag over a defined shoulder and strode toward a stretch of trailers near the end of the parking lot.

Three steps into the pursuit of Yazminka, Hollister said, "Remind me, are we supposed to know who this Jenna chick is?"

"The publicity manager," I said. "She was the woman with the camera at the preview. Now, come on. We have to hurry."

Yazminka hadn't slowed her pace; she was nearing the most distant trailer. We quick-stepped it to the end of the path just as she entered a trailer marked "Costume Shop." I knocked.

The door swung open, revealing a young, lanky woman of South Asian descent who looked like she'd front a band with a name like Public Menace or Itchy Parts. Her deep-purple Doc Marten lace-up boots stood firmly planted in the elevated doorway at my eye level. I raised my gaze to her pierced septum and green-dyed crewcut. "Hello, hello," I chirped cheerily.

"Yeah?" she replied with the geniality of a bouncer.

"We're here to interview Yazminka Smilova." Smiling, I added, "We're from the *Examiner.*"

"No!" Yazminka shouted from inside the trailer. "Tell them to go away, Zell!"

The green-haired woman, Zell, apparently, looked amused. As she shut the door in our faces, she smirked. "You heard the woman. Beat it."

The woman's rudeness had riled Hollister up. She reached past me, knocked again. More insistently.

This time Zell flung open the door. "Are you two deaf? I told you to get lost. You don't want to piss her off. Trust me."

I leaned forward and shouted past Zell, "Ms. Smilova, Jenna said to tell you that interviews are in your contract. We need only ten minutes. We can ask our questions while you're . . ." I said to Zell, "What is it you do?"

"You're interrupting a fitting," she spat as if her job were a curse. "I'm on a tight deadline here. So like I said—"

"Got it." I leaned past Zell again. "We'll be quick, Ms. Smilova. We can conduct our interview while you do your fitting. Two birds, one stone sort of thing."

Yazminka grumbled like a teenager denied the car keys. "You got ten minutes before Zell tosses your asses out!"

Zell gave me a look that suggested her preferred move would be to connect her boot to my chin. With a sneer, she stepped back and opened the door wider for us to enter. Unlike Kit Durango's trailer, Mysterium's costume shop was a study in order, variety, and all-out splendor. Bolts of fabric—from shiny and sequined to gauzy and ghostlike—dressed two walls from floor to ceiling. Fringes, furs, wigs, and hats—most notably a duplicate of the tall pink top hat that Kennedy had worn—filled the many shelves, and atop a large table sat two sophisticated-looking sewing machines, their digital displays intimidating even from a distance. Five dressmaker mannequins circled the table, each wearing a costume, all of which were in various stages of completion. Two of the outfits looked military of some kind (the epaulets a dead giveaway); one had periwinkle leather fringe that screamed Kit Durango; another appeared to be the full-body leotard for a very fit man; and the fifth was an exquisite black satin tuxedo-dress that I recalled the French ring mistress had worn at the VIP preview.

"Jenna is so on my list," Yazminka complained from the corner of the room. She stood on a carpeted platform before a trio of mirrors that showcased her slender physique at every angle. Judging by Hollister's look and the level of her gaze, she hadn't noticed Yazminka's knee-high socks with colorful illustrations of comic-book heroes.

"Zell, make sure the seams are triple strength at the crotch this time. Remember what happened last spring in Montpelier." Zell nodded and unrolled a bolt of deep blue fabric. "There's no ticket price high enough to cover that show."

I shot Hollister a glance to see which of us dared to begin the interrogation of the feisty, scantily clad acrobat.

Glaring in our direction, Yazminka barked, "Nine minutes."

The reminder of a ticking clock shook Hollister from her reverie. She stepped forward. "Ms. Smilova, were you in your room the night your friend was brutally murdered?"

Had Yazminka been taken aback by the question's abrupt-
ness, she gave no indication of it. Instead, she looked annoyed.
"Friend? Who told you we were friends? Oh God. Does Jenna
know what you were going to ask? How many times do I have to
talk about Kennedy? Boo-hoo. Poor Kennedy. I'm sick of it. How
about poor me? I'm the one who has to keep reliving that fiasco.
I'll tell you what I've told everyone. No, I was not in my room.
I was out with members of the cast. I didn't know anything had
happened until I arrived at the hotel around eleven. The cops
wouldn't let me upstairs. To my own room! I didn't get to bed
until hours later. I blame Kennedy for the hangover I had the next
morning. Eight!"

Taking my turn, I asked, "Do you or anyone else with the
show have any idea who might have killed Kennedy?" I poised my
Bic above my notepad and raised a brow in anticipation of hearing a newsworthy headline.

"Are you impaired? That's a serious question, by the way.
They arrested some woman right then and there. I mean, *hello!*
What more evidence do you need?"

"The kind that proves a person's guilt," Hollister quipped.

Yazminka snapped her head toward Hollister and gave her a
scathing look.

Wishing to get things back on track, I said, "So . . . I was asking if you suspect anyone in particular? Perhaps someone working
here at Mysterium?"

"No. Well, maybe. Who knows. I mean, who doesn't have
enemies? Kennedy made more than her share by spouting off
about how the show wasn't up to *her* standards and needed to be
more upscale. I mean, the *nerve* of that woman. All her talk of
change was freaking people out. Everyone was worried sick about

whether they would have a job the next day. My brother told me she planned to cut some of our most popular acts. Many people around here, myself included, aren't mourning the fact that Kennedy Osaka is permanently out of the picture. And although you didn't ask, I didn't get the artistic director job only because of sibling rivalry. My pathetic brother couldn't stand the idea of me being his equal. News flash—I will never be that dumbass's equal. I have been and will always be his superior. In every way. Six."

"You last said 'eight,'" I pointed out.

"Five!"

Zell, wielding a pair of enormous tailoring shears, began making a long cut from a bolt of sheer fabric. I had to hand it to Mysterium's wardrobe manager; she was giving an Oscar-worthy performance of pretending not to be hanging on our every word.

"And how did *you* feel about Kennedy's proposed changes?" Hollister said. "'Elevating the elegance' was how she'd put it." She turned to me. "Do I have that right, Chet?"

"Elevating the elegance," I agreed. "Kennedy intended to stamp the show with her personal brand. More sophisticated. More refined. More—"

"I swear to God, I'm going to barf if you two don't shut up!"

Had Yazminka been fully clothed, I might not have noticed her suddenly shaking. She crackled with anger. Unable to help myself, I said, "She was going to give the show her enchanting Kennedy flair."

"Get out! Now! And tell Jenna her ass is grass! Zell, get these two idiots out of my sight!"

Zell sprang toward the door. She held the Jurassic Park–sized shears at nose height, sharp ends up. Passing close by her, I caught a glimpse of my distorted reflection in the steel. Zell made an abrupt snip of the blades. I jumped, bumping into Hollister, and we stumbled down the trailer's steps and onto the sidewalk.

"I told you not to piss her off," Zell snarled. "Now I have to deal with her." The door slammed shut behind us.

"Hey! You two!" A woman marched toward us at double time.

"And here comes Jenna," Hollister whispered.

I sighed. "Out of the frying pan . . ."

Hollister held up a hand. "I got this, little dude." She started toward Jenna, matching the woman's determined stride. I trotted alongside to keep up. As the two women neared each other, Hollister pointed a finger at Mysterium's publicity director. "You must be Jenna. Great. Your timing couldn't be better. Yazminka is waiting for you. She wants to thank you personally."

Neither Jenna nor I had seen that coming. The steam that seconds before had hissed from Jenna's ears suddenly dissipated. She looked utterly confused.

"Thank me? Thank me for what?"

Hollister lifted her camera. "For the front-page feature, of course. Chet here"—she pointed the long lens down at me—"scored some Pulitzer-level copy on Ms. Smilova."

"You're too kind, Bernice. You're the one knocking this one out of the park." Beaming at Jenna, I said, "Wait till you see Bernice's cover photo of Yazminka. *Cosmo* would be so lucky."

"Of Yazminka?" Jenna sputtered. "You can't be serious. Yazminka Smilova? *Our* Yazminka Smilova let you take her photo? But there was no stylist. And her makeup artist is still in LA."

"No need," I declared proudly. "Bernice here has serious photo creds. Dog shows, bar mitzvahs, retirement parties, junior high proms . . ."

Jenna closed her eyes and shook her head.

"We need to run," I said. "Deadline, you know."

Hollister and I hustled toward the exit, leaving Jenna, her mouth agape. Unable to stop myself, I shouted over my shoulder. "If you hurry, you might catch Yazminka just as we shot her. Right down to the socks."

Chapter Nineteen
Someone's in a Hurry

"I thought we were going to Slice," I said in response to Hollister abruptly pulling Mo into a gravel parking lot next to a small community of weathered houseboats. She brought the Porsche to a stop, its nose just inches from a row of makeshift weathered signs, each painted with a resident's name and pointing toward one of the two docks. I'd driven past this Lake Union enclave, across the water from the university, countless times. On only one previous occasion had I been on a houseboat: a friend's birthday party put on by her physician mother, who lived in a two-level floating home near Eastlake with unobstructed views of the Seattle skyline. This was not that.

The *chirp-chirp* of Mo's locked doors met my ears the moment my eyes landed on the words "J. Gemalto, dock A," stenciled in red paint across a slab of driftwood. Hollister headed toward the dock on the left. Halfway up the wobbly floating walkway, a lithe orange tabby sauntered across our path. My attempt to entice the cat with an ear scratch was aloofly rebuffed. We continued up the goose poop–spattered dock.

Hollister explained that Jess Gemalto had suggested hosting us at his home. Selfishly, I was glad. I was curious to see if Jess's and my uncanny physical resemblance extended to our personal surroundings. The initial impression was mixed. While both of our homes were modest at best, my apartment sat above an identical layout occupied by a retired mail carrier, and Jess's floating home bobbed in a small cove on Lake Washington.

"Here it is," Hollister said, stepping onto the porch of a tiny houseboat. A sleek silver kayak lay alongside the wood-frame cottage clad in darkly stained shingles and green shutters.

"You found me." Jess waved cheerfully from the open doorway. As on previous occasions, he was dressed for the office, but today he had rolled his white sleeves up to his elbows and wore no tie; his open shirt collar revealed a thin silver chain. "I hope you don't mind coming out this way." He grinned, displaying a winning smile. "Sarah Lee said she has never been inside a houseboat. So I figured it was my duty to right that wrong. That is my business, after all." He tipped his imaginary cap.

At that precise moment, I decided I liked Jess Gemalto.

Burley and Sarah Lee were already inside. So snug was the houseboat's interior that Burley was in the entryway, kitchen, and living room all at the same time. Even at my size, I had to shimmy between the back of Burley's chair and a compact refrigerator just to get inside the place. With no chance of doing the same, Hollister said, "Burl, honey, unless you want me sitting on your lap for this confab, I'm going to need you to scoot."

Burley stood and promptly smacked her head against one of the beams crisscrossing the low ceiling. Rubbing her scalp, she shifted to an adjacent chair. The floorboards creaked as the entire house listed to the port side. Burley was like a parent squeezing inside a child's playhouse—any sudden movement threatened to overturn the whole structure.

"Is your head all right?" Jess winced in empathy. "I'm sorry. I should have considered . . ."

"Not your fault," Burley said with a chuckle. "When you're my size, you get used to knocking your brain box against the rafters."

Sarah Lee had put on a bit of makeup, but there was no hiding her look of fatigue. The weight of Kennedy's death, along with not knowing if the police were getting any closer to making an arrest and at the same time knowing that the police had yet to rule her out as a suspect in her friend's murder had worn her down. Burley reached out to drape a large hand over hers and looked beseechingly at Hollister and me. We understood the message. Every day of the week but Monday, Burley and Sarah Lee worked side by side in the bakery, just the two of them. They were colleagues but also close friends. The emotional toll Kennedy's murder had taken on Sarah Lee affected Burley too. At that moment, she reminded us that she was counting on us to clear Sarah Lee as a suspect.

Jess perched on a stool, spread his hands. "Shall we begin?"

We all nodded in agreement.

"Burley says you two have been busy," Jess addressed Hollister and me. "I said I didn't want to hear about your investigation, but as Sarah Lee's lawyer, I'd be remiss in not being open to hearing what you've discovered. In other words, as much as I don't want to know *how* you came across your information, I still have to ask *what* have you learned?"

Hollister and I wasted no time, taking turns recounting our time spent at Mysterium. I took particular enjoyment in describing Kit's performance. Jess reacted with wide-eyed amazement and a well-timed gasp. Burley grinned proudly at Hollister's bravery. Sarah Lee's attempt at a smile just made her look sadder. Hollister then described our encounter with Yazminka and Zell, the costume manager.

Three pages of scribbled notes later, Jess summarized, "So both the cowgirl, Kit, and the Russian"—he flipped a page of his notepad—"Yazminka Smilova, believe that Kennedy's proposed changes to the show created a lot of consternation among the cast and crew."

"That's the long and the short of it." Hollister sat back, seemingly pleased with Jess's summary. "A new unpopular boss and dozens of disgruntled employees. Seems there's no shortage of people at Mysterium who might be happy Kennedy was out of the picture. And let's not forget the unusual weapon or the mysterious blond woman in the hotel at the time of the murder."

"I wonder if the scissors used in the crime are the same type that Zell uses in the costume shop?" I mused aloud.

Jess tapped the end of a ballpoint pen against his hairless chin. "Good question, Hayden."

I smiled at having provided a bona fide insight into our investigation.

"The costume shop is probably accessible to many employees, though," Jess said. "It's possible that anyone could have swiped a pair of scissors."

I nodded, pleased Jess and I were in sync. Jess asked, "Sarah Lee, if we showed you pictures of the scissors, could you identify the ones you . . . held?"

"I'm not sure," she answered. "So much of my time in the bedroom is still a black hole. I know it would be much easier on everyone if I could remember. If I could tell the police what I saw. What I did. What I *didn't* do." As she spoke, she started to cry.

Dismayed, Burley wrapped an arm around her. "Now, let's have none of that. This is not your doing, you hear? Hollister and Hayden are working hard to prove that you were just at the wrongest place at an even wronger time. Meanwhile, Mr. G is keeping the coppers at bay."

Jess tried a different tack. "What if you closed your eyes and held the scissors, Sarah Lee? Could you tell us if they *feel* like the ones used in the crime?"

Sarah Lee blinked several times. "I might. I could try."

Jess said softly to himself, "If only we had a way of obtaining a pair of scissors from the costume shop."

Seeing Hollister's eyes light up, I said, "Jess was only thinking to himself." But it was too late. Like a school bell signaling the day's end, there was no going back once rung.

Realizing his mistake, Jess said, "Please, do not take that as a suggestion. I was simply thinking it could be helpful to know. The police have surely followed up on that element, but since Sarah Lee has not been charged, they haven't shared that particular information."

"Nothing to worry about, Counselor," Hollister said. "Hayden and I are on it."

Jess, now knowing Hollister well enough to see any argument was futile, lowered his head and pinched the bridge of his nose. "I wish you wouldn't. As Hayden says, I was only thinking aloud."

My stomach twisted as I envisioned a second encounter with green-haired Zell.

As if to change the subject, Jess set a charcuterie plate of assorted meats, cheeses, and crackers on the table. "I'm left curious about . . ." He again consulted his legal pad. ". . . Sasha Smilov, head of operations."

Covering my mouth full of cracker and Emmentaler, I mumbled, "He looks like a cross between a metalhead and a Brooklyn hipster." Swallowing, I continued, "He has tons of pics on every platform. Loves to pose with everyone and everything. His life appears to be one long series of Instagram moments. His likes include women, man-bling—chains, rings, diamond ear studs—tattoos, piercings, that sort of thing. His go-to camera pose is flashing the rock sign with his pinky and index finger. His dislikes make a much shorter list: buttoning a shirt and modesty."

Picking a piece of prosciutto from the platter, Jess said, "Sasha is Yazminka's brother, I presume. But the last names? They don't quite match."

"Smilov and Smilova," Hollister clarified.

Although my mouth was again half full of cheese, I couldn't help showing off my Jerry-sourced knowledge. "Most Slavic surnames are gender-specific. When the last name ends in a V, the female form adds an A to the end."

"Curious," Jess said. "A very binary approach."

Having no reply to that, I pushed on. "The father, Boris, owns the whole operation."

"Interesting." Jess started to pace. Given the kitchen's tiny size, he essentially walked in a tight circle. "Kit Durango, Yazminka Smilova, and Sasha Smilov. All three are associated with Mysterium. And all three of them are staying in suites at the end of the hallway near Kennedy's room. The police will undoubtedly focus on the three of them, seeking to rule each out."

I brushed crumbs off my chin. "But again, we can't rule out Zell in the costume shop or anyone else at Mysterium. And if that weren't enough suspects, there's the still unidentified woman in the hotel."

"Speaking of which . . ." Hollister pulled a flash drive from her pocket.

Moments later, the video file she'd copied, while supposedly retrieving her phone from the hotel's security center, opened. We huddled close to Jess's laptop. What transpired on the screen was a replay of what Gwyneth Lang had shown Hollister and me: a woman with messy blond hair entering the hotel, taking an elevator to an unknown floor, then leaving through the lobby six minutes later at 7:07, roughly the same time hotel security entered Kennedy's suite and discovered Sarah Lee. Jess replayed the video several times, pausing every few seconds to scrutinize the scene. The blond woman never shifted her gaze from the exit—not a single frame showed her face.

"That woman appears inebriated." Jess rewound the video and slow-motioned the woman's wobbly, rushed exit.

"Drugs?" I wondered aloud.

"Could be." Jess shrugged. "High and in a hurry. In my line of work, I see it all too often."

Hollister tapped the screen. "Yeah, but is Blondie in a rush to get somewhere? Or in a hurry to get away?"

A new thought struck me as I stared at the frozen image on the screen. "And is that her real hair? Or a wig?"

Chapter Twenty
Mates on Dates, Post No. 24

MATES ON DATES: Plus Counts!

A friend and a friend of hers are going through a rough time. How rough? Let's just say the friend of a friend is in the type of trouble that requires the services of a lawyer. That said, this post is not about my troubled friend. Instead, it's about her lawyer, who I'll call Jedd for anonymity's sake.

The first incredible fun fact about Jedd is that he looks like he could be my identical twin. Take that in for a moment. One day I'm blithely going about my day when into my life (or into my friend's kitchen, to be precise) strolls a person who looks just like me. To be clear, this is not an "Oh!-You-must-be-brothers" type of situation. I mean—*exactly like me!* Same size, eye color, freckles, hair—though his hair is A-plus, whereas mine is delinquent. The whole package that is Hayden suddenly appeared before me as a duplicate version in a pressed dress shirt, with a different name. Trust me, it's *Twilight Zone* bizarre. And that, my readers, isn't even half the story.

Jedd, who could fool many of my family members, coworkers, and friends into believing he is me, is transgender. Before meeting Jedd, I had never crossed paths in any way other than in passing with a transgender person and honestly had never given it much thought. Getting to know Jedd has been an eye-opener. What strikes me most about him (after his freakish resemblance to me) is that he is just another person going through the daily motions of his life. I need to pause here and point out that I intentionally avoided the word "normal," as in "he seems like a normal person." I hate that word. For starters, how boring! Two: it suggests a norm that is usually code for cisgender, straight, and straight acting (the last, another term I detest—please, if you use it, *just stop*).

What we humans share—and I have in common with Jedd— is having worries, regrets, hopes, and aspirations. Of course, the specifics vary, but that we all have them is undeniable. Not a day goes by that I don't wish my mom were still alive, that my hair was not so untamable, or that I could add even just two inches to my height (my tennis serve would improve immeasurably!). But I also look forward to the day I meet my future husband, beat my friend Jerry at backgammon, and learn how to see things as half full instead of destined to be drained.

Among those thoughts, there's another to which only roughly five percent, depending on the generation and the study, of my fellow humans can relate. Not a day goes by that someone or something in this world doesn't remind me that I'm not straight. I don't know what's on Jedd's mind, but going out on a limb, I imagine his transness is not something that preoccupies his every thought. But I'm guessing his being trans is something other people constantly remind him of, whether overtly or subtly.

Where am I going with all this? I like Jedd, and I'd like to be his friend. I'm determined to see Jedd for *all of who he is*. While I can't ignore he's trans—nor should I—I also know there's much, much more to him than just that. For starters, Jedd is a defense attorney, an intelligent and nice person, a kayaker, a houseboat owner—and more that I intend to discover. Speaking for myself, I'm gay, but I'm also a teacher, a writer on the topic of gay dating, an animal lover, a friend, a tennis player, and—reluctantly—something of an amateur detective. Hollister is my best friend, a furniture designer, Porsche enthusiast, daughter, wine aficionado, and romantic soul with girl troubles. Burley is my sweetest friend, a queer baker, emu raiser, pot grower, and karaoke MC extraordinaire.

Let me spell it out if you've yet to get my point. Whichever part of LGBTQ+ most applies to you, *you* know that one single character does not fully define you. Remember that the next time you're about to make the mistake of defining someone else by a mere letter or a label. Let that plus sign be a reminder, people!

Till next time, I'm Hayden
And remember, if you can't be good, be safe!

Chapter Twenty-One
Back in a Flash

I didn't go out to the clubs all the time, but when I did slip on a cute shirt and venture out for a bit of nightlife, Hunters was my place. Tonight was the once-a-month drag edition of karaoke. Burley, the regular MC, had threatened to break her streak of sixty-four straight weekly appearances with the excuse that Sarah Lee needed to be kept company. Hollister and I waged a counterargument that she should bring Sarah Lee along. What better way to lift one's spirits than an evening of drag kings and drag queens belting out show tunes? We'd also invited Jess Gemalto, but last we heard, he was noncommittal, citing work overload.

Burley, as her musical idol Bruce Springsteen, wore a short black wig and pasted-on sideburns. Otherwise, save for the short-sleeved denim shirt and black leather wristbands, she looked pretty much the same. Hollister, naturally on the masculine end of the spectrum, pushed it further by adding a goatee and bushy eyebrows. Where she scored a vintage male airline pilot uniform was a secret she refused to divulge. Her usual jovial mood whenever at karaoke was blunted by the nonappearance of her sometimes girlfriend, Mysti. While I sympathized with Hollister, I didn't miss the femme fatale. As much as Hollister longed for Mysti's presence, she only succeeded in making Hollister miserable. As Hollister's and my friendship grew stronger, I voiced my opinion: she deserved better. Hollister would reply with a knowing nod before making excuses for Mysti's slight of the day, whether it was a needlessly cruel remark, a missed date, or a snide comment about yours truly. Why Hollister—confident, dynamic, glorious Hollister—continued to put up with up Mysti's crap was mind-boggling. And yet, it wasn't. As wildly misplaced as her affection seemed to be, Hollister loved her.

Sarah Lee had agreed to come, but only if she didn't have to "dress up." We'd assured her there was no requirement that you be in drag to attend. Were there one, I'd be blocked at the door. As much as I flirted with the idea of doing drag, drawing attention to myself was something I usually avoided at all cost. Camilo gave me grief for my reluctance. "What's the big deal?" he'd say, confident and comfortable in his own skin, whether or not he was wearing beard cover, a wig, and red L'Oreal lipstick. Camilo had offered to paint my face, but I feared the intimacy of the experience would sink me deeper into my infatuational abyss. And both Hollister and Burley grimaced at a department store makeup counter as if it were an electric chair.

From the edge of the dance floor, I sipped my go-to brand of hard cider and scanned the crowd, hoping to spy an attractive fellow to sweep me off my feet.

"Hey, buddy." Camilo sidled up beside me, looking like a gazillion bucks in a lemon chiffon mini dress and matching heels.

His waist-length Cardi B wig was a dazzler, straight, shiny black, and parted in the middle. He lazily draped an arm over my shoulder. The sweat from his arm felt damp against the back of my neck. I thought my knees would buckle.

"Hey," I shouted back over the dance music. "How's it going?"

As usual, the presence of my unrequited crush triggered conflicting emotions. Taking a deep breath to muster resolve, I readied myself to tell Camilo that his more-than-just-friends innuendo was making me crazy and that he had to knock it off.

"Listen, Camilo—"

"Hayden, check it out." Something had caught Camilo's attention on the other side of the dance floor. "That queen looks how I imagine you'd look in drag. Like *exactly* . . ." As the person approached, Camilo's eyes grew giant. "Whoa." He drew out the word as Jess stepped up—in full glorious drag.

Camilo stepped back and gave his head a Scooby-Doo shake. His mouth gaped like a halibut's.

"Wow," I said, never meaning a syllable more.

"I'll take that as a compliment," Jess said.

The soft-green, sleeveless cocktail dress was cut to perfection. The ribbon-like straps accentuated Jess's smooth, freckled shoulders, and its knee-length skirt was sexily slit up the side to his hip.

"Va-va-voom," purred Hollister, joining our little circle.

Seeing Jess so spectacularly transformed, I was hugely conflicted about my drag prospects. On the one hand, I was inspired: Jess—or for the night, Jessica—modeled what was possible—we were, after all, working with the same basic ingredients. On the other, Jess set the bar as high as the speakers suspended from the ceiling.

Bruce had just killed it with an energetic rendition of "Born to Run" and was introducing the next singer to the stage. Given the name, The Sisters Flip, they must be a duo at least.

Over the din of chatter, bar orders, a screech of feedback, and a smattering of applause, two queens, both knockouts, clacked up onto the stage in six-inch heels. I leaned forward and squinted, trying to bring them into better focus. I couldn't be sure. And yet . . . I was.

It was Vlad and one of the other guys from Adrenalin!

The crowd started clapping to the rhythm of "Can't Hold Us Down" by Christina Aguilera and Lil' Kim. The guys sounded even better than they looked and moved in their pink skimpy tops and miniskirts.

Hollister nodded, bunching her lips—the equivalent of a nine on a ten-point scale. Camilo rocked seductively, his shimmering hair swaying against his muscular back. Jess, who had no idea who they were, leaned over to me. "Now that is how you do it."

I didn't disagree. Moreover, I pitied whoever was to follow them. But as unexpected as their appearance on Hunter's stage was, it was Vlad's wig that locked my attention. Big and blond, it looked a lot—*a lot*—like the woman's hair in the video shown to us by Gwyneth Lang at the hotel. I glanced at Hollister. Had she noticed the similarity?

The place was packed. As soon as The Sisters Flip left the stage, I lost sight of them. I did a few laps around the club but couldn't find them. Had they performed and immediately left?

As the evening neared its end, I found myself standing alone while the others were off ordering a final round of drinks.

"You know her?" Camilo—or Miz Vixen this evening—had quietly appeared at my side.

"Who?"

No sooner had I asked than she stepped up. "Hey, remember me?"

If I'd needed a reminder (I didn't), the Romanian accent would have tipped me off.

"Vlad, right?" I said.

"The one and only. Though tonight, I'm Vladmilla." He bowed slightly, his grin all the more attractive up close. "And you are Hayden. I remember."

"Good to see you again. This is my friend Camilo. Sorry—Miz Vixen."

As if Camilo intended to convey a more intimate relationship, he returned his arm to my shoulders. Despite the move, Vlad continued to ignore him. He asked me, "What are you drinking?"

I held up my half-empty bottle of cider. Vlad examined the label. "Back in a flash."

Camilo glared at Vlad as he walked away. "'Back in a flash,'" he said mockingly while attempting to cross his eyes.

I scowled. "What's your problem?"

"She's full of herself if you ask me." Camilo scowled. "You going to tell me how you know her?"

"It's a long story—"

"Okay. I see where this is headed. Just tell me this"—he gave me a sly look—"boxers, briefs, or commando?"

"Funny you should ask."

In an instant, Camilo's face went from smiley to frowny.

"But it's not at all—"

"Whatever." He shook his head. "I'll let you two catch up, then. Later."

Before I could explain, Camilo stomped away. For a split second, I considered chasing after him, but we weren't dating. I didn't owe him an explanation. And his making fun of Vlad was a turn-off.

Vlad returned with two bottles of cider, slippery with condensation. We clinked them together in a toast. "To Hunters," he chirped happily.

I chuckled. "Yeah, it's an okay place."

"Okay? I'd say it's pretty awesome."

"You think so?" I gave the familiar space an appreciative look.

"I found you here. So yeah, I do. Most definitely."

My mouth opened, but I rejected each reply as it formed in my brain—none of them a sufficiently smooth line.

"I have to say, man, I was pretty disappointed you never stopped by my room. I thought we, you know, had a connection. So naturally, I expected . . ."

If I didn't come up with something good, and fast, I would likely send a second guy marching off into the crowd. "Sorry about that. I wanted to. Really I did. It's just that—"

"Boyfriend?"

"As I said, Camilo is just a friend."

"Someone else?"

"Oh. No. No boyfriend here." Hearing the words spill from my lips, I couldn't help but wonder if the message sent was a good thing (I'm available!) or not (*still* available).

"Good. I thought that you and that hot Latino might be together. But I figured nothing ventured, nothing gained."

I took a sip of cider, grateful for an excuse not to have a comeback. While some guys might be put off by such boldness, I found it a thrilling change from Camilo's mixed signals. More than that, Vlad filled my head with images of unzipping the back of his dress.

"Lucky I came here on your night off," he said.

Again, I fumbled for words. Vlad thought I was a hotel employee, and I nearly corrected him. I'd gone along with his misunderstanding before, and now, unable to come up with another reasonable explanation, I found myself stuck in a lie. I took a long drink.

"You're going to drain that before the song ends."

"Two-drink limit. I'm driving."

"Responsible." He raised a brow. "I like that."

"You do?" I stammered.

"Yeah. It's the boys that are shy and quiet in public that end up surprising you the most in private."

I grimaced before I could stop myself. "I'm not sure about that."

"I guess I'll just have to find out."

At this point in the conversation, the next question was only a line or two away: *Do you want to go to my place?* I knew Vlad was staying in a hotel, so he had no roommates or a visiting friend crashing on the sofa. Odds were he'd invite me to his room. As much as a part of me wanted to go, I didn't know this guy. He could be a killer for all I knew—or didn't know. There was something real about "bad boy attraction," but it had its limits. I took yet another sip and tried to settle my nerves.

"So . . ." He gripped my shoulder and stepped closer. My knees turned to jelly. This was actually going to happen. A half hour earlier, I'd swung open the door to Hunter's, hoping to meet someone cute. I'd have been happy with a friendly, flirty chat, never expecting to go home with one of the sexiest guys I'd ever met. I set my bottle down on a nearby table.

"This is terrible timing, I know," Vlad said, "but I need to get going."

Wait. What? I might have misheard the "I need to get going," but "this is terrible timing" was unambiguous. The words sank in. Vlad was leaving all right. *Without me.*

"There's an early technical rehearsal tomorrow. New acts, new routines, new equipment to test out. Sorry, man. But I don't have a choice. We preview this Wednesday, and opening night is Thursday."

I nodded and turned back to where I'd set my cider just as the barback whisked it away. How appropriate. Vlad had bought it for me, and it, like him, was easy come, easy go. Even though I decided I couldn't trust him yet, I still wanted the invitation. I nodded, trying to hide my disappointment.

He returned a puzzled look. "Really?"

"Um . . . what do you mean?"

"You're not curious? I know what you do. But not even the intrigue of 'new acts' or 'new routines' makes you interested in what I do?"

Crap, crap, crap. Not only did Vlad think I worked at the hotel, but he didn't know I'd attended the preview show—I'd seen part of his act. I was stuck in a whopper of a lie. My pause in replying was too long. I blurted, "Yes. Sorry. Please, tell me. What is it you do?"

Not skipping a beat, Vlad announced, "The seemingly impossible!" He waited for my smile, then said, "It's hard to put into words. Better to show you. Any chance you're free tomorrow? Come by where I work. I can show you around. You can see what I do. Then we can hang out. Grab dinner. Make a night of it, if you're free. If you want to."

"Yeah. Sounds good." I was dizzy with the ping-ponging of emotion. One moment, I felt as low as the sticky concrete beneath my sneakers; the next, I was as high as Lizzo's voice pumping from the club's speakers.

"Sweet." He moved a strong hand to the back of my neck and squeezed almost too forcefully. "Have you ever heard of Mysterium? It's sort of like a circus for adults." He grinned; I shivered with excitement. "We're in Seattle for a month. We've got the tent set up south of the sports stadiums. Can't miss it. I'll give the guard at the employee entrance your name. He'll call me when you arrive, and I'll meet you at the gate. Say four o'clock?"

"Yeah. Okay."

"Yeah?"

"Yeah." I smiled.

"Okay, I gotta jump. Florin is waiting." He leaned in and kissed me lightly on the cheek. "See you tomorrow. *Don't* disappoint me again." He pressed both hands to his ridiculously defined chest. "I don't think my heart could take it."

Chapter Twenty-Two

No Turning Back

Hollister didn't pick up her phone. But as soon I had left a voice-mail recounting my conversation with Vlad, she did exactly what I thought she would: she called me right back.

"That Vlad guy just gave you the perfect way inside, little dude. Remember what Jess said? We need a pair of scissors from the costume shop to see if Sarah Lee can match them with the murder weapon."

"You're leaving out the part when he said we shouldn't take it as a suggestion that we're the ones to get them."

"That's one way to read it."

"That is the *only* way to read it."

"Exactly. Suggestion. As in, 'I suggest you do something.' Jess's words, not mine."

I shook my head. "You're impossible."

"You said Vlad is putting your name on the visitors' list. You go early, slip inside the costume trailer, and snatch the scissors. If you're lucky, you might even stumble on more clues while you're on the inside."

On the inside? I didn't like the sound of that one bit. I was and had always been quite at home on the outside. Such relentless testing of my boundaries lay at the heart of my friendship with Hollister. From the moment I'd first met her, she had yanked me out of my comfort zone and never let up. Being around Hollister pushed me to do things I would never in a gazillion years consider doing on my own. Had I gained confidence along the way? Admittedly, yes. But hardly had I been transformed into some swaggering tough guy unafraid to enter dark basements, throw down with a menacing villain, or in this case, trespass into a circus and steal a pair of fabric shears from an intimidating, green-haired costume manager.

Sensing my need for reassurance, Hollister said, "You got this, Hayden. What could possibly go wrong?"

Like the windup before a pitch, I took a deep breath. "To start—"

"Please don't."

A pause.

"Don't do that either."

"I didn't say anything!"

"You didn't have to. The dramatic sigh said enough. What time did Vlad say to meet him?"

"Four," I said with mixed emotions. What should be only excited anticipation for meeting up with the cute acrobat was countered by the prospect of breaking the law, as minor as it was.

"You can't be certain the coast will be clear when you get to the costume shop. You may need some extra time. You better show up by three. Just to be safe."

"Extra time? For what exactly?" I said cautiously. "You do realize that if Zell or anyone else is around, it's game over."

"Be creative. Be spontaneous. You'll think of something."

"None of this is helping. But thanks for . . . the cheerleading."

The brief silence on the other end of the line gave me immeasurable pleasure. This was one arrow in my quiver that always proved reliable. During last summer's adventure, a crazy set of circumstances had led to Hollister confiding that she had been a cheerleader in high school. I didn't mention her short-skirt-wearing, pom-pom-flailing past often, but it never failed to knock her off balance when I did. After a low groan, she signed off with, "Go, Hayden! You're our man! Show us that you really can! Gooooo, Hayden!"

After a night of tossing and turning, I awoke agitated, stressed, and feeling picked on by the universe. What if I got caught? Getting thrown off the property would be embarrassing, but I'd live. But what about Vlad? Would management hold him responsible for my trespassing and theft? Could I get him into trouble? Fired even? I thought about calling and dumping my anxieties on Hollister, but I knew what she'd say: *"Don't get caught!"*

My sleeplessness wasn't due solely to worries. Imagining a barely clad Vlad played on an endless loop in my brain. I didn't have "a type" per se, but there were attributes I considered deal-breakers. Mega gym built didn't do for me, nor did much younger, way older, too tall (when you're five four that rules out many guys), or pot-bellied. There were other more specific attraction killers from my past—the dude with a dragon neck tattoo with an eyelid-licking fetish, the barefoot guy with a puka shell choker who reeked of patchouli oil, or the otherwise perfect guy who dissed *Drag Race*.

Granted, Vlad didn't live in Seattle—just passing through—but he would be in town for a monthlong run of the show. If our first date went well—and if I could be sure he wasn't involved in Kennedy's murder—we had plenty of time for others. *Stop it, Hayden. Stop it!*

I was already getting ahead of myself, putting too much expectation on a first date with a guy I didn't know. Despite my earnest attempts to find someone special, I was still boyfriend-less in a city chock-full of young gay men. How many times had I tamped down my hair and checked the pits of my shirt before grabbing my wallet and heading out to Hunters? Too many to count. Once when I was twenty-two—for the record, nearly four years ago—I went out every night of the week for three weeks straight. I was hoping to make a connection, a real one. As that had yet to happen, whenever a guy seemed promising, I overin-vested in hoping he would be "the one."

Seven hours later, I approached Mysterium under the pro-tection of my prized, oversized, and breathtakingly overpriced Wimbledon-branded umbrella—a gift-shop splurge during my one overseas vacation. As I puddle-hopped in the downpour, I regret-ted not wearing more suitable shoes. My soaked white Converses, now a dirty dark gray, squished water into my thick double socks at each step. Approaching the employee entrance, I saw a different guard from the other day. She sat huddled on a metal folding chair beneath the overhang of a tiny booth. Her long yellow rain-slicker, its hood raised, had been pulled tightly around her face.

"Hello, my name is Hayden. I should be on your list. I'm here to meet a friend in the cast."

The woman, clearly more interested in the game on her phone than verifying my claim, waved me in without taking her eyes off the screen. So easily had I entered the grounds that I questioned whether I'd just expended all my luck. Heading straight for the farthest trailer, I hoped to find the costume shop empty, grab what I'd come for, and wait out the rest of the hour back in my car before meeting up with Vlad.

I had just splashed my way past Kit Durango's trailer when a door opened ahead of me. I ducked into the space between Kit's trailer and the next. The clomping of boot heels on wet asphalt rapidly approached. I moved behind the tiny building on wheels. Burley and Hollister would have had to crouch to stay below the window's height, but standing tall, I remained beneath the sill by a good two inches. I heard the trailer's door open. One thing I knew: Kit wore Western boots.

Once inside the trailer, she opened and closed cabinets and drawers, making a racket as she rummaged around the room. Was the cowgirl magician trying to find something? Recalling the room's state of disarray, I wasn't surprised.

More clomping of boots. The front door opened. Cautiously, I poked my head out from around the trailer. My breath caught. I'd been wrong. It wasn't Kit. It was Sasha Smilov. I watched him descend the trailer's steps, hurry to the end of the pathway, and disappear into the distant costume shop.

"Hey, you! What are you doing?"

I spun around, nearly losing my footing.

"I said, what are you doing?" The security guard on duty when Hollister and I had first visited Mysterium stood behind me in a bright orange jacket slick with rain. His long, thin hair appeared pasted to his skull; rivulets of water meandered down his forehead.

"Oh, hello." I peered up from beneath my massive purple and green umbrella. "Kit thought she heard something behind her trailer. I didn't see anything. Did you?"

"Yeah. I'm looking at him."

Ignoring the remark, I pressed on. "It was probably a feral cat or raccoon. You must have scared it off. Kit will appreciate knowing you're on the lookout. You know how she is about security. I'll be sure and tell her that you're making the rounds. She'll put in a good word for you with management."

The guard's expression didn't soften. "I don't know you. I've never seen you . . . Wait, a second. I *have* seen you. You were here the other day. You were here with that big Black lady with a Mohawk. Reporters. You back to do a story on Kit?"

I nodded, relieved that the guard was doing my work for me. "And I better not keep our star waiting." Still not entirely convinced, the guard followed me around the corner. Under his watchful eyes, I stood in front of Kit's trailer. There was no turning back. I shook the water from my umbrella, swung open the door, and stepped inside.

Chapter Twenty-Three

Behind the Scenes

In the few minutes that Sasha Smilov had spent rummaging around the small, messy space, he'd turned it completely upside down. Fringed vests and jeans lay strewn about the floor, the wardrobe door hung open with boots in a mismatched jumble, and cowboy hats that hadn't toppled to the floor dangled precariously from wall hooks. Sasha had been looking for something and didn't care about leaving a mess—or wet boot prints—behind. Had he found what he'd been looking for? There was no way to tell.

I peered around the short curtains covering the window next to the door, noting the southwestern pattern of the canvas material. Kit was country inside out and, apparently, all about. To my disappointment, the guard had gone only as far as the next trailer. Sheltered beneath a metal awning, he sat on the steps, smoking a cigarette. It was too soon to leave without drawing suspicion, so I turned my thoughts to Kit Durango. The cheerful cowgirl hardly seemed like a killer, but what did I know? I had to consider the possibility that she might have plunged a pair of tailoring shears into her coworker's chest—unquestionably an H.R. violation if ever there was one. Kit could be dangerous, making my lurking in her inner sanctum ill-advised. I'd give it five minutes, then, whether or not the guard had moved on, I would.

Clomp, clomp, clomp.

Someone was coming. Sasha? No. These footfalls were different. More staccato, shorter legs. A faster pace. They belonged to the owner of the enormous white cowboy hat that, on a whim, I'd decided to try on in front of the floor-to-ceiling mirror. The boot steps grew louder. I tossed aside the hat and scanned the room for a place to hide. As I closed the bathroom door, the trailer's front door opened. It shut with a bang.

Taking slow, deep breaths, I tried not to hyperventilate. For the first few minutes, I heard nothing. Had Kit seen the disarray and left? If she was still inside the trailer, she hadn't moved. I imagined her silently surveying the wreckage and wondering who had ransacked her home away from home.

"It's me."

I jerked, startled to hear Kit's voice so close by on the other side of the thin door.

"Someone's been in my trailer. This place is about as secure as a henhouse with a picket fence. I'd like to know what you plan to do about it?" After a short pause, she said, "For starters, how about posting some real guards, Alexander? This batch is too lazy to fan their own farts." Then after a long pause, Kit continued, "Yeah, well, you can say that till you're blue in the face, but it won't change a galdarn thing. I don't feel safe. The next time a fox struts into my henhouse, he's gettin' his giblets snipped, and yours truly will be holding the scissors." Another long silence; then: "Yeah, well, excuses only satisfy those who make 'em. And I've used up my last whit of patience. Might serve your interests to do more than just handlin' the produce. I may be well past what you consider an expiration date, but that hasn't stopped you from ogling my melons, and I want it to stop. Word gets back to the big man . . . well, that'll be your barn to clean."

Clomp, clomp . . . Kit was approaching the bathroom.

Having no other place to hide, I scurried into the shower, praying the plastic curtain wouldn't reveal my silhouette. The door opened. The lid to the toilet lifted. Clothing rustled.

"Regrettable, what happened. But one thing's sorted. This girl won't be downgraded to rope tricks at the concession stand. And as for Miss Priss, that one's got her own set of issues. Paranoia in heels, that one. She thinks everyone is out to get her. Like we don't have better things to do." Another long pause. "News flash. Family can be a real bitch." Kit farted loudly and cackled. "Was that reference clear enough, or do you need me to be more explicit?"

The minutes that followed were among the longest of my life. I might have wept with relief at the whoosh of the flushing toilet had my eyes not already been tearing. Moments later, I heard Kit's boots stamp out the door and splish-splash into the distance.

Back in the main room, I noticed that, while talking on the phone, Kit had picked up several items from the floor and secured the hats to their wall pegs. Otherwise, the room appeared to be as much of a chaotic jumble as ever. *"I don't feel safe,"* Kit had said. Had she referred to a specific threat or Mysterium's general lack of security? I peered out the window again. Fortunately, the guard had moved on not a minute too soon. My trusty

Spider-Man watch told me I had thirty minutes before meeting Vlad. I still had time to snatch the scissors.

Approaching the costume shop, I was relieved to see Sasha Smilov step out. He acknowledged me with a casual bro-to-bro head nod as he strutted past. I went around to the back window of the costume shop, to see if anyone else was inside. There was no need. A sound like a miniature jackhammer signaled that, unless a sewing machine was running itself, Zell was inside at work. Channeling my inner Hollister, I acted before considering the consequences. I knocked on the door and steeled myself for the encounter. Nothing happened. The sewing machine kept clacking, uninterrupted. I knocked again, louder. This time, the machine stopped abruptly. The door swung open.

"No one's here," Zell said, as if I refused to believe her. She appeared angry and flustered as she pulled a strap of her coveralls over her shoulder.

"I came to talk to you," I lied. "Jenna had the most fantastic idea. To round out our story in the *Gazette*, she suggested I interview the people responsible for making Mysterium hum—the incredibly hard-working professionals behind the scenes. I think our readers will enjoy a glimpse into everything it takes to put on an extravaganza like Mysterium."

My attempt at flattery landed flat. If anything, Zell looked even more annoyed. "Like I have time for that." She glanced behind her at a clock on the wall and swore under her breath.

"It won't take long, just a—"

"Tell Jenna she's not my boss," she said before slamming the door. The sewing machine started up again.

The Hayden of last year would have contented himself with *"Oh, well! I gave it a shot."* But this was something I could not walk away from. I was on a mission—there could be no turning back. I checked my watch. I'd need five minutes to race back to my car and stash the scissors before meeting up with Vlad. That left me with twenty minutes.

I knocked again. Louder.

The machine went quiet. The door flew open.

I raised my hand to stave off the verbal onslaught. "Five minutes," I blurted. "Five minutes, then I'll do anything you want for fifteen."

"What?"

My unexpected proposal caught Zell off guard. She twisted her face, showing suspicion.

"I know you're busy. But my job's on the line here. Give me five minutes to ask my questions. Then I will do anything you want for fifteen minutes. It's a three-for-one offer. You can't go wrong."

"What are you talking about?" Zell said, scrunching her nose ring against her top lip.

"I have twenty minutes before I need to race back to the office and write up my story before the deadline. You're my last interview. Give me five minutes—just five minutes—and the rest of my time is yours. That's a quarter-hour of free labor."

Encouraged that Zell hadn't slammed the door a second time, I went for the close. I produced what I hoped came across as a sad puppy dog face and said, "Please, Zell. You would really be helping me out."

"Anything?" She looked skeptical.

I nodded. "Yes, ma'am. Anything."

"Seriously? *Anything?*" The corners of her mouth lifted in the suggestion of a smile.

Suddenly my impromptu offer didn't seem like such a bright idea. "Seriously," I confirmed, trying for a steady tone. And with that, Zell ushered me inside.

Before when Hollister and I had visited the costume shop, the room had smelled of Yazminka's perfume. That pleasing fragrance had been replaced by an odd mixture of locker room muskiness and heavy cologne. Zell picked up a heap of costumes from the floor, along with spools of thread and a measuring tape, and set them all on the spacious worktable that dominated the room. "Better start asking. The clock's ticking." She surveyed the room as if searching for something she'd misplaced.

Once the pretend interview for a fictional story for a nonexistent news site had concluded, Zell wasted not a second of her fifteen minutes. She instructed me to "drop the duds" and "for God's sake, keep your skivvies on."

Standing on the raised platform before three angled mirrors in the corner of the trailer, I modeled a tight-fitted spandex bodysuit of a leopard print. I don't mind saying I didn't look half bad. The costume designed for Yazminka was behind schedule. The famed Russian aerialist had missed her fitting for this particular costume for the second time in as many days.

"'ol' still," Zell mumbled, a pin clamped between her lips.

"I am holding still."

She gripped and squared my shoulders.

"'o'nt move."

Examining my shape in the mirror from many angles, I could see how my body might be confused for that of a slim and fit, flat-chested woman. Professional that she was, Zell had recognized my potential as a Yazminka stand-in.

Trapped in the pin-riddled bodysuit with nothing else to occupy my thoughts, I was free to formulate a plan to snatch the scissors, which rested on the large cutting table. All I needed was five seconds alone in the room, and I could temporarily hide them beneath the pile of my clothes; then later, when I dressed, I would tuck them between the two pairs of thick wool socks I'd worn for that exact purpose. But how to get Zell out of the trailer? Scanning the room in the reflection of the mirrors, I searched for inspiration.

"What was that?" I jerked.

Zell stabbed my thigh with a pin.

"Ow!"

"I told you not to move."

"I saw someone outside." I pointed to the window.

Demonstrating her lack of concern, Zell took a half step back, cocked her head, and examined her work. "Dozens of people work here," she said dismissively. "Could have been anyone."

Zell had nearly finished Yazminka's costume. I was running out of time.

"It's a man! With a camera!"

"Camera?" She whirled around toward the window. "Where?"

"He ducked below the sill!" I urgently jabbed my finger toward the window. "I'm pretty sure he took a picture."

"Bloody hell," she hissed. "He probably thinks he got a pic of Yaz. She'll freak." Zell raced the few steps to the door, stopped abruptly, and turned back. "He's got a surprise coming." She snatched up the large shears from the table and hurried out of the trailer.

Are you effing kidding me!

I had to act fast. I yanked off the bodysuit. *OW!* More than a dozen pins jabbed into my flesh. I gritted my teeth and wiggled out of the body-hugging fabric, releasing a flurry of F-bombs. Draping the costume over a chair, I caught my reflection in the mirror. Blood oozed from tiny puncture wounds on my chest, shoulders, and torso. I muttered a fresh round of curses. Outside, the crown of Zell's green hair, glistening with rain, appeared at the bottom of the window. She'd find no one behind the trailer and return inside in no time. I threw on my clothes. As I reached for my sneakers, Zell entered the trailer, shears in hand.

"He got away," she grumbled. Seeing me lace my sneakers, she said, "Hey! I wasn't finished."

"Yeah, well, we had a bargain. Your fifteen minutes are up." Failing in my mission, I had run out of patience.

Zell dropped the scissors onto the table. "I got to go alert security. They might be able to find that creep before he leaves the grounds. See yourself out, will you?" And just like that, Zell left me alone among the bolts of fabric and wall of wigs, and with the prize I'd done all this for.

Chapter Twenty-Four
Adrenalin!

The time was 3:58 PM. I carefully descended the costume shop's slippery steps. I couldn't exactly tour Mysterium with nine inches of rigid steel stuck between my socks, and surely Vlad would ask why I was walking funny. But I had only two minutes before I was to meet him.

Waiting at the gate for my date, four o'clock became four twenty, and then four thirty. I chose not to pester the guard a second time. When I'd first asked her to let Vlad know I was waiting, she'd seemed put out to make a call, telling me, "The stage manager says things are running behind. Could be a while."

Initially, I'd welcomed the delay—the extra time allowed me to hobble to my car and stow the scissors beneath a blanket in the trunk. But a half hour of standing in the cold rain had made me grumpy. How long did Vlad expect me to wait? Checking my watch—again—I promised myself five more minutes. That was my absolute limit.

Twenty minutes later, with no sign of my date, I was halfway across the parking lot when the splish-splash of rapidly approaching footsteps preceded a voice shouting, "Hayden, wait up!"

Vlad jogged up beside me. Despite the rain and chilly temperature, he wore only a tank top and very short shorts. He stood barefoot in a puddle.

"So sorry, man. You have no idea. We lost a key performer, and the new equipment is tricky. It's thrown everything into a tailspin, and I mean everything. I couldn't text. I was tied up. Literally. And suspended thirty feet in the air."

I stepped closer to Vlad to share my umbrella. His brown Marine-short hair shimmered with water droplets; his damp shirt clung to his pecs and biceps.

"We still hanging out?" he asked.

"Yeah," I replied. "Okay." Was I being too forgiving? Although I believed Vlad, I had stood out in the cold rain for nearly an hour. What signal did that send? That I didn't value my own time? That I was exceedingly understanding? That I was desperate? The reason that I had come here—the only reason that should matter—was to swipe the scissors, which I'd done. So why had I stayed? The answer twisted my gut. Not since last summer, when I'd first seen Camilo dancing on the pool table at Hunters, had I been so taken by a guy. While the realization should have made me gleeful with anticipation, I felt emotionally exposed.

Vlad led me back through Mysterium's gate and toward a row of trailers, on the backside of the main tent, that I hadn't seen before.

"Home sweet home." Vlad pointed to a door with four names. The last one read: "Vlad Halep." The first three names, Florin,

Marku, and Stefan, were each coupled with a surname heavy on consonants. Vlad explained simply by saying, "Romanian. Myself included."

Once inside, I got a sample of what I'd missed by playing high-school tennis instead of a team sport—like football or basketball—that began and ended practice in a crammed locker room filled with muscled athletes. Blue-eyed and fair-skinned, each guy had a sculpted acrobat's body and wore some combination of a jockstrap, smile, and wide-eyed look of surprise.

I was greeted by thick Eastern European accents, the smell of Old Spice, and handshakes that nearly crushed my fingers. I made a concerted effort not to let my gaze drift south of the equator. My trusty gaydar picked up no reading on these guys whatsoever, including Florin, the other half of The Sisters Flip. Did this trio of Slavic Adonises know Vlad was gay? If they were curious about how Vlad and I knew each other or why I had crashed their already cramped trailer, they showed no sign of it. Had Vlad said something to them beforehand? Or was the appearance of an unfamiliar guy alongside him so common that it needed no explanation? Suddenly I was hit by a dreadful thought: *What if I'm just another guy in just another city?*

Thankfully, all three spoke English, but not entirely. There was a good bit of banter in what I assumed was Romanian. Over the next thirty minutes, the guys dressed after taking turns showering in the tiny adjacent bathroom. The colors of their T-shirts and brands of jeans differed, but every stitch of clothing was tight. Footwear, however, varied and was curiously suited to what I gleaned from each guy's personality. Stefan, the smooth operator, had expensive-looking loafers (no socks). Florin, Mr. Outdoorsy, wore techie hiking shoes, and Marku—Bucharest's equivalent of a frat boy—wore flip-flops. Vlad—the guy next door—met my silent approval with his choice of clean white sneakers.

I was particularly interested in observing Florin and his inter-action with Vlad. I wondered whether he and Vlad might have something going on the side. Although I was antsy to get on with our date, time hadn't been wasted. While waiting, I learned a great deal about Adrenalin! (although some of it I already knew from seeing them perform at the preview). In addition to their high-energy group performance, each of the guys also supported a solo performer. Florin spotted a female Chinese contortion-ist who swung high above the crowd while striking seemingly impossible poses. Marku and Stefan provided trapeze support for a torch song singer from France; and Vlad provided the mus-cle and eye candy for Yazminka Smilova's head-spinning aerial acrobatics.

I couldn't help but romanticize these guys' lives. They enjoyed comradery, applause, housekeeping services, and a new city each month. And there was the bonus of achieving a shredded phy-sique. My job satisfaction would improve considerably if grading papers and lecturing eighth-graders gave me a defined chest, a six-pack, and an impressive set of guns. Envious of the bodies surrounding me, I vowed to hit the gym more regularly. Glanc-ing at myself in the mirror, I was reminded that a half hour on the elliptical trainer while watching the Sci-fi channel does not a ripped body make.

"Hungry?" Vlad gripped my shoulder.

Marku sprang to his feet; his bare heels smacked against the rubber soles of his Havaianas. "Yes. Where to? I vote for burgers."

"Pizza, pizza, pizza," Florin chirped excitedly, reaching for a waterproof jacket I wouldn't mind having for myself.

"You chose last time," Stefan argued. "I'd kill for some good sushi."

Vlad grinned at me and shrugged. I couldn't tell what he intended by the gesture. Did his friends amuse him? Or—the very idea crushed me—were the five of us going out together?

Minutes later, the question was answered when Vlad and I dashed across the parking lot and climbed into the back seat of an awaiting SUV next to Florin. Marku had the wheel; Stefan sat next to him. My disappointment was somewhat softened by being among a fun-loving and ridiculously attractive group of guys. Besides, I told myself, I still wasn't sure whether it was safe to be alone with Vlad. Suddenly, another thought struck: the murderer could be any of these guys. Or more than one of them.

Chapter
Twenty-Five
Stay Safe

Marku navigated the white land yacht to a popular downtown pizza place. Our host, a cute twink (my gaydar picking up a clear reading on the slim twenty-something), escorted our party to a large round table at the center of the dining room. The poor guy was so befuddled by the handsome cast of Adrenalin! that he fumbled his words while handing out the menus. "Have a good menu . . . I mean, it's good to have you . . ." He blushed, turning his cheeks the color of a ripe tomato. I smiled encouragingly, and he managed to mutter, "Enjoy your dinner," before skulking away.

The waiter took our drink orders—no alcohol for these guys. Sensing my opportunity, I said, "So, how did you four get together?"

"There is a famous gymnastics institute in Bucharest," Marku said. "We met there."

I followed up with, "But what made the four of you decide to form a group?"

"It was my idea." Stefan suddenly looked serious. He set his iced tea on the table and sat up straighter, as if readying himself for a difficult conversation. "It was a cold January day. I remember this well."

"It was January in Bucharest!" said Marku, "Of course, it was cold!"

"Shh," Stefan scolded. "You're ruining my story. As I was saying, it was January. Very cold in the gymnasium." He gave a theatrical shiver. "I looked around very carefully at all the other male gymnasts, and I thought to myself, *Now which of these guys can I be sure, absolutely sure, will never ever outperform me.*"

Florin nearly spit out his Pepsi. Marku gave Stefan a playful shove and said, "You wish, ass-bite. It took you three months to learn a double back."

"Ha. You're one to talk," scoffed Stefan, "I was nailing quad layouts while you were fumbling handstands."

Ten minutes later, I regretted what I'd started. However, I did need to bring up the subject of Kennedy Osaka, and once I'd triggered a conversation about work, the guys couldn't talk about anything else.

Between slices of Meat Lovers Supreme, the members of Adrenalin! confirmed that Mysterium's owner was Yazminka's and Sasha's father, a wealthy Russian named Boris Smilov. While no one involved with Mysterium denied her talent, many in the cast and crew resented her special treatment. They questioned whether her marquee status had been earned or gifted by her rich father. Yazminka seemed to despise everyone—with the lone exception of the wardrobe manager, Zell, whom she appeared to at least tolerate. About Sasha, Marku summed up the guys' feelings: "He's interested in only one thing. Women. Rumor has it Papa Smilov has had about enough of his son's sleeping around. He causes too much drama among the cast and crew. It's bad for business."

"He ought to be fired," hissed Florin. "The man is no good. He does nothing but smell up the place."

The other three guys, mouths full of dinner, grunted in agreement.

I hadn't forgotten seeing Vlad and the guy I now knew was Marku peering through the costume shop's window moments before Sasha had come outside. At the time, Hollister and I had chalked it up to a dare of some sort or innocent horseplay. But given their animosity toward Sasha, I wondered if there were more to it.

At the other end of the popularity spectrum was Kit Durango, who was "beloved." Surrogate mother to some, sister to others, and amiable colleague to all, Kit was the heart and soul of Mysterium. According to the guys, when Kennedy Osaka had been hired as artistic director, everyone had been disappointed that the job hadn't gone to Kit. Then, when word got around about Kennedy's planned changes, that disappointment turned to discontent and anger. As Stefan put it, "Kennedy waltzed into Mysterium thinking she was better than everyone else. As if the show wasn't good enough. That we needed—"

"A facelift," Florin interjected. "Can you believe that crap? Literally, her words. A facelift. She wanted velvet seating and valet parking. Even the ushers were supposed to wear tuxes. You'd think Mysterium had hay on the floors and the audience sat on folding chairs by the way she talked. I mean, the event is already high end. Tickets start at four hundred bucks, and the chef has a fricken Michelin star."

"And sorry if this sounds arrogant," Vlad said, "but Adrenalin! has performed for six different heads of state and won five international acrobatics competitions. In the aerial arts world, we are superstars. Rather than show us proper respect, Kennedy stopped our first rehearsal just three minutes in and said we needed to 'rethink our music.' According to her, our band was 'abrasive.' Then she said, and I quote, 'My six-year-old niece can do a somersault. You boys need to try a bit harder.' Unbelievable."

I was about to bring up the topic of Kennedy's replacement when Marku, mouth half full of crust, mumbled, "Thank god, they should be announcing the new artistic director soon."

"Please, don't let it be Yaz," Stefan groaned, wiping sauce from his chin.

"Ought to be Kit!" Florin said loudly, drawing looks from nearby tables. We'd been the subject of attention since arriving, so it wasn't as uncomfortable as it might be.

As our time at the restaurant wound down, it became apparent that no one else was going to ask the question that had been on my lips throughout our meal. I had to ask, "You guys have any ideas about what happened to Kennedy?"

Stefan and Florin froze mid-chew. Marku held his water glass pressed to his lips. Vlad's eyes bugged. It appeared that I'd said the unthinkable. Mortified, I wanted to slip beneath the table. After a long silence that felt like a century, Florin came to my rescue. "How could any of us possibly know? I mean, it was a thief, right? Someone in the lobby posted a video of the cops arresting some chick."

Hearing the remark, I swallowed hard, nearly choking on a bite of crust.

"Yeah," quipped Vlad, "but I read they let her go the next day."

"Still though," Florin said between chews, "it had to be a thief. Some rando lowlife hoping to score some cash or valuables. They must have thought no one was in the room. Doesn't make Kennedy any less dead, but at least it's no one we know."

I wasn't itching for an argument, but I disagreed. That it might have been a thief didn't add up. What would compel a hotel burglar to escalate to stabbing a stranger to death? Why not run? What thief prowls about with giant tailoring shears? I'd learned firsthand what a pain they were to conceal.

"Kennedy must have caught the thief in the act," Marku mused. "He couldn't leave behind a witness."

"That's a bit extreme, don't you think," I said, "You can't think—"

"Can't think what?" Marku snapped. "You have another idea?"

"Hayden's got a point," Vlad said calmly. "Someone who paws through drawers for cash isn't the type of person to kill another human being in cold blood."

"How would you know?" Marku's voice matched his irritated expression.

"Think about it," Vlad said. "You're saying any criminal could commit any criminal act. But that's like saying any acrobat can perform any acrobatic act."

"That's absurd," Stefan said, looking offended.

"Precisely my point." Vlad sat back in his chair and crossed his arms over his broad chest.

"Way-way-way-wait." Florin waved a finger. "You're saying it might have been someone we know? Someone with the show?"

"Oh, right," Marku said jokingly. "I forgot to tell you guys. I killed Kennedy."

"That's not funny, Marku." Vlad gave him a hard look.

"C'mon, guys." Marku rolled his head. "You really think someone in the crew is a killer?"

"Let's not forget the cast," Florin said. "She did piss off a lot of people."

"What do you think, Hayden?" Vlad asked. "You don't know anyone at Mysterium, so personal relationships won't cloud your judgment."

"He knows us," Florin corrected.

The question took me off guard. All four guys stared at me expectantly. It's a funny feeling to hold the rapt attention of four gorgeous guys, but the topic was hardly a turn-on. I took a long swig of water and selected my words carefully. "If the police thought they had anything on the individual they initially arrested, that person would still be in custody. I think whoever murdered Kennedy Osaka works at Mysterium."

"So, it could have been you," Florin grinned slyly at Marku.

"Or you," Marku replied with a maniacally raised brow.

Joking aside, my stomach was doing cartwheels. There was no love lost between Kennedy and Adrenalin! How badly had one—or more—of them wanted her forever silenced from having any say over their act?

I threw in a twenty and a ten to cover my portion of the bill and tip, and the five of us made our grand exit, drawing the attention of every other table in the restaurant. Passing the young host, he said, "Thanks for coming in. You all be safe out there." I did a double-take, thinking for a split second that he was speaking directly to me. His words were well chosen despite the impossibility of him knowing my situation. Any one of the guys who was giving me a lift back to my car might be a killer.

Chapter
Twenty-Six
Mates on Dates, Post No. 25

MATES ON DATES: Free to Love

As some of you know, I'm secretly in love (I'm pretty sure I am, anyway) with a friend. However, I have serious doubts that he feels the same way. Despite his flirting with me in ways that suggest we're more than friends, he always stops short of actually doing anything that would clarify his intentions. For months on end, the situation has made me crazy. Then just when I resolved to tell my friend to knock it off, along comes a new guy. New Guy is a few inches taller than me (surprise, surprise), a professional performer, and has beautiful, slightly crossed eyes the color of a swimming pool. To pile on, he works closely with a few other guys, also in their twenties, each of whom is attractive in his own right. Together, they form a bonfire of hotness. I'm not ashamed to say that when around them, I can't help but bask in the glow of their good looks.

Alas, there's a problem. Isn't there always?

Also aflame are my can't-quite-stamp-them-out-though-I-wish-I-could feelings for my friend. Although I'm attracted to both guys, there is a critical distinction between them. New Guy is available and shows interest in me, while my friend just messes with my head. Given that, you'd think the matter would be clear-cut. You'd be wrong.

Despite my friend continually causing me emotional turmoil, given a choice, I would still choose him over New Guy. It defies all reason.

However, not all is lost. New Guy's arrival brings into sharp relief how much I've allowed myself to be tormented by love unre-quited. Whether or not New Guy is the one (too early to tell, and he doesn't even live in my city), I have to find the wherewithal to stop holding out hope for a relationship with my friend.

And so, back to New Guy. I will do my best to enjoy his company, take things less seriously, and live in the moment. Even if it doesn't work out with New Guy, I am determined to use the experience to work myself out of my current romantic logjam.

The hippies of the 1960s practiced Free Love. I'm not opposed to the idea, though for me, a variation on the theme hits closer to home: Free *to* love. Don't forget, guys, you heard it here first on Mates on Dates! Free to love is the idea that before you can love someone else, you must be free to be loved in return. You might have selected your undies with the care of a farm-to-table chef and gelled that pesky cowlick into submission, but I ask you: Are you equally prepared on the inside?

If you're carrying the baggage of having feelings for someone else, do yourself a favor and push "Pause" on that next date. If not for yourself, do it for the other guy. After all, would *you* want to go out with someone stuck on someone else?

Till next time, I'm Hayden
And remember, if you can't be good, be safe!

Chapter Twenty-Seven
No Time for a Hissy Fit

I'd seen enough television crime shows to know that the police have sophisticated means to track down weapons used in crimes and thereby narrow a list of possible suspects. I could only assume detectives were doing that with the scissors used to murder Kennedy Osaka.

The five of us had reconvened again at Jess's houseboat. After recounting my time hiding in Kit's trailer, overhearing the strange conversation with someone named Alexander, and modeling Yazminka's outfit for Zell, I proudly set the hefty shears from the costume shop on the middle of the table and pulled from my pocket a folded printout of a web page that described them in detail.

"Those, ladies and gentleman, are Clauss nine-inch steel fabric shears. They'll run you about seventy bucks. Though not rare, they are a specialty item. It's safe to say that only a professional tailor or someone who takes their clothes-making very seriously would own a pair."

Hollister picked up the scissors and examined their smooth finish in the window's light. "Substantial." She passed them to Jess.

Gauging their weight, he said, "Surprisingly heavy. I don't imagine these are easy to conceal or wield as a weapon." He turned to me. "Do *not* tell me how you obtained these."

Burley asked Sarah Lee. "What do you think? Are they the same?"

The four of us exchanged excited looks. Sarah Lee took them with a trembling hand and appeared to gauge their weight. She closed her eyes. After a long moment, she wordlessly returned them to Jess. "I wish I could be one hundred percent certain. But, yes, I think they might be."

Jess stood and started pacing the tiny space as if addressing a jury. "Investigations follow a common set of steps. Evidence is gathered, forensics performed, witnesses' statements are taken, and leads pursued. If a prosecutor believes there is sufficient evidence to get a conviction, they'll bring charges. So far, I haven't heard anything from the detectives working the investigation. The scissors seem more crucial than ever to lead us to the killer. Again, there's no obvious reason for Kennedy to have had any scissors other than, say, cuticle scissors in her room. Which takes us back to where we started. The murderer must have arrived at Kennedy's suite with the scissors. Presuming they did come from the shop, who took them?"

Chapter Twenty-Eight
Moving Parts

Realizing that I'd not checked my mailbox the previous day, I made a U-turn on the steps up to my apartment. At Orca Arms, mailboxes for each apartment block were clustered near the carports on stout white poles. At first glance, the half-dozen letters addressed to me or "Occupant" appeared to be junk. But between a credit card offer and a big box store coupon was a yellow envelope containing a small, solid item. Someone, a woman by the looks of the loopy cursive handwriting, had addressed the letter "Mister Hayden McCall" in blue ballpoint pen. I didn't recognize the return address, nor did I know the sender, Harriet Heffelfinger.

Once inside my studio, I ripped open the curious envelope. A plastic keychain depicting Oregon's famous Multnomah Falls fell onto the table. I unfolded the page.

Dear Mister McCall,

Please accept this small token of gratitude for your most gracious assistance in helping me catch Alice in the park earlier in the week. Alice is high-spirited but good-natured. She is most dear to me. Had I sent this note just days earlier, I would be signing off with a final expression of gratitude. However, as with so much in life, things change. For a host of reasons I won't go into here, I have decided it is best for me to move in with my daughter and son-in-law and grandchildren in Salt Lake City. This, however, presents a problem I find most upsetting. I must give up Alice. One of my grandchildren is allergic to pets, and I've been told that Alice is not welcome. And so, much to my anguish, I must find a good home for my dearest Alice. Mister McCall, I know nothing of your circumstances or if you have ever considered owning a dog, but as I searched my cupboards for a small gift to send you, I fondly recalled how immediately Alice had taken to you. And you to her? Should you be at all interested in taking her, I would like to speak with you at your earliest convenience. I must make a suitable arrangement for her soon. The thought of a shelter is unbearable. If it is not meant to be, perhaps you have a friend or family member who might be interested? If not, I certainly understand.

Warmest regards,
Harriet H.
206-555-9889

An hour later, I reread the letter aloud at Jerry's kitchen table. When I finished, I said, "Okay, go ahead. Ask me."

"Ask you what?"

"The question you're dying to ask."

Jerry paused setting up the cribbage board. "Why not just tell me the answer?"

"Dalmatian."

Jerry nodded as if he'd seen that coming. "Attractive dog. I've always found them a bit high-strung. Still, that wasn't what was on my mind. Isn't a far more interesting question whether you're going to take her?"

"You're out of milk." I turned back from the open refrigerator door. "I would have stopped at the store if I'd known. Why didn't you tell me? Not thirty minutes ago, on the way over here, I called to see if I should pick anything up."

"And that was appreciated, Hayden. But it's not urgent. There will be milk at the store tomorrow."

I stared at Jerry. He had always been honest with me. Although nothing he'd said was a lie, he was being purposefully evasive. I knew why. His need to pinch pennies only reaffirmed the idea that had blossomed in my brain when I'd first read Harriet's letter.

"Tea without milk is a sadder existence than I'm willing to live," I said.

Now it was Jerry's turn to stare at me.

I closed the fridge door and switched on the burner beneath the kettle. "In case you don't recognize those words, they are a Jerry Millstein original. So you're not fooling anybody."

Turning my attention to the cupboard, I gasped and whirled around, holding a box of cheap, discount-store tea bags. "No, no, no. No frigging way, Jerry."

"Harney & Sons is too expensive. You don't understand."

I pulled up a chair next to him. The tears pooling in the corners of his eyes nearly did me in.

"Listen, Jerry. I've been thinking . . ."

It took two hours to convince Jerry of my plan's soundness, hammer out the details, and re-convince him that I was okay with it. I was moving in with Jerry. Not only would a new place shake things up for me, but by sharing the cost of his townhome, Jerry would be better off than he'd been in years and able to afford his new prescription and then some. I would also be money ahead. The entire top floor would be mine (Jerry wasn't good with stairs). I'd set up one of the two second-floor bedrooms as my own little living room-slash-office, and I'd have a bathroom to myself. We would share the kitchen. Jerry didn't own a car, so I'd have full use of the double garage. Best yet, the townhome had a fenced backyard for Alice.

Jerry, being Jerry, hadn't hesitated to raise an issue I'd worried about. "You're a young man, Hayden. If this is going to work, you can't think twice about bringing someone home. For what it's worth, I turn in at eight o'clock, and my hearing is crap. So whatever you might get up to up there"—he pointed a bent finger at the ceiling—"I won't have a clue, and don't care two cents. You're an adult. What you do in your own home is your own business."

I pointed out that I would be a tenant, not an owner, but Jerry would have none of it.

"No, sir. I won't have you thinking that way. Sure, on paper, I am the proud owner of this grand estate, but if I'm going to agree to this, you need to think of this place as yours as much as it is mine. You're giving up too much. Say what you will. Spin it how you like. But we both know you're saving my ass."

The truth was, I wanted Alice, and the ability to save twice as much money each month was undeniably appealing. I knew Jerry well enough to know he'd let me live my life and involve himself only when invited. Still, there were two major setbacks to the plan. First, the commute to my Federal Way school would take twice as long. The second was far more concerning: Jerry's next-door neighbor was my Aunt Sally.

"What if we don't tell her?" Jerry joked. "She spends all her time either at Bible study or with her eyes glued to that religious television station. It may be years before she catches on."

I laughed and wondered for a moment if we might not get away with it. But the dog would reveal the truth soon enough. Jerry was in reasonably good health, considering his age, but he was no match for the young, energetic, and extremely fleet-of-paw Alice.

Setting ground rules with Aunt Sally would be imperative. No impromptu visits. No questions, such as "Was that a boy I saw you come home with last night?" And when she came to collect Jerry to drive him to a doctor's appointment, under no circumstances would she be permitted upstairs.

"Don't worry about that, Hayden. I'll threaten to throw myself on the staircase if she tries to intrude on your lair. At my age, that will scare the living daylights out of her. She won't want a Kamikaze mission to occur on her watch."

After a round-trip to the grocery store, I hugged Jerry gently (his bony frame suggested the need for careful handling). As it was nearing his bedtime, and I'd done next to nothing to prepare myself for the next day's classes, I headed back to West Seattle. That I had a dwindling number of trips home to Orca Arms did bum me out. I told myself to concentrate on the upside of moving in with Jerry. I could finally have a dog of my own. And I could start putting away enough money that it would actually amount to something in a few years.

Although my mind was filled with thoughts of moving boxes and chew toys, worries about our investigation muscled their way in. More than a week had passed since Kennedy's murder. If the homicide detectives had made progress in identifying her killer, they hadn't told Jess about it. But would they? Surely they would share such information with Sarah Lee's lawyer.

As for Mysterium, Smilov Entertainment Group had made no announcement about Kennedy's replacement. With the clock ticking down to opening night, I started to think there would be no press release. Were that the case, the public would learn who had assumed the role by reading about the appointment in the program on the night of the show's opening.

Returning home, I jumped onto the bed, phone in hand. For months I'd habitually monitored my screen for a text from Camilo, and only on a handful of occasions had I not been disappointed. Today, things were different. Not because Camilo had come through but because another sender had. I texted a reply: *WOW! That's super generous. Thanks.*

The rest of our exchange:

Vlad: *NP. Looking forward to seeing you.*
Me: *Me too! I guess I shouldn't say break a leg.* ☺
Vlad: *Ha! See you after. About 11:30?*
Me: *Yeah sounds good.*
Vlad: *Cool. Enjoy the show. Night.*
Me: *Night, Vlad.*

Tomorrow was Mysterium's opening night. I had assumed I'd find out whether there was a new artistic director in the following morning's news. But that had just changed. Vlad had gifted me a two-person, front-row table for tomorrow's performance. Hollister and I were returning to Mysterium. But we would not be sitting in row Z. No, sir! This time we were going as VIP guests of Adrenalin!

Chapter Twenty-Nine

Showtime

Hollister dropped onto the tattered passenger seat of my gutless compact car. Although she'd initially offered to drive, the monstrous nail on Seneca Street that had punctured her Porsche's tire had had its own ideas. Before I pulled away from the curb outside her place, a nifty live-work setup, in Seattle's Central District, where she ran her high-end furniture design business, I established the rules of the road: no back-seat driving, no eye-rolling, no muttering under her breath, no rapping her knuckles on the dashboard. Five minutes into the drive, she had violated each of these conditions—multiple times.

I decided to ignore her criticism of my respect for speed limits, stop signs, and the number of designated lanes on the road. What I couldn't ignore were Hollister's long nails. Usually all one solid color, tonight each nail had been painted in a different animal print.

"How'd you do that?" I marveled.

She shot me a look. "Apple Pay."

Her hair was also different. Despite repeated glances, I couldn't figure out what exactly she'd done to change it and didn't want to ask.

After arriving at Mysterium, we shuffled along with the crowd into the big tent. The buzz of excitement was palpable. The show had been the talk of social media and local news for weeks; tickets were impossible to score unless you were willing to pay double the price from a reseller.

"Check him out," Hollister said, pointing a tiger-striped nail toward Sasha Smilov, who stood at the entrance greeting guests as they entered the tent.

I couldn't help my eye roll. Tonight Mysterium's head of operations was even more of a caricature of himself. Dressed like a biker with a Hollywood stylist, he wore a loose-fitted leather and suede jacket, no shirt, black jeans, and motorcycle boots. As we stepped closer to him, I inhaled a waft of cologne that tickled my nose with the subtlety of Stilton cheese. When it was our turn to enter the tent, he welcomed us in a thick Russian accent and shook my hand; his chunky silver skull ring jabbed into my palm.

Hollister sniffed the air. "The dude smells like Helen," she said, a reference to the matriarch of Burley's mob of backyard emus. "Good lord. And he's the boss of his sister?"

"Partially," I replied. "In arts organizations it's common for one person to head up the creative side of things—that was Kennedy—while another handles the business end; that's Sasha's job." I had picked up this kernel of knowledge during a two-week dating spree with a ballet dancer. Just when I'd started to think things might actually be going somewhere, he did. Accepting a promotion to soloist with another company, he moved to San Francisco.

Hollister said, "To that point, there's still no word about who, if anyone, has replaced Kennedy. Right?"

"As far as we know. But if someone did, we're about to find out."

We were escorted down to our front-row table by a young usher wearing official Mysterium staff garb, which seemed like pirate outfits designed by Tim Burton: a crisp black suit with comically oversized shoulders; high-water, cuffed bell-bottom trousers; and a Victorian-era pearl-white blouse with a frilly high collar beneath the jacket. To emphasize the jaunty intent, the staff wore pink bowler hats. We hadn't even sat down, and I was already loving it. As we passed by rows H, G, F . . . descending closer and closer to the stage on our way to row A, I felt an odd rush of superiority. Of course we hadn't paid the nearly thousand dollars the pair of tickets would have cost. And even if we had, that would be a gross reason for feeling self-important. Nevertheless . . .

Most audience members had been required to preselect their main course—saffron mushroom risotto, pan-seared halibut, filet of beef tenderloin, or chicken. Hollister scoffed, "Chicken? Given the choices, who would order the chicken?"

"Perhaps it comes with a side of five-dollar bills."

As VIP guests, we would order that night off the velvet-bound menus. House wine or a signature cocktail—a gin-based concoction named the Twisted Acrobat—was complimentary. Being a wine connoisseur, Hollister sprang for a pricey bottle of Sancerre to complement our fish, rationalizing the splurge since the tickets had been comped.

The lights dimmed as staff cleared dessert plates from the one hundred or so candle-lit tables. A hush settled throughout the tent. The show was about to begin. A second stage behind the ring silently began to rise, revealing an orchestra of a dozen musicians, all dressed in Mysterium outfits—white sneakers to pink hats. At first slow and subdued, the music gradually built to a frenzied crescendo. *Clang!* The cymbal clash died out. A single spotlight flashed on. A lone figure stood in the center of the ring. Wearing a sexy part tuxedo, part gown with a revealing slit to show off her pole-vaulter legs, the woman bowed and doffed a beret matching her black bowtie and lipstick.

As I'd become familiar with the Mysterium lineup, I knew this was Nicole Armand, a French chanteuse and trapeze artist.

"Ooh la la," Hollister whispered.

Nicole Armand sang a beautifully melancholy song in French as Stefan and Marku danced around her with a sensuality that would make a Brazilian blush. The guys slowly removed Nicole's tuxedo dress, leaving only a black bikini. Like the old Maypole dance, the guys skipped around her, wrapping her torso in colorful ribbons. Once bound in strips of cloth, Nicole stepped onto a trapeze that ascended to the tent's full height. Below her, Stefan and Marku rolled a colorful net matching the ribbons binding Nicole's body onto the stage. As the guys danced around the net, Nicole performed a series of elegant and complicated moves while swinging high above our heads. When the music climaxed, Nicole let go of the trapeze bar, tumbling back to earth in a kaleidoscopic blur of unraveling ribbons, landing into the net hidden behind Stefan and Marku. The crowd held its breath. With a dramatic flourish, the guys parted to reveal Nicole—only Nicole had vanished. In her place stood a small girl (Nicole's daughter, maybe?) wearing a beautiful dress made of the same colorful ribbons. The audience went nuts.

"Damn," Hollister said. "That was worth the price of admission right there."

I neglected to remind her that we'd paid nothing for our tickets. If what was to come was half as good as what we'd seen, the night would be amazing.

Next up was Lady Valentina, an Argentinian juggler. To spirited salsa music, Lady Valentina juggled flaming torches while spinning on a large disc—sort of a ginormous lazy Susan—that gradually increased its speed to the point that I became dizzy just watching.

As Lady Valentina took her bows, I whispered to Hollister, "Don't go getting any ideas."

Four acts later, the lights above the audience signaled intermission. Hollister and I were already on our feet, continuing the ovation for Yazminka Smilova's performance, which had just closed the show's first half. I'd read about the ornery Russian acrobat's work, but no description could do it justice. The tight round bun into which she'd coiled her golden hair must have hidden a connecting mechanism. Vlad had attached a cable suspended from high up in the tent's rafters to Yazminka's bun seconds before she had been lifted off the ground—*by the hair on her head.*

Once airborne, Yazminka commenced ten minutes of mind-boggling contortions while circling low over the crowd like some crazed drone. The musical accompaniment, an orchestral rock opera featuring squealing violins, had been perfect. The whole thing was thrilling, oddly arousing, and indescribably loud.

In the lobby, Sasha Smilov held court by a life-size cardboard cutout of himself. He was offering pictures with both of him to audience members, and there was a line.

"He's not even in the show," I grumbled to Hollister.

"People must figure he's somebody important. These days, that's all it takes. What are you waiting for?"

"How do you mean?

"Go get your picture with the bad boy boss. Chat him up. We need to stir the pot. Go get to stirring. I'll get in the drinks line."

I couldn't help but scowl. During the first six acts, she'd polished off all but my one glass of Sancerre. Then again, she had an unnatural tolerance for alcohol, we'd had a rough week, and I was driving.

Minutes later, I stepped from the line and stood in the designated spot between heavily cologned Sasha and his cardboard likeness. Figuring he was the type of guy to eat up flattery, I said, "Love the show, man. You're killing it."

Sasha flashed a twenty-thousand-dollar smile. "Wait till you see what I have in store for the second half. I'll blow your freaking mind."

I'll? He wasn't a performer. He was the head of operations. Was the Russian hipster so conceited that he was taking credit for everything that happened under Mysterium's big tent?

"Everyone is giving a fantastic performance," I said. "It couldn't have been easy considering what happened to Kennedy—especially since she was going to improve the show."

Sasha kept smiling, but the edges of his mouth twitched beneath his bushy mustache. "I don't know what you're talking about. Mysterium needs no changes. It's perfect as it is. Anyone who says any different doesn't know a damn thing about circus arts. Look around." He gestured broadly to the packed lobby. "Does it look like we need a new artistic direction?" No sooner had the photographer snapped our photo than Sasha gripped my shoulder roughly. "Now then, who's next?" He shoved me to the side and motioned for a group of middle-aged Japanese women to take the spot between him and his equally one-dimensional other self.

"Learn anything good?" Hollister handed me a tall tumbler of clear liquid with a slice of lime bobbing on the surface.

"Thanks, but I still have a glass of wine at the table. I can't possibly."

"Relax, little dude. It's sparkling water. I didn't feel right getting something only for myself." We raised glasses in a toast. Returning to our seats, I told her about my chitchat with Sasha Smilov, mentioning his remark about the show not needing any new artistic direction.

"Guess we can confidently add Mr. Blackbeard to the list of suspects," Hollister said.

"As if we needed any more."

From the program's description of the five acts in the show's second half, we were in for a wild ride—starting with Kit Durango. I was eager to watch the cowgirl shoot at a moving target just inches from someone's head while tossed about in the saddle. And there was another act—immediately following Kit's—for which I was even more excited. Stefan, Marku, Florin, and Vlad would take the ring. Finally, I would see Adrenalin!'s full act.

Chapter Thirty
A Little Trick
My Mama Taught Me

Kit took the stage, and after performing the trick she'd rehearsed with Hollister, she exchanged the professional assistant for another, a guy who immediately got my attention, along with the women in the audience. Even Hollister let out a soft whistle, giving me a nudge.

"Well, lookee here, folks!" Kit hollered to the crowd. "We got ourselves a bona fide cowpoke, ain't we? What's your name, fella?"

"Dakota," the hunky man answered.

"*Magic Mike* is missing its cowboy," I whispered. The thirty-something guy was ruggedly handsome and totally cut, with mussed rusty hair and a short, well-trimmed beard. He wore an over-the-top cowboy outfit: boots, chaps, a fringed shirt, a big ol' hat, and a silver belt buckle the size of a rib-eye steak.

"Welcome to the stage of Mysterium, Dakota!" Kit shouted. "You ready to help me with a little trick my mama taught me back home on the ranch?"

Dakota tipped his hat. "Yes, ma'am!"

Kit arched a hand above her eyes and looked into the crowd. "I'm pleased as punch to announce my very own mama is here in the audience tonight. She's visitin' all the way from Colorado. You doin' all right out there, Mama?"

From a front-row table, five over from our own, an older wiry woman in fancy rodeo attire gave a wave and shouted, "Doin' good, baby girl!"

Kit giggled and turned back to Dakota. "You ready to show us what you got, Dakota?"

The four increasingly rowdy moms at a nearby table—littered with as many empty chardonnay bottles—shouted their approval and cackled mischievously.

Kit nodded appreciatively. "Now, Dakota. When I say I need you to help me with an ol' Durango family trick, I don't mean just any ol' sleight o' hand. No sir! I mean a trick that you'll be tellin' your young'uns about for years to come. You ready for that, Dakota?"

"Yes, ma'am!"

The first assistant returned to the stage and placed one end of a slender, foot-long stick between Dakota's teeth before handing a bullwhip to Kit. It quickly became apparent that Kit would use the whip to snap the stick in Dakota's mouth in two. Kit's confident whooping and joking were counterbalanced by the look of sudden mock terror firmly planted on Dakota's face. If it weren't obvious that this was a well-rehearsed schtick, I might actually have been concerned.

"Dakota, you'd best not move now. Trust me on that, partner." The low rumble of a timpani drum commenced. Kit did a little jig in her white boots and spun a full circle.

Crack!

Half of the stick flew through the air and landed on the lap of a young woman sitting in the second row. The other half remained clenched between Dakota's chattering teeth. Hollister and I joined the audience in applauding our appreciation for Kit's skill—along with relief that Dakota still had a nose. The stagehand reappeared and placed a different stick between Dakota's lips. It was half the length of the first. The crowd muttered nervously. Again, the drums rumbled, and Kit shimmied around the stage. Then, to the amazement of all onlookers, she performed a perfect cartwheel.

Crack!

The stick snapped in half.

With exaggerated relief, Dakota bent over and gripped his knees. As the audience clapped, the stagehand reappeared and handed Kit a shotgun—or at least that was what it appeared to be.

"Now, Dakota," Kit said. "Seeing that you and I are all warmed up, what say you help me out with a bit of target practice? How about it, ladies and gents? Would you like to see Dakota here help ol' Kit practice her sharpshooting?"

Hollister and I did our part in contributing to the crowd's shouts of approval.

"All right, then. Sounds like we ought to proceed!"

Next, the assistant rolled onto the far end of the stage a bit of wall roughly the size of a commercial refrigerator. Someone had painted a full-size replica of Dakota's entire outfit on its front. Surrounding the figure's outline, at approximately a foot distance, were four silver stars, similar to those worn by western sheriffs. An oval hole was positioned near the top, just under the illustration of his ten-gallon hat. Dakota strutted over and stepped behind the wall to reveal that the single cutout was the perfect size for his face.

"Now, Dakota. Here's what's going to happen. While riding Thunderclap"—two assistants pushed a mechanized bull onto the stage's opposite end—"and with you standing over yonder, I will fire my grandpappy's rifle and hit those silver star targets, one by one."

Dakota aped a terrified look. The crowd oohed and aahed.

"Oh, and one last thing," Kit said, as if she'd just remembered. "Dakota, sweetie, I do truly mean it when I say it's best you hold good and still."

The audience muttered nervously as Kit mounted the bull. An assistant switched it on. It began to rock, and Kit raised the rifle. Surely she had done this trick thousands of times before, but I couldn't suppress a twisting of my stomach. I sat forward in my chair, palms pressed against my cheeks.

A drumroll.

Pop!

For a split second, the crowd was so silent you might have heard my gasp. I clapped a hand over my mouth. Kit's bullet had not only bull's-eyed one of the stars but also triggered the bit of wall depicting Dakota's boots to explode into confetti, revealing his naked shins and feet.

"Now that's a surprise!" Kit laughed.

Seeing where this was headed, the mood in the tent shifted from apprehensive to eager.

Kit repeated the routine twice, revealing the top of Dakota's head and then his bare torso and arms. Only one star and his chaps and belt buckle remained. The four moms at the nearby table were about to lose their minds. While the stage show remained PG, their catcalls had crossed the line to an R rating. I feared one of them might rush the stage.

Another drumroll, louder, more intense.

Kit raised the rifle.

Pop!

As much as I saw it coming, the sight of the hunky cowboy wearing only a big silver star—just big enough to keep the show respectable—was a satisfying end to Kit's act. Judging by the audience's reaction, they wholeheartedly agreed.

After a brief musical interlude that settled the crowd, Nicole Armand, serving as the evening's ring mistress, returned to the stage. To a chaotic sweep of spotlights across the stage, she announced, "And now, mesdames and messieurs, ladies and gentlemen, please welcome to the Mysterium's center ring *Adrenalin!*"

Chapter
Thirty-One
Flying Blind

Hollister and I had seen a portion of the Adrenalin! act at the preview. As before, The rock band Estonia! replaced the Mysterium Orchestra on the raised stage. They served up a screeching metal riff as the four members of Adrenalin! entered the tent, cartwheeling down the aisles, and somersaulted into the ring. They'd had a wardrobe change. Instead of the black harnesses and short shorts, they wore pale skin-tone singlets, like wrestlers. The effect was both sexy and oddly creepy—they looked like Ken dolls with no clothing. Strangest yet, whoever had conceived their "look" had included bald skullcaps but with a single micro ponytail sprouting from the top of the head, each a different brilliant color: Stefan's, red; Marku's, blue; Florin's, yellow; and Vlad's, green.

After performing the acts we'd previously seen, the stage went black. That close to the stage, we could make out the silhouettes of a dozen or so assistants racing around to set up the trapeze segment.

Two bars lowered to the stage. Marku and Stefan each grabbed one and were whisked to a height equal to that of a three-story building. They took turns flying from one bar to the next and swapping bars by passing each other midair. Meanwhile, Florin and Vlad had ascended a narrow ladder leading to a platform. They joined in displaying an impressive series of aerial twists and flips by swinging and flying between bars. Two assistants pulled a large trampoline onto the stage below. The ring of fire returned and was positioned horizontally above the trampoline. From the trapeze, one guy after another swung over the fire, released the bar, executed a complicated aerial contortion, and fell through the blazing ring onto the trampoline.

It was a heart-stopper. Each guy had to let go of the bar at precisely the right moment to fall through—and not into—the circular inferno.

Once all four had made it safely to the stage, the four performers reascended to the platform. The audience muttered. Hollister and I shifted in our seats in anticipation. At seeing what was coming next, Hollister squeezed my hand. I winced at the tightness of her grip but understood. The guys were taking turns tying blindfolds on one another.

"Seriously?" she muttered.

The music downshifted to a low, ominous theme that sounded like a combo of cello and ghost whispers.

First up was Marku. After three passes over the ring, he let go of the bar and executed a perfect double flip through the fire. The crowd cheered, seemingly as much for saving them from the grizzly sight of what would have otherwise occurred as for the stunt's brilliance. Florin followed with a twisting somersault, then Stefan did a pike-like dive straight through the ring. While I appreciated the other guys going first to prove the death-defying act could be done, my foreboding had grown. Vlad was up next.

With his three comrades and three hundred people looking upward, Vlad passed over the flame *once . . . twice . . . three . . . four times.*

I glanced at Vlad's comrades, who had removed their blindfolds and stood beside the trampoline, looking up. Like a passenger examining the face of a flight attendant during turbulence, I gauged their degree of alarm. Gratefully, they showed none. *Five . . . six . . .* I couldn't stand it. I was about to cover my eyes when he let go of the bar.

Head tucked, knees pressed to his chest, Vlad spun three perfect rotations and fell straight through the ring onto the trampoline.

I was standing and applauding before the crowd could breathe sighs of relief.

Over the next hour, Nicole presented three more acts: a risqué slapstick mime troupe, a wacky ballet company whose members continually switched between female and male roles (hard to describe, but wildly entertaining), and the night's finale that brought back the entire cast for mini-reprise of each act.

The last performer to be featured in the spotlight was Yazminka Smilova. Once again, she swung by bun alone, soaring over the audience. Everyone in the crowd was on their feet and—considering that most in attendance had spent the past three hours drinking—raucously following along in a group dance that Nicole had introduced at the onset of the finale. Reserved as I was, I couldn't help but get swept up in the crowd's energy. Hollister was surprised to see me let loose. I had above-average rhythm (thanks, gay genes!), but I had nothing on Hollister. The woman could get down. Feeding off her moves, I danced with a freedom usually reserved for my studio apartment after two hard ciders.

We returned to the lobby, still buzzing, in a slow shuffling line to the exit. I was excited to introduce Hollister to Vlad. We joined the several dozen audience members milling about to meet the performers after the show. Twenty minutes later, the cast started dribbling in. Nicole Armand arrived with Yazminka Smilova, followed by Kit Durango and the four Adrenalin! performers.

I waved, but with my height and the crowd, Vlad couldn't see me. However, he did hear Hollister's whistle. Vlad led his comrades over to us and surprised me with a quick kiss on the mouth. The guys appeared unfazed. My eyes jumped to Florin for a reaction. But Florin's utter disinterest in the kiss reassured me that he and Vlad were only coworkers and friends—and The Sisters Flip.

I introduced Hollister to Vlad, who introduced her to Marku, Florin, then Stefan. The guys were gracious in accepting our praise for their performance. In return, they seemed genuinely impressed by Hollister. I'd seen this reaction before. With a towering, solid stature, black curve-hugging clothing, and a fuchsia-tinted Mohawk, Hollister exuded rock-star cool.

"You guys were totally amazing," she said, "Thanks again for the tickets. That was incredibly generous. I've been pestering Hayden to introduce me ever since I learned he knew you."

This was not an entire lie. Hollister was happy to meet the guys, but she was far more interested in observing their character. As she'd put it earlier that evening, "I need to get the vibe of the Romanians. Maybe we've got it wrong. Maybe Kennedy's killer is *killers*."

If pressed, the theory that four guys had entered the hotel suite on that fateful night wouldn't hold up. But I got her main point. One of these guys could have done it. The possibility that it could have been Vlad was like the universe shoving me to the ground before kicking dirt in my face. Could it be possible that I finally meet a great guy, and he turns out to be a violent murderer?

Sasha Smilov approached and bumped shoulders with Marku as he passed. Stefan's growl was audible as he took a step in pursuit of the hard-charging Russian. The others moved in perfect unison to grab him and hold him back.

"Not now," Florin scolded.

Furious, Stefan shrugged free of their grasp. "I hate him so much. I swear, one of these days."

Hollister and I shared a look.

"Not the time," hissed Vlad. "Slap that smile back on your face. We are here to thank our fans for attending. Not settle scores."

This time, Hollister couldn't resist the bait. "So I take it you guys have a beef with the boss?"

Marku smiled tightly. "It's nothing. Who doesn't have an occasional disagreement with management?"

The long silence that fell over the six of us quickly became awkward. As it happened, Hollister and I intended to keep the meet and greet short for another reason. Vlad still thought I was a hotel employee. And others in the cast might recognize us as Chet and Bernice with the *Seattle Gazette*. The more we talked, the greater the chance we would slip up and say something to unmask our lies. I hated to continue the fiction. The longer it went on, the messier it would be to come clean. But what choice did I have? Sarah Lee considered us her true friends. What's more, she was Burley's rock at the bakery. Had I any ambivalence, Hollister had erased my misgivings when she'd said on the way to the show, "Remember, little dude, boys come and go, but friends stay to clean up after the party is over."

But what if Vlad was the one? What if I'd finally, *finally* found a guy who would not only help chuck the empties in the recycling bin but also surprise me with a grand-slam breakfast the next morning?

We exchanged goodbyes and left the popular cast to turn its attention to its gaggle of fans—all women—jostling to get photos and their programs signed.

Hollister and I stepped into the chilly rain and started zigzagging around puddles en route to the exit. Picking up on my abrupt mood shift, she said, "What's up, bud? You seem upset all of a sudden."

Risking a lecture I'd heard before, I answered truthfully. "Perpetuating the lie with Vlad will ruin any chance I might have with him. And I say that knowing he'll go traipsing off to the next city in a month, regardless."

"Where does he live, anyway? London? Moscow? Monte Carlo?"

I shrugged. "I don't even know. We've never had enough time to learn even the basic stuff about each other. And before you ask, no. I don't think he did it. Nor one of the other guys."

We started walking again. Hollister wrapped an arm around me. "For what it's worth, neither do I. But for right now, how about we not think about the investigation? Tomorrow will happen tomorrow. There's no good in worrying about what it might bring."

"Get off me, you stupid idiot!"

We both spun around toward the woman's voice.

"You need to listen to me, Yazzie," her brother snapped in reply.

Several trailers away, Yazminka and Sasha were engaged in a heated sibling squabble. Before I could object, Hollister was run-walking toward them, staying off the path so as not to be seen.

I cursed under my breath, inventing expletives that would shock even my middle schoolers. As Hollister had done since the night I'd first met her; she forced me to choose: wait for her in the warm safety of my car, or trot after her like a spaniel acting solely on dumb loyalty.

Chapter
Thirty-Two
Smilov Versus Smilova

"In here," Hollister whisper-shouted. She gestured for me to join her inside a large cabinet. I recognized the big box on wheels from Kennedy's act during the VIP preview—the same one in which she'd made Hollister disappear. Now it was parked in a steel storage building at the end of the circus grounds, where Yazminka and Sasha had taken their argument.

Hollister pressed a finger to her lips as if I needed shushing. I replied with my best eye roll, regretting it would be lost in the darkness.

"I know what you did, you glupyy pridurok." Hearing Yazminka's voice brought to mind a cartoon villainess with a thick Slavic accent. I pictured her pressing a long-tipped cigarette holder to her glossy red lips.

"You know nothing," Sasha spat in reply.

Having no sibling myself, when I imagined filling that void, I romanticized the relationship: riding bicycles, gleefully teeter-tottering, whispering, and giggling about Great-Aunt Who-ever's whiskers at family dinners. Had little Yazminka and Sasha ever played companionably as children? Overhearing the vitriol they were flinging at each other, I couldn't picture it. But to be fair, I was hearing two grown-ups with several decades of history between them. Adults had a capacity for anger and grudges that children could shake off with a popsicle or the latest Disney video. These two needed a time-out that didn't seem to be on the agenda.

"Pridurok!" Yazminka repeated. "You thought you'd get away with it? That no one would find out? How could you think that is remotely possible? You will be found out. And when that happens, I will not try to save you. You! You, Sasha! You have done this to yourself."

"You are still angry about Kennedy," Sasha argued.

A silence followed. I was growing desperate to shift my position in the crate but couldn't risk causing a squeak.

"Don't change the subject!" Yazminka roared, "You did that because you can't stand the idea of me being your equal."

Another long pause. Hollister's stomach growled so loudly I feared they might hear.

"That makes no sense," Sasha said, as if sounding out the words. "Kennedy was a woman."

"Please. Kennedy was an amateur. You thought you could control her, but discovered you couldn't. I'm sick to death of talking about her. It's the other matter, Sasha, that you need to take care of. Do it or else."

"Do not threaten me, Yazzie."

"Then do not test me. Do it. And do it soon. Or I will have no choice but to tell—"

"You can't. You know what will happen."

Yazminka chuckled menacingly. "Oh yes. I know. Father is extremely predictable."

Moments later, a door opened and shut. Hollister and I waited another full minute to ensure the coast was clear.

"Finally," I said. "That drama was thicker than homemade borscht."

Hollister joined me in running my hands against the wall of the crate, searching for a door handle or latch or some way to open the door.

"Do you even know what borscht is?"

"A soup. Very beet-forward. Thanks, Cooking Channel. It was the only cultural reference I could come up with."

The seconds ticked by as our roaming hands discovered nothing to trigger the door.

"How'd you get out before?" I asked.

"I didn't do anything. There were assistants. I was told to do precisely one thing: nothing."

The sound of the building's door opening caused us to freeze. The thinnest strip of light appeared on the crate floor, indicating that whoever had just entered had flipped on the lights. Two voices, both male, were debating the merits of the latest Bad Bunny album.

"This one?" one guy said.

"Must be," said the other.

"Thank god it's on wheels."

Before Hollister and I could react, the crate started to move. We flung out our hands, bracing ourselves against the walls.

"Heavier than I expected," said one of them.

"So, what's your call? Best Puerto Rican rapper ever? Or best Puerto Rican singer ever?"

The guys' banter continued for several minutes as they rolled the crate and us outside—the patter of rain and sudden chill leaving no doubt—to somewhere that seemed outside the circus grounds.

"Leave it here? You sure?"

"That's what Sasha said. Some junk haulers are supposed to pick it up later tonight. He wants it out. Says the sight of it is bumming everyone out."

We listened as the squish-squash of footsteps in the rain receded in the distance.

"Okay," Hollister said. "We need to get out of this thing."

"Yeah, I hadn't thought of that."

"Not helping."

I fished my phone from my pocket and activated the flashlight app.

"Okay, helping," Hollister granted.

Several minutes passed, and I started to panic as I realized that the crate might have been designed to open only from the outside. We could find no way out. I kicked the wall, trying to break through. Hollister joined in, and we quickly discovered we had to take turns or risk overturning the thing.

"Dammit. Talk about overbuilt," I said. "This only needed to hide someone visually, not entomb them for eternity."

"Again, not helping."

We froze. The sound of an engine. A truck was approaching.

Frantically, we kicked harder. I pitched my head back in exasperation when I saw it—a faint seam defining a square hatch above our heads.

Beep, beep, beep. The truck backed up. Very close.

With her help, I climbed on Hollister's shoulders. With all my might, I pressed upward on the hatch. My hands punched through the light ceiling material with ease. Hollister grabbed my ankles and pushed me up through the hold. Once outside, it took me no time to find the latch and open the door.

"And now for my next trick . . ."

Driving Hollister home, we discussed what to make of the conversation between Mysterium's resident brother and sister. Had we overheard a murder confession? Or something else we didn't understand? Whatever the case, Yazminka and Sasha were keeping a secret that had them at each other's throats.

Chapter Thirty-Three
Hello, Ginger!

After making a pit stop at Slice for a caramel macchiato for Jess Gemalto and my usual single-shot cappuccino, I arrived at Jess's houseboat a few minutes early for our ten o'clock get-together. He was tidying some files on the kitchen table and humming along to some acoustic Indy band on the stereo.

"Good morning, handsome," he said with a wave and smile. He had traded his usual dress shirt for a grass-green polo shirt.

"That's a nice color on you," I said.

"I know, right? As a fellow ginger, you'll appreciate that green is my go-to." Acknowledging my pullover, he added, "Navy is another solid choice."

"More than half my wardrobe is blue." I set the cardboard container holding our drinks on the counter, along with a surprise bag of chocolate croissants. Jess reached for his wallet. I waved him off. "It's on me. It's the least I can do."

We took sips of our drinks. "I was starting to think all you owned were white dress shirts and dark pants. Well, that and a killer green cocktail dress."

"It's important to look professional whenever meeting with clients. I hope you don't mind me dressing more casually today. It being Sunday, I thought—"

"Stop," I said, giving Jess's shoulder a friendly squeeze. "I was only joking."

Jess shot me a conspiratorial grin. In that instant, our friendship took hold. Perhaps a tiny foothold, but it was a good-feeling start.

Minutes later, as we brushed pastry crumbs from our hands and finished our coffees, Jess said, "So, you're sure? You're ready to do this?"

At this moment, I was ready. I was sure. I was even excited.

"Yes!" I declared.

Jess laughed. "Okay, give me a few minutes to get things set up."

At karaoke, when I had seen how beautiful Jess looked as Jessica, I knew he would be the ideal person to transform Hayden into Ginger. Not only did he possess obvious skill, but he understood how to make a face like mine look *stun-ning*. When I'd texted him about it, he'd suggested we do a trial run at his houseboat some time when there was nothing at stake. That was now.

"First, we shave your eyebrows," he said.

As I sputtered my objection, he laughed. "*Kidding.* I'll show you a work-around."

For the next hour, Jess went about his work, explaining each step in the process and entertaining my questions with a patience

I envied—and I was a middle school teacher! Never having spent any one-on-one time with him, I was eager to get to know him. Just because we both found ourselves at home within the big colorful LGBTQ+ tent hardly meant we automatically had loads in common. Find me a dozen gay guys, and I'll show you twelve different opinions on Pride parades.

Jess and I chatted about jobs, dating (he liked girls), and hobbies. Whereas I spent the workday shaping young minds while withstanding shockingly improper remarks from thirteen-year-olds, Jess represented adults in criminal proceedings. He seemed genuinely interested in my job. I was in the classroom to teach, not to be a gay mentor or guidance counselor. Still, if a kid did come to me with an issue, I wouldn't turn them away.

When I told Jess that I managed a subreddit and wrote about gay dating, he asked, "Have you ever written a post about a trans person?"

I told him I'd lightly touched on the issue, but never really discussed it. "I wouldn't know what to say. I don't have anything interesting to offer. I'd probably just get something wrong and piss someone off."

That's when it struck me. "Hey, Jess. I've got an idea. You don't have to say yes. But what if . . ."

Jess appeared to consider my idea of him writing a guest post with the intensity he might give to weighing a plea bargain for a client. After a long moment, he nodded. "Yeah, okay. That could be cool."

I told him I was a tennis fan, soon to be a dog owner, and enjoyed backgammon with my elderly friend Jerry, with whom I was moving in. Jess, in turn, said he was interested in aviation, kayaking, and loved animals. A year ago, when he had bought the houseboat, he had brought along his cat, Amy, named after a famous *Jeopardy!* champion. A week later, Amy disappeared. Jess still hadn't gotten over the loss.

"Have you considered getting another cat?" I asked.

"I want one so badly, Hayden. But I never found out what happened to Amy. I can't risk getting attached again, only to have a repeat."

Appreciating Jess's predicament, I nodded but felt the need to say something encouraging. "It could have been a one-time freak occurrence. I saw an orange tabby on the dock the first time I was here. So it would seem the area is safe for at least one cat."

"That's Morris. He's a sweetheart. Belongs to an old fool in the first houseboat on the lane. I get your point, though, Hayden. If Morris is around, why not another cat? But I need to be sure. I can't take a chance. I've lost too much in my life as it is."

Loss, I understood, as I did putting up walls. After my mom's passing, I'd kept to myself, avoiding new relationships with the potential to cause me any pain. I got the feeling that beneath Jess's self-assuredness, he was like me—like most people—with his fair share of vulnerabilities.

"I know there are cat people, and there are dog people," I said, "but you're welcome to hang out with Alice and me. We could all go to the park or something. Or you could come over to Jerry's one of these days."

"That would be cool. Yeah."

Jess stepped out of the room, to retrieve a wig from his bedroom closet, when my phone rang. It was Hollister. Not wanting to risk smudging my makeup, I put her on speaker.

"Burley is never late," Hollister blurted. "She likes to be early. Says being late upsets the rhythm of her space in time."

"And you're telling me this why?"

Jess reentered the room holding a glorious dark red wig of long, lustrous, *straight* hair.

I gasped.

"What's wrong?" Hollister said.

"Nothing," I answered. "The opposite. So much the opposite."

"So as I was saying," Hollister continued, hinting at her annoyance for being interrupted, "Burley is late. She wasn't even at her place. I was supposed to meet her there."

"And you're telling me this why?"

"Hayden! Are you listening to me?"

At this moment, I realized that something I didn't yet understand was wrong.

"Listening," I said, and I was.

Jess shot me a look of concern.

Hollister said, "I called. She didn't pick up."

"Why didn't you leave—"

"It's full. I've told her a thousand times to delete old voicemail. I swear, the woman can memorize the names of ten different flour distributors, but she's hopeless when it comes to remembering that garbage pickup is on Tuesdays."

"So what am I missing? You're too worked up just for her missing a big-girl playdate."

Hollister launched into a minutes-long monologue, concluding with, "So there you have it. Splitsville. Sarah Lee's Beetle is in Burley's driveway. I don't like this one bit. Big Miss has done this before. Several years back, when another friend was feeling stressed and overwhelmed, Burley took her to Sedona on a whim. When I tracked them down three days later, she explained that they 'went off the grid to better hear the counsel of their spirit animals.'"

I leaned close to my phone. "I thought Helen was Burley's spirit animal."

"No, Helen is Burley's animal *sister*. Apparently, there's a difference—something to do with emus being omnivores. I found her and this other chick in a camping tent stockpiled with gallons of apricot nectar and three cases of Costco peanut butter. The woman was elated to be rescued, while I'd never seen Burley happier. I think we may have a repeat of sorts on our hands. Burley has taken Sarah Lee someplace, thinking it will cheer her up. Frankly, I'm as concerned for Burley's mental health as Sarah Lee's."

"Hate to interrupt," Jess said, directing his voice toward the phone, "but the police requested an interview with Sarah Lee first thing tomorrow morning. If you're right and she's gone off somewhere with Burley, I can't stress enough how important it is that she return in time to meet me downtown at eight o'clock. Sharp."

Before calling me, Hollister had made a flurry of calls, starting with Camilo and then moving down the list of Burley's other friends. None of them had seen her or knew where she might have gone with Sarah Lee. She had not arranged for anyone to care for Helen and the other emus or the basement ganja farm, and both required daily attention. And Burley had only one sibling, a man with whom I'd be glad never to cross paths again.

"Did you call Roy?" I asked hesitantly.

"Ding, ding. Now we're on the same page. I keep trying him, but the call goes straight to voicemail, and his mailbox is full. Just like his sister. Ridiculous. So it looks like you and me—"

"No way, Hollister."

"Yes, way, little dude."

"How about we just drive by?" I tried. "See if we spot Burley's Bronco."

"You've been to Roy's. It's impossible to see anything beyond the mess of overgrown bushes and trees. We have to find out if Burley's there. If she isn't, Roy might know where she is."

Roy Driggs was a creep who made his living illegally selling guns out of a trailer. Hollister and I had visited the Driggs' compound one night last summer, and the memory still haunted me. I'd since learned he and some of his numbskull friends had instigated a disruption of a drag-queen story hour at a local library.

"We won't be in the dark this time around," Hollister said encouragingly. "We pop in. We pop out."

Chirp, chirp.

That sound I recognized. I leaned forward in my chair to see out Jess's front window.

"What are you doing here?" I said into the phone, as I watched Hollister bound up the dock. I wasn't prepared for a visitor. Not yet.

Reading my expression in the mirror, Jess nodded and placed the wig on my head, shifting it slightly this way and that.

I ended the call. She was nearly to the porch.

"You ready for your close-up, Ginger?"

"Ready or not."

Jess opened the door to Hollister's hand, poised midair to knock. She stepped inside. Saw me standing there and jumped. The expression on her face was extraordinary. In that instant, she was confused about which one of us was which. She looked at Jess, then again at me.

"Hayden? Holy shazam! You look amaze balls." She said to Jess, "You did this?"

He nodded proudly.

"Damn. You're gorgeous, Hayden."

Jess said, "Not Hayden. Ginger."

After a few deserved minutes of oohing and aahing, Hollister broke the spell. "So . . . we really need to get going. I'm anxious to get over to Roy's to find out if he knows where his sister"—she shifted her gaze to Jess—"and your client went."

"I didn't go through all this to look fabulous for five minutes," I complained. "And it's hardly fair to Jess. He went to all this trouble."

"It's okay," Jess said, though I could tell he was crestfallen that we'd not have a chance to show off his handiwork at the brunch out we had planned in the gayborhood.

That decided it. "I'm not changing," I said. "I may never be half this stunning ever again. Besides, this hair. OMG, do I love this hair! I may never take it off."

"You do realize we're going to Roy's?" Hollister said.

I hugged Jess, careful to keep my heavily painted face away from his. He again stressed how important it was to find and return Sarah Lee in time for her police interview the next morning. Walking to dry land, I was glad my drag was only from the neck up. There was no way I could have handled heels on the wobbly dock. Morris crossed our path, and I thought of Amy, Jess's missing cat. Could Amy be out there somewhere, curled up and safe on someone's lap? And what about Burley? Was she safe? What had caused her to take off with Sarah Lee? Was she all right? What were the two of them thinking? They must know we'd find out they were MIA and be worried.

I dropped into the Porsche's passenger seat. Hollister reached to start the car, then paused and looked over at me. "You know, Hayden. You are a beautiful person. Both in and out of drag."

"Dammit, woman!" I waved a hand in front of my eyes. "Don't you dare make me cry and ruin my makeup!"

Chapter
Thirty-Four
Big Brother

"When I insisted you come along with me to Roy's, I was expecting Hayden. With you as Ginger, I'll understand if you want to wait in the car."

I appreciated Hollister's concern, both for my safety and how my being in drag might impact our success in getting information from Burley's younger brother and living, breathing poster boy for conspiracy theorists of America. After I'd gotten home from meeting Roy last summer when Hollister and I were searching for Camilo, it took me hours to get to sleep—that's how much the encounter had scared the crap out of me. Although he seemed to have a good relationship with Burley—performing occasional acts of brotherly kindness (and I didn't doubt he'd do anything to protect her)—I couldn't look past him dressing up in camo and bullying little kids and my gay community.

Hollister and I stood side by side outside the chain-link fence bordering the Driggs' property. I had assumed the scene would appear less sinister in daylight than it had late at night. I was wrong. Before, it had been what we couldn't see that had stirred fear. Now, it was the menacing clarity of densely thicketed grounds, silence, and a chipped tin sign with an explicit message: "Warning: This property guarded by attack dog—no responsible for injury or death."

I studied the sign. "As we know all too well, there are *two* dogs. The sign ought to read 'attack dogs,' plural. Also, Roy forgot the T on 'no.'"

Hollister rolled her eyes. "Yeah, well, I'm sure Roy will appreciate you pointing that out. Him being such a stickler for grammar and spelling." She glanced at me, then the gate. Then back at me. "So?"

"So what?"

"You opening that gate, or are we standing here all day?"

Vividly remembering how this had gone last time, there was a zero percent chance I was entering the property without first knowing the whereabouts of Roy's two beasts from hell. The impossibility of Hollister leading the way negated any worry I might have had on her behalf.

Fortunately, I was an ideas man. Surveying the gravel strip between the road and fence, I selected a midsize rock and tossed it over the gate, aiming for the cracked concrete path. It landed with a loud thud.

Hollister spun around. "What the hell?" She threw her hands in the air.

I answered with a smile and tossed a second rock.

"Seriously, little dude. You're going to—"

The dogs bolted from the bushes with frightening speed, barking viciously. Slobber flew from their fangs. They threw their muscular bodies at the fence.

Hollister and I jumped back. She looked at me wide-eyed. "Why'd you do that? If Roy's home, he'll be out here in seconds." She stopped abruptly. "Oh. Gotcha."

From around the bushes, Roy marched into view, looking like an XXL cover model for *Militia Digest*. Surprise, surprise—he toted a shotgun. Recognizing Hollister immediately, he rolled his cannon-ball head on his tanklike shoulders, causing his foot-long beard to sway across his sweat-stained shirt. "You! This some kind of joke?" He made a show of looking up and down the street. "Somebody out there filming this? Am I going to see this later on YouTube?"

She shouted over the dogs, "We're looking for your sister, Roy."

With a single sharp voice command, Roy silenced the dogs, whose names I recalled as a testament to his breadth of imagination: Winchester and Bullet. "What about my sister?" He looked suddenly alarmed. "She all right?"

"We'll know that once we find her," Hollister repeated.

"We?" He aimed his oddly tiny eyes at me, squinted, and stepped closer to the chain link between us. "Not shy about the makeup, are you, girl?"

Suddenly having even greater respect for Jess's talent, I said, "Just a dab of lipstick I slapped on in the car on the way over."

Hearing my voice, hardly deep but neither feminine, he cocked his head like one of the dogs that flanked him.

Hollister tried to get us back on track. "Has Burley been around to see you recently? As in today?"

"Always looking for somethin', ain't you? Last time you come around here, you was looking for that Mexican boy—"

"Venezuelan," I corrected, though with Roy it hardly mattered. To him, everyone with brown skin was Mexican and somehow responsible for him not being a millionaire.

"Have I seen you somewhere before?" he asked.

Roy tried to work out who I reminded him of, but my drag was complicating matters considerably. Coming up short, he glowered and turned back to Hollister.

As she explained, it was evident that Roy had no idea about Burley's proximity to a murder, though he had "heard about some oriental girl getting knifed downtown." A sad state of affairs that was bound to happen since she ventured out at night "without a gun in her purse." I started to point out that Kennedy was a woman, not a girl, and that she was murdered in a luxury hotel suite, not in some seedy back alley. But I needed to stay on message.

"As I was saying, Roy," Hollister said, "has Burley been by to see you?"

"She mighta come by yesterday."

Hollister gritted her teeth. "And? Do you mind telling us why?"

"Burl didn't look quite right to me. But I'm not one to pry. She asked me to swing by her place and feed the animals and water all that pot she got growin' in the basement while she's away."

Eager to do my part, I asked, "Did Burley say where she was going?"

"Or for how long?" Hollister added.

"Just muttered something about that town in Japan. Not Tokyo, the other one."

Hollister stopped my forthcoming geography lesson by touching my arm and said, "You mean Osaka?"

"That's it." He added a finger snap. His two dogs, hearing what they recognized as a command, dropped to a lying position.

"That's where she said she was going. To pay respects. Hell if I'll ever understand my big sister. She won't fly on a plane, so how the woman plans on getting across the ocean is a mighty good question."

Hollister asked, "Did Burley say anything about parents?"

"Might have." Roy shifted his weight. "Come to think of it, yeah, I think she did mention that."

By the look on Hollister's face, she understood something. Having apparently gotten what we'd come for, we thanked Roy through the chain-link fence.

"Next time you're thinkin' 'bout comin' round here, don't."

Hollister started up Mo and had shifted into third gear before I'd had time to buckle my seatbelt. An hour later, I'd removed the wig and makeup, and we sat side by side on my small sofa, my laptop resting on my knees.

"It's a thing with Burley," Hollister explained. "She believes that when a person dies, you must offer condolences to their next of kin and share a happy memory. If you don't, you rob them of fully celebrating the life of the person they lost."

"But she didn't know Kennedy. They were supposed to meet the night of the fundraiser."

"It's not about Burley, little dude. Remember, Sarah Lee and Kennedy grew up in the area and were college roommates back east. Sarah Lee had to have known Kennedy's parents. Burley must have got it into her head that Sarah Lee needed to visit them. How Burley convinced her that was a good idea is another question."

It took a bit of digging, but we eventually found what we were looking for.

"Bonney Lake?" Hollister said. "Isn't that somewhere south of here?"

I nodded and read aloud from the screen. "Nearly forty miles southeast of Tacoma. Not accounting for traffic, that should take what? About an hour?"

Hollister made a face. "The suburbs give me the heebie-jeebies."

"I'd say we're lucky. Bonney Lake isn't that far." My computer's clock read 12:25 PM. "Assuming that's where Burley and Sarah Lee went and that they left this morning, they should be there by now. Finding Kennedy Osaka's parents' home address is one thing, but finding a telephone number for them is another."

Hollister stood and stretched her hands over her head, brushing her fingertips on the ceiling. She let her head fall back, her mohawk pressed between her shoulder blades. "I should know better than to skip yoga. I'm tight everyplace." She bent in the opposite direction, touching the tips of her yellow nails to the toes of her black boots.

"That's all fascinating, but are we hitting the road or what?"

"Geez. Chill, will you? I appreciate the urgency, but tomorrow morning is still a long way off. I'm just stretching a bit before being stuck behind the wheel for an hour." Still folded at the waist, she walked her hands out in front of her, posing in downward dog. She craned her neck and looked up at me. Victim to the power of suggestion, I kicked a leg out in front of me to stretch my calf muscle, which was tight from a recent run.

Hollister stood abruptly. "All right. Let's ride."

"So once again, you're driving. No negotiation?"

"You really want to do this?" She stuck out a fist. "Having an unblemished losing record, you're resilient. I'll give you that."

I replied with a fist of my own. "The past is the past. The odds are, as they forever will be, fifty–fifty."

"Then how do you explain the fact that I always win?"

"Sorcery?"

"Close." She grinned. "Black magic."

Chapter Thirty-Five
Road Trip

After double-checking for keys, wallet, phone, and Dramamine, I slipped my backpack over my shoulder and bounced down the outdoor staircase to the carport. Despite the reason for the trip ahead, I was looking forward to it. I could use a change of scenery.

Hollister lowered the window and eyed my backpack. "You do know we'll only be gone a few hours."

"That's the plan, absolutely. But a smart superhero is always well provisioned. I packed a phone charger, energy bars, umbrella, light jacket, heavier jacket, and sunglasses."

She furrowed her brow. "We may be going south, but we'd have to cross two state lines before you might need those shades."

She pointed toward Mo's sloping front hood. The trunk lid popped open with a soft click. Two paper sacks filled with colorful women's clothing occupied most of the small cargo space. I peered around the hood. Hollister fiddled with the car stereo with one hand and drummed her fingers on the dashboard with the other. After some adjusting, I managed to fit my pack along-side the bags.

"Care to explain?" I asked, settling into the passenger seat.

"Explain what?"

"Mysti's clothes in the trunk of your car."

"I'd rather not."

"You're impossible."

Hollister turned up some Mary J. Blige, and we set off. Merg-ing onto I-5, Hollister suggested we play the game I'd invented, in which we took turns making up outlandish stories about the passengers in nearby vehicles. My tale of a band of bank-robbing ventriloquists in a rusted Volvo wagon was bested by Hollister's grim odyssey of an Israeli assassin in a black BMW M5 with smoked windows, who, posing as a high-end gigolo, ended his appointments with a postcoital aperitif laced with strychnine.

When she'd finished, I said, "Remind me to skip the musical."

"Oh, really? Two words for you: *Sweeney Todd*."

"Still not convinced."

"And if it starred Timothée Chalamet? You're saying you wouldn't kill for a front-row seat?"

I clutched my heart at the mention of my Hollywood crush. "Not fair."

"Or that cute British dude who played Spider-Man?"

"Okay, okay. Point to Hollister. But you could cast either of those guys in an eczema commercial, and I'd be glued to the screen."

"There's a joke in there somewhere." She chuckled, shifting lanes and pressing her foot to the accelerator.

After allowing several minutes to pass, I again tried ask-ing about the assortment of pastel clothing in the car's trunk.

Hollister answered with a drawn-out sigh. I turned down the radio in anticipation.

"I gave Mysti a choice. Pick them up, or I was donating them."

When it became clear that no further explanation was forthcoming, I said, "You're no doubt aware that you fast-forwarded to the ending, leaving the listener unsatisfied."

"You've heard it all before."

"Actually, I haven't. You don't talk about your girlfriends. And don't say I don't ask you because we both know that's untrue. You always change the subject. If I persist, you shut me down. I respect your privacy. I do. But it's weird that we are such close friends and can't talk about something so important. I tell you all about my boy troubles, but I know nothing of—"

"My girl troubles?"

"No. Not just the troubles, but the fun stuff too. Surely it can't be all bad. I'm pretty sure you're not a masochist. There must be some good parts to your relationships."

I'd known Hollister for about nine months, and Mysti had been with Hollister when I'd first met her. They'd broken up and gotten back together three times. On each occasion, I'd learned about it after the fact, and Hollister seemed relieved the relationship had ended each time. This time, however, she seemed sad.

"What happened, Hollister?"

Her silence suggested she was sifting through various answers. Or maybe she was finding it difficult to put her feelings into words. Or perhaps . . . "If you don't want to talk about it because I'm a guy—"

"Don't be stupid." She gave me a hard glance. "You should know it's not that. I suppose it came down to her and me wanting

219

different things. You know Mysti. Never satisfied. Nothing lives up to her standards. I can deal with aspiration or ambition. In fact, I like that in a person. But Mysti didn't just want more, she believed she deserved more. Nicer apartment, higher-profile job, fancier car." She glanced over at me again, this time with a rueful smile. "More impressive girlfriend."

I scoffed. "Gimme a break. You started your own business. Your furniture is in high-end design magazines. Movie stars and business moguls can't get enough of it. You are supremely awesome in more ways than I can count. *She* is lucky to have *you*."

Undeserving was the word I wanted to use, but I was pushing it as it was.

Hollister reached over and gave my knee a gentle squeeze. "You're my friend. You have to say that. Though I don't doubt you believe it, Hayden. You're good that way. But Mysti wants to be with someone who wants to be somebody as badly as she does. She wants a partner that turns heads at restaurants—the kind of person profiled in the celebrity rags lifestyle section and invited to A-list parties. It matters to Mysti—a lot. I tolerate that hubris, but it is not my thing. Won't ever be. Don't get me wrong. I like nice things. It's not lost on me that I'm driving a Porsche or that I wear good clothes and live in a nice loft. But I don't need more. Mysti got tired of me settling for what I had, and I got fed up with her trying to convince me that I was wrong being happy."

"That sounds definitive."

Hollister spurted a laugh. "It does, doesn't it? So what about you? What's new on the Vlad and Camilo fronts?"

I wasn't a champion at exercising selflessness, but for today my drama wouldn't suck up all the airtime. "Nothing of note to report," I said. "So I take it Mysti never came to get her stuff?"

Hollister answered with a slight nod.

"Are you planning to keep her clothes in your trunk forever?"

"It's pathetic, I know. But as long as they're there, it's not completely over. As soon as I drop them off at Goodwill, that will be the end of the longest relationship I've ever had."

Wait. What? I remembered Hollister once saying she'd started dating Mysti a few months before I met her. Hollister was thirty-six, and in all her adult years, her longest relationship had lasted less than a year? My track record was far worse, but I had a decade to improve on it.

"I have a new game," I announced with my slyest grin.

"Oh boy." Hollister rolled her eyes.

"It's called five things that make Hollister magnificent."

She smirked. "Not even my family will buy that."

"It's a one-time-only free special edition, requiring only one player—me. You ready?"

"What am I supposed to do?"

"Listen."

"All right." She chuckled.

"What makes Hollister magnificent? One: the Mohawk." I raised my hand in defense before she could argue. "I know it's superficial, but it truly is magnificent. Few other humans could pull it off with such aplomb."

"Aplomb?"

"I've been working on my crossword game with Jerry. Two: your courage. You're not afraid of anything or anyone. Including Roy Driggs."

"Yeah, but his dogs terrify me."

"They're not of this world. They don't count. Three: your loyalty. You're the best friend a ginger pocket-gay and middle school teacher could have. Four: you named your car after Toni Morrison."

"You still haven't read any of her books, have you?"

"Irrelevant. The point is, *you* are well-read, creative, and . . ." I looked at her expectantly.

"Magnificent?"

"Magnificent! Five: you have superb taste in best friends. Game over. I win!"

"You're nuts."

After a moment, I returned to the topic of our investigation. "Here's something that's been bugging me. Why did Kennedy take the job with Mysterium when she was so critical of the show? All the talk about it needing big changes only seemed to antagonize everyone. Why would she bother?"

"A million reasons," Hollister said, not skipping a beat. "Think about it from Kennedy's perspective. You're an Asian female magician. How many good jobs could she have come across? Let alone such a sweet gig. Mysterium offered her a five-star venue to showcase her talents, along with a million-dollar salary."

"So cause and effect," I said. "It has to be more than coincidence that Kennedy was killed so soon after being named artistic director."

Hollister gave the steering wheel a double tap to emphasize her words. "However you look at it, all roads lead back to Mysterium. Money, scissors, wigs. That circus may be high-end, but it's like a telenovela—a very dangerous, high-flying telenovela."

An hour later, we passed through the entrance to Cascadia Falls, a well-scrubbed, suburban private community of a half-dozen home styles stretching down the block in varied colors. Hollister turned onto Meadowlark Lane.

"I don't see the falls?" she said.

"According to the online brochure, it's a water feature behind the clubhouse."

Cascadia Falls was an over-fifty-five community with hundreds of homes and zero children. I read aloud from the brochure, "*Grandchildren are welcome for visits, but stays are limited to one week.*"

"Harsh," Hollister said.

"Unless you have demons for grandchildren." Feigning an older-sounding voice, I said, "Sorry, son, I would *love* to have little Beelzebub and Lucifer stay the summer, but darn it all if the community won't allow it."

"Thank God," Hollister muttered, seeing Burley's Bronco in a driveway up ahead. "Now let's hope Sarah Lee is in there with her."

We'd reached 6262 Meadowlark Lane, home of Kennedy's parents.

"How long do you think they've been here?" I wondered aloud.

Hollister eased Mo to the curb in an unprecedented display of gentleness. "We're about to find out."

Suddenly, I couldn't move. The idea of walking up the sidewalk and knocking on the Osakas' door seemed too much. "I don't know, Hollister. These people just lost their daughter. And in a particularly horrible way. I'm not sure how to act or what to say."

"You don't have to say anything, Hayden. Just introduce yourself. If you do feel compelled to say something, a simple 'I'm sorry for your loss' will suffice. This isn't intended to be an extended social call. We only came here to make sure our friends are both all right and see them home safely."

I nodded and stepped out of the car. By outward appearances, the Osakas' home looked as pleasant and tidy as all its neighbors. But I suspected the mood would shift dramatically once we stepped through the front door. And what about Burley and Sarah Lee? How was their arrival received? Even more curious, why were they still here?

Chapter Thirty-Six
Amen

Minutes after the doorbell's chime announced our arrival, Hollister and I found ourselves seated at a polished oval table in the Osakas' formal dining room. Mrs. Osaka insisted we join Mr. Osaka, Burley, Sarah Lee, and her for breakfast. Mrs. Osaka couldn't have known we were coming, yet she had prepared more than enough waffles, eggs, and bacon. The awkward tension I had anticipated wasn't completely absent, but the atmosphere wasn't as uncomfortable as I'd feared. Kennedy's parents hardly appeared cheerful, but neither were they debilitated by grief. They projected an undercurrent of sadness masked by what seemed a habit of hospitality. While Burley appeared delighted to see us, Sarah Lee looked bothered. Perhaps she felt we were intruding on a private encounter? Or did our presence pull her thoughts back to the criminal investigation?

I suspected Hollister was as antsy as I was to get back to the city. As I lifted my glass of orange juice, the Osakas joined hands while each extending a hand to the person sitting next to them. With our hosts' eyes closed and heads bowed, Hollister and I risked exchanging glances. I couldn't be certain about her thoughts, but mine were conflicted. My own beliefs didn't include saying grace, but I was a guest in this home, and considering what they were going through, respecting their ritual was the least I could do. The prayer offered by Mr. Osaka was sermon-like long. He gave thanks for the health of those present and the immeasurable and incomprehensible love of his savior before turning to the topic of "forgiveness for those who had yet to experience God's abundant grace." A long silence followed. Curious about whether the prayer had finished, I squinted at our host just as he nodded decisively and declared, "Amen."

During the long breakfast, we learned that Burley and Sarah Lee had arrived earlier that morning. I sensed that their visit had given the Osakas a welcome distraction. Sarah Lee had once meant something to their daughter and vice versa. Despite Sarah Lee's grievances with Kennedy, the two women shared a past. As Mrs. and Mr. Osaka told it, their daughter had not an enemy in the world and first displayed her gifts as a performer at the age of six, singing and dancing to a medley from *The Little Mermaid* while sloshing water from a small tank holding a goldfish. Their description of an open and loving woman didn't match the Kennedy Osaka that I had met at the preview, nor did it agree with how Sarah Lee or anyone at Mysterium described her. Still, Burley had been correct in believing the visit would be a healing experience—at least it seemed to be for the Osakas.

Once the breakfast plates were cleared, we coaxed Burley and Sarah Lee out of the house as quickly as possible without appearing rude. Although we had plenty of time to return Sarah Lee to Seattle, we were anxious to phone Jess and set his mind at ease.

On the front porch, the Osakas surprised me with a warm hug, before embracing Hollister, then Burley. Saving their daughter's friend for last, they both held her tightly for a long while. As they pulled away from each other, Sarah Lee started to cry. "I'm so sorry. I'm so, so sorry." Her emotion wasn't a shock—perhaps it was even helpfully cathartic—but I winced at the outburst. Not only did I fear a ripple effect touching our hosts, but we had nearly escaped the encounter without tears. Burley was quick to wrap an arm around Sarah Lee and hurry her to the Bronco. Gratefully, the Osakas didn't break. They just stood looking sad and worried, waving from the steps.

We had a brief word with Burley through the driver's side window before we set off. We explained the need to get Sarah Lee home and that we'd let Jess know we were all on our way. As the three of us talked, Sarah Lee continued to weep, saying over and over. "I'm so sorry."

As soon as Hollister and I left Cascadia Falls, I said, "Sarah Lee is pretty upset."

"Uh-huh," Hollister replied. "Understandable, don't you think?"

"Why do you think she kept saying she was sorry?"

"Hayden . . ."

"I'm just saying. She was furious when she left the fundraiser that night. She can't remember the crucial moments when she was in the hotel suite. And she was caught holding the scissors."

"Stop it. You and I both know Sarah Lee isn't capable of such a thing. Back there"—she flipped a thumb in the opposite direction—"that was about the Osakas' loss."

I nodded, wanting to believe she was reading it right. And I did—mostly. But that tiny sliver of doubt had wormed its way back into my brain. As much I was disappointed in myself for thinking it I couldn't help but wonder: *Could she have done it?*

Chapter Thirty-Seven
Mates on Dates, Post No. 26

When talking with Jess Gemalto at his houseboat, he'd asked whether I'd ever devoted a post to anyone or anything trans. I'd replied that I never had—what did I have to say on the subject? But his question had given me an idea. Happily, Jess had agreed, and just now he'd made good on his word.

MATES ON DATES: Special First-Time-Ever Guest Post
Hello, readers. My name is Jess Gemalto. Hayden asked if I might be interested in writing a guest post. Why me? Because I'm transgender. There. I've said it. Now, no one needs to wonder whether I am, or if it's okay to mention the word, or if I am comfortable addressing it. Every letter in LGBTQ+ represents a particular group, true, but some transgender persons are also gay or bi. For those curious, I am a straight, transgender man. My buddy Hayden is a cisgender gay guy, so we have our queerness (read: letter Q) in common. Complicated? Confused? Don't be.

I'm only saying we all have our differences and similarities, but in simple terms, we are who we are. And however we identify, each of us deserves to be accepted and respected for who we are.

Moving on . . .

The reason I agreed to write this post is not that I saw an opportunity to give a cisgender person meaningful insight into what it means to be transgender. There is no single insight I can share about being trans to which anyone might respond: "Oh, *now* I get it. Now I see where you're coming from and what you're all about." That will never be for the simple reason that being trans does not fully define me. I am—as we all are—many things. I'm a lawyer, but your knowing that doesn't unlock some hidden world within my brain. I like to wear nice clothes, but that fact hardly tells you everything else there is to know about me. I also live on a houseboat (way more maintenance than I'd bargained for!), enjoy doing drag (didn't see that coming, did you?) and love animals—cats especially. Taken alone, none of those things swings open the door to Jess's inner mental sanctum. Rather, only when every last quality of me is combined does the real me start to take shape.

I'm not about to claim that being trans is no more important than my red-orange hair or freckles. Yes, it's a bigger deal. As Hayden would say, "One thousand percent bigger deal!" But if you still haven't gotten my point, here it is as plainly as I can say it: I am trans, yet I am so many other things too. And so is every other trans person on the planet. Just as is the case for every cis-gendered individual.

Oh! I nearly forgot. I recently bought a sweet new kayak. If anyone reading is interested in joining me for a paddle around Lake Union or through the Arboretum, give me a shout. Also,

I'm crowdsourcing a name for my vessel. Silly puns welcome. Don't be shy. Send 'em my way.

For this special guest post, I'm Jess.
And remember, if you can't be you, who else are you going to be?

Chapter
Thirty-Eight
Chew on That

I arrived at Jerry's place a half-hour early to visit with my Aunt Sally next door. When I told her I would be moving next door, she pulled me into a tight hug, filling my nose with rose-petal perfume. Curiously, she skipped any questions about why a twenty-six-year-old, single gay man would give up his own apartment in favor of sharing a townhome with an elderly man on the opposite side of the city.

"Oh, Hayden! Praise the Lord! Now I can see you all the time."

Aunt Sally had just voiced my greatest concern. Still, I cut her some slack. I owed her big time. She had been there for me when my mom, her only sister, passed away eight years ago. Going through the worst possible kind of experience together creates a unique bond between people. Beyond that, we had nothing in common. Aunt Sally believed in Jesus Christ as her personal savior; I'd write in RuPaul if forced to vote. Aunt Sally loved garage sales, flea markets, and resale shops; I liked things fresh out of the box, with assembly instructions. Aunt Sally prayed for my soul; I remained unconvinced that my soul needed saving.

"It won't be just me moving in," I said slyly, knowing she would wrongly assume I was bringing a guy with me.

"I see. (She didn't. Not at all.) And Jerry is okay with that, is he?"

"I can say with one thousand percent certainty that Jerry loves the idea. I'm not sure I would have given it serious thought had it not been for Jerry." I had just crossed the line from having a bit of fun to misbehaving, but I couldn't stop myself. It was too easy. And too much fun.

"And does this friend of yours have a name?"

"Alice."

Judging from the look of surprised delight on Aunt Sally's face, you'd think I'd just told her I'd joined a Pentecostal church and was marrying the pastor's daughter—out of necessity. Knowing the joke had run its course, I told her, "Alice is a dog. I'm adopting her from a woman I met in the park who has to give her up."

Aunt Sally couldn't hide her disappointment. That made two of us—it didn't feel great to confirm her wish that I be Christian and married to a lovely girl. But I had brought this on. I should have let sleeping Dalmatians lie.

The mood next door was decidedly better. Jerry was in fine form. He'd never admit the real reason for his upbeat mood. As excited as he was to have a dog in his life, the financial relief enabled by having a roommate had put a spring in his shuffle. I had to watch my dollars, but I was in my twenties. I had decades of earning years ahead of me—a thought both comforting and dispiriting. On the other hand, Jerry faced increasing expenses on a fixed income. It must suck to be in your tenth decade and still be stressed about money.

Lasagna was on the evening's menu, along with Caesar salad and garlic bread. I opened the bottle of red I'd picked up at the market. Not counting tea or our recent margaritas, Jerry wasn't much of a drinker. However, he did enjoy toasting and didn't mind taking a few sips during dinner.

"That wine isn't going to pour itself," he said with a mischievous grin.

"Someone's feeling his oats."

"Ha! I can't believe someone your age has ever heard that expression."

"I have grandparents."

"Proving my point."

Jerry's sharp, inquisitive mind was one of the qualities I admired most. The speed with which he solved crossword puzzles, answered *Jeopardy!* questions and recalled historical facts was a marvel. The mystery of Kennedy Osaka's murder presented a problem to solve, and he took to it with the determination of Alice chasing a squirrel.

Between bites of pasta, I pointed out that our working hypothesis must be wrong. Kennedy's killer wasn't another performer gunning—or, in this case, stabbing—for her job. No one had been named Kennedy's replacement as artistic director. Who would kill someone for a job they didn't have a reasonable expectation they would get with the other person out of the way?

"You're quick to draw a conclusion," Jerry said after taking a surprisingly large swallow of wine. "But even so. Let's presume our theory was incorrect and that jealousy of Kennedy's high-paying job in the spotlight wasn't what got her killed. So we were wrong. So what?"

I dropped my fork; it hit the plate with a clang. "So what? We were wrong. That's what!"

"You should realize, Hayden, that it's most often the case that before anyone gets anything right, they first get it wrong—usually, more than once. You're a schoolteacher. You, of all people, shouldn't need reminding of that fact."

"I see you like the wine."

"You're changing the topic."

"It's just so frustrating. I have spent hours searching the Internet, reviewing hotel video and guest records, and sneaking around Mysterium. I even trespassed and stole those stupid scissors. All for nothing. All that work only to find out we were wrong."

"Good lord. Would you listen to yourself? None of that effort, not one single second, was a waste of time. At every step of the way, you learned something."

I ripped a hunk of garlic bread from the baguette and chewed on his words.

Jerry sighed loudly. "Let's review, shall we?"

"Okay, where do you want to start?"

"It's always been my experience that the beginning usually works."

I began by telling Jerry everything I knew about Kennedy. After noting qualities suitable and often requisite for a famous entertainer—talent, self-confidence, good looks—I emphasized her unpleasant personality and the changes she was rumored to plan on making at Mysterium. I then described Yazminka, the high-flying Russian sexpot.

"Sounds like quite a pill. Let's move on to Kit Durango," Jerry said. "I hope she's more popular."

"Other end of the spectrum. Everyone seems to love her. Professionally speaking, she's got amazing rope skills. Next-level aim. Big personality. One of those people you can't help but like immediately."

"In every way the opposite of my first wife. But I digress. Please. Go on."

I told Jerry that Kit came from a humble background. The daughter of a single mom, she had grown up in a small Colorado town. With talent and ambition, she had worked her way up to be a Mysterium headliner, where she was loved by everyone—the Adrenalin! guys had said so, anyway. Her mother had attended opening night, which had obviously delighted Kit, as she'd pointed her out in the crowd.

Moving on to Sasha Smilov, my eye roll was reflexive, triggered by the thought of any guy who believed he was too big for his boots, applied cologne as if it were body lotion, or posed with a cardboard likeness of himself. "Sasha's a piece of work. He exudes jerk in that *'just parked my Harley in the handicapped zone, and what are you going to do about it?'* sort of way."

I went on to tell how I'd been on the Mysterium grounds and discovered him searching Kit's trailer and that afterward, while hiding in the bathroom, I overheard Kit tell someone named Alexander on the phone that she didn't feel safe.

"What do you know about this Alexander character?"

"Not a thing. I have no idea who he is."

"Anyone else of interest?"

Nodding, I named Zell first. "She's the wardrobe manager. According to Vlad and the guys, Zell is the only person at Mysterium who Yazminka doesn't despise. Whether or not the two of them were really friends is an open question. My impression of Zell is that she is short-tempered and cranky, but with the demands of her job, who wouldn't be?" I gave him the rundown on Vlad, Marku, Stefan, and Florin and concluded with a reminder of the blond woman rushing through the hotel lobby before returning to Zell.

"Zell is the only one with immediate access to all the supplies in the costume trailer, including scissors and wigs. I keep coming back to her. You know, an Occam's razor sort of thing."

Jerry nodded. "In layman's terms, the easiest explanation is most likely."

"Just saying."

"However"—he raised a bent finger—"you proved that once inside Mysterium snatching pretty much anything from the wardrobe trailer could be done quite easily."

"Well, I wouldn't say *easily*."

"Seems to me you're going to need to flush out the killer. There are just too many people with a probable motive or acting suspiciously to focus on just one. And, as you say, that circus is full of performers Kennedy might have made into enemies."

As much as I wanted to see an end to our investigation and a murderer put behind bars, I'd secretly hoped that the police would beat us to the finish line. Flushing out a killer wasn't something I was eager to do, yet curiosity compelled me to ask: "And how do you suggest we do that?"

"Remember when I told you about my grandfather, Archibald? The tent revival preacher and his sermon about the devil's chew toy?" Registering my nod, he continued. "He also had a theory about proselytizing. Had he tried to spread the Good Word by going door to door, he would have exhausted himself. As a side note, he couldn't have passed the plate either, which I think was the real reason he traveled with a tent. But regardless of his motive, he successfully drew the townsfolk to him. Not the other way around. He offered music and free lemonade in addition to eternal salvation. It's a business model that works to this day."

Seeing my look of bewilderment, he explained, "Bring them to you, Hayden. That's the message. Offer the killer something they want. Draw them out. Make them come to you."

"What, like lay a trap?" I said slowly, trying out the idea.

"Make them think you know who they are. If you're convincing, they'll try to shut you up. But in so doing, they'll reveal who they are. But be careful. Hollister will have your back, but I don't want to lose my new roomie before he moves in. Plus, I've been promised a spotted dog to spoil. Now, how about you pour me another glass and not be so stingy this time."

To my amazement, Jerry had drunk all his wine. Should he be drinking alcohol with all the medications he was taking? I knew better than to ask. I'd only get a lecture on him being old enough to do whatever he liked. And who was I to argue? At ninety-one, he could drink the entire bottle if he wanted. I just didn't want to encourage it.

For the next hour, right up to Jerry's bedtime at eight o'clock, we discussed the plan for my and Alice's arrival. It had been years since I'd last moved; the to-do list was head spinning. Suddenly, I felt as weary as Jerry looked. As he shuffled toward his bedroom, I flipped off the kitchen light and grabbed the keys he had made for me.

"You'll be interested to know," he said from across the room, "in Russian, Sasha is short for Alexander."

Chapter Thirty-Nine

Bombshell

In thirty-three minutes, the final bell of the day would ring. I'd then have an hour until rendezvousing with my best friend and crime-fighting partner to initiate my plan. Presenting ourselves as Bernice Morrison and Chet Blaze, reporters from the *Seattle Gazette*, we would spread the word that we were about to break the story: we knew the identity of the Mysterium murderer. If Jerry was right, that would bring whomever it was out of hiding. More specifically, they would try to silence us and our story. When they did, we'd be ready for them. My props, such as they were, were already in the trunk of my car.

It was a Monday, the one day of the week that was traditionally dark for live performances. But that didn't mean the cast and crew had the day off. During a text exchange with Vlad, I learned that everyone associated with the show was required to be on-site for an exhaustive safety review. He'd added that he and the other

Adrenaline! guys had planned a rehearsal, regardless. *"Stay sharp or break your neck"* was how he'd put it.

Hollister and I were timing our arrival, we hoped, for when things had begun to wind down for the day, but before people started to leave. And with my classroom duties, I couldn't get to the Mysterium tent any sooner.

Dressed in a rain slicker and ball cap, I watched Hollister approach the gate in a simple black pantsuit, perfectly calibrated for that mid-management space between a private office and the boardroom.

"Good evening, Bernice." I handed her a set of personalized business cards I'd made in the school's art room while my class watched a Civil War video.

"Chet." She nodded. "You're looking a little casual, don't you think?"

"We're supposed to be freelance reporters. What do you think they wear? If anything, you're overdoing it."

"You two here to see someone?"

We spun around. The security guard—the third guard in as many visits—had quietly appeared at the gate. She raised a clipboard. "Your names?"

As luck would have it, this particular guard appeared to understand the job entailed more than blindly waving people past. We handed over our cards, complete with our office's telephone number (in reality, Jess Gemalto's landline with a new and temporary voice recording) and our office address (Jess Gemalto's houseboat). The guard slowly traced her finger down the top sheet of paper. She flipped the page and repeated her scan. She looked up, shaking her head slowly. "Chet Blaze? Bernice Morrison? Neither of you is on the list."

"Clerical error." I smiled and shrugged.

Hollister followed my lead. "You wouldn't believe how many times this happens."

"So many times," I added. "Interviews get scheduled last minute. But do the big shots ever delay the deadline? Nope, never. So Bernice and I race off to an assignment, often arriving before the paperwork has a chance to spit out of the printer."

Unconvinced, the guard returned my card. "Say again? Who are you here to interview?"

"Kit Durango," I answered. Hollister and I had previously decided that our first visit would be with the cowgirl sharpshooter for several reasons: Kit already believed we were members of the press, she was amiable, and—most important to our plan—a real talker and liked by everyone.

While the guard dialed Kit, I fought to maintain eye contact and appear relaxed. I hated to lie, even considering what was at stake. It shouldn't bother me that some stranger might think I was a sketchy character, but it did. On the other hand, Hollister had no qualms about using deception when she sensed injustice. Once, when I had questioned her nonchalance about thwarting the rules in such situations, she'd replied, "Let me get this straight. Your argument is that I should be playing by the rules, even when those rules are rotten by design? Interesting take, Hayden. That kind of thinking would set back gay rights, social justice, animal interests, environmental protection, and everything else worth pursuing by—oh, I don't know—say, *forever*."

I hadn't challenged her on the point since.

After thirty long seconds with the phone to her ear, the guard said, "Kit's not answering. I'll go get Jenna or see if I can find

Sasha." Like a power-tripping traffic cop, she raised a hand with a curt, "Wait here."

By the time the guard had turned the corner toward the canteen, Hollister was already thirty feet down the path toward Kit's dressing room. I caught up with her as we passed the trailer assigned to Adrenaline!

"Hold up, Hollister. That guard is bound to wonder where we went."

"News flash—don't care," she said over her shoulder.

Because Kit hadn't answered the guard's call, we were surprised when she swung open the door to her trailer. Wearing a thick pink bathrobe, she invited us inside. Her hair was bundled atop her head in a white towel. She smelled of sandalwood soap. Steam seeped into the room from the adjoining bathroom—a room I was all too familiar with.

"Sorry, you two. I wasn't expectin' company. Jenna does a dang good job of keepin' me in the loop about interviews, photo shoots, and the like, but I guess this'n slipped through the cracks."

Kit removed a lariat and fringed vest from an overstuffed chair. Hollister took the seat; I perched on the arm. Kit sat on a small white stool before a vanity encircled by white frosted light bulbs. "So then, what can I do for ya?"

We ran through five innocuous warm-up questions before turning to the main event. "Well, that about does it." I flipped closed the cover of my spiral notebook and retracted the point of my pen with a click. "Thank you so much for your time, Ms. Durango."

"Now, you should know by now to call me Kit. Please."

Hollister made a show of slowly climbing to her feet as she said, "Just more thing, Kit. Tomorrow's edition of the *Gazette* promises major news on the tragic event that befell Mysterium recently. Do you have any final comment before that story hits?"

Kit's eyes telegraphed surprise. "Major news? What sorta major news?"

I did my best to look apprehensive. Kit needed to believe we knew the killer's identity for our plan to work. But we had to be careful because the killer might be Kit! Were Kit innocent, we needed her to spread the word among the cast and crew that two reporters were about to break the story. However, if Kit were the killer, she had to think we were toying with her, seeking one last quote before we revealed her guilt in the next morning's newsfeed.

Kit Durango was nothing if not effusive, so seeing her look utterly floored was unsettling. Her mouth gaped, but having no words, she shut it before trying again, with the same result.

"Thank you again, Ms. Durango." I stepped past her and opened the door.

Kit spun around. "Wait!" She extended an arm, fingers outstretched. "You know? You know who killed Kennedy?"

Hollister and I made sure our exchange of uneasy glances didn't go unnoticed.

"The police? Do the police know? Did they tell you who it was? Is that how you found out?"

Hollister smiled tightly. "Again, thank you for your time, Ms. Durango."

A shiver shot up my spine as I closed the door behind us. One way or another, Hollister and I had just put a target on our backs. That was our plan—half of it, anyway. When the villain emerged from the shadows, we'd be ready. Not only did we have the advantage of anticipating what was to come, but being around Mysterium had taught us a trick or two.

Chapter Forty
Spread the Word

With one interview completed, we randomly decided to start at the last trailer and work our way back toward the entrance. And so, we found ourselves standing among bolts of fabric, wigs, shoes, half-dressed dress forms, and a pissed-off wardrobe manager.

"Jenna can bite me." Zell tossed our business cards onto the sewing table. She had made it clear from the moment she opened the door that she had no time for the press. When I'd dropped the name of Mysterium's marketing director, I had only further riled her up. If I had been alone in the trailer, I'd have cut to the chase, dropped the bombshell, and scurried away. Hollister sat and crossed her legs, looking settled, as if to prove a point. "We're just trying to do our jobs, Ms. . . . ?"

Zell answered with a tit-for-tat crossing of her arms along with a glower that called attention to her nose ring, which was hard not to notice as it was.

"Right, then," I said, trying for a softer approach. "We hate to take up more of your time, but we have a few follow-up questions from the other day. Just to round out our story. I promise, just five speedy questions—then we'll leave you to your important work."

Zell didn't warm, but neither did she throw us out. She replied to each of our perfunctory questions with clipped answers and a tone reflecting either bother or boredom. Finally, the moment arrived, and we repeated the routine we'd just pilot-tested in Kit's trailer.

"Hold the hell up," Zell snapped. "What are you saying? That you know who Kennedy's killer is?"

"I'm sorry," Hollister said, "but unless you have anything to say on the record, we must get going. We'll be working on the story late into the night as it is."

Zell stepped between us and the door. "Tell me. Now."

"Bernice is right. We've taken up enough of your time." I moved to step around Zell, but she shifted, blocking my path. Hands on hips, legs at a shoulder-width stance, she meant business. "I said, tell me what you know. You're not leaving here until you do."

Being roughly one hundred and fifty percent larger, Hollister didn't hesitate; she pushed past Zell, clearing us a path to freedom. As we clamored down the steps, Zell stood in the open doorway. "You two are a joke. I don't believe a word you say."

With nothing to be gained by arguing, Hollister and I turned and hurried away, nearly colliding with Sasha, aka Alexander, Smilov. Hollister had seen and overheard Sasha, but never spoken directly with him. I doubted he'd remember me from opening night and our brief conversation in the lobby. Naturally, he wanted to know who we were and what business we had on the property. Naturally, we handed him our cards and presented ourselves as Bernice Morrison and Chet Blaze, freelance reporters on assignment for the *Gazette*.

Sasha raised the cuff of his loose-fitted hoodie to consult a fat gold Rolex. "I'll give you five. Walk with me." He turned away from the wardrobe trailer and began marching down the path, his worn Soviet soldier–style boots smacking the wet concrete. Sasha was a strutter with long legs; I struggled to look casual while keeping up, while Hollister maintained a half step ahead of him. Like two side-by-side sled dogs, they vied for the lead position. As we ran-walked up the sidewalk, we repeated our five warm-up questions for the third time.

Sasha stopped suddenly. "You know who did it?"

"We didn't say that, Mr. Smilov," Hollister said calmly. "We simply asked if you have any comment before our story comes out in the morning."

"Who? Tell me! Tell me who killed Kennedy. I'll kill them myself."

I had anticipated a range of reactions to our news, from surprise to disbelief, to relief that a dangerous criminal had been identified. I had not, however, imagined someone hell-bent on vigilante justice. When for the third time we explained to Sasha that for no amount of money, VIP tickets, cases of vodka, or boxes of Cuban cigars would we divulge the identity of who murdered Mysterium's short-lived artistic director, he grabbed Hollister by the shoulders. Leaning so close that their noses nearly touched, he snarled, "You tell me now. Who did it?"

Sasha was the type of guy who pressed all my buttons. He was entitled, arrogant, and over-cologned. But still, I couldn't help but feel a bit sorry for him for making such a clueless move. I held my breath. To my surprise, Hollister closed her eyes and said quite calmly, "Dude. Take. Your hands. Off me."

Fortunately for him, Sasha did as he was told. "Sorry, sorry. It's just . . . the show. My father . . . you have no idea." He swept an arm toward the dark and empty grounds. "This is all my responsibility. It's a lot of pressure."

"We understand," I offered. "But justice will be served by the system."

Hollister gave me a double-take before shaking her head. "Excuse me?"

"Anyhoo," I said, returning her look, "we need to get going." I pulled Hollister away and pointed us toward the canteen.

As we left Sasha standing on the walkway, he shouted after us. "Whoever did this will pay!"

"Curious, don't you think?" I said softly so only Hollister could hear. "He seemed as upset about the financial loss and his dad being mad as he did about the death of a performer.

Hollister pinched two fingers together, leaving a sliver of space between them. "That dude came this close. And as for you saying—"

"You need to chill, Hollister. We have a job to do. It doesn't include teaching a macho straight dude a lesson."

"Never is it not the time—"

I yanked Hollister off the pathway and behind a large dumpster.

"What the—"

"Shh."

"Adrenaline!" I whisper-shouted to Hollister. "Vlad doesn't know what we're up to. He still thinks I work at the hotel."

Crouched and silent, we waited as the chorus of cheerful Romanian banter receded. With the coast clear, Hollister stood. "You never told him? He's bound to find out eventually, and when he does, he'll be pissed you didn't tell him sooner. What were you thinking?"

"Are you kidding me? Look around us! We're creeping around a circus, after dark, spreading a lie to ensnare a murderer. Sorry if I didn't dot all my i's. *Sheesh.* You might think I'd get an 'atta boy' for getting us this far."

Hollister gave me a long, steady stare. "You get that out of your system?"

I rolled my eyes. As steamed as I was at the criticism, I appreciated her willingness to let my outburst pass. Our night's elaborate plan was still in its initial phase, and we needed to maintain team cohesion.

For our plan to work, the message had to reach the ears of our villain. Kit, Zell, and Sasha now knew our not-so-secret secret. We'd planned to drop in on Yazminka, but after running into her brother, we figured he'd fill her in. Hopefully, word of our knowing the killer's identity would soon spread among the rest of the cast and crew. Still, it couldn't hurt to hand out at least one more card.

"Nicole Armand?" I suggested.

"You read my mind. As Mysterium's ring mistress, Ms. Ooh La La should have her finger on the pulse of all that goes on around here."

We assumed correctly that Nicole Armand would have a private trailer near those assigned to Yazminka and Kit. I hadn't noticed hers before because the doorplate carried just the initials "N. A." instead of her full name. Nicole was on her way out just as we arrived. Appearing even taller than she'd looked on stage, the French performer had wrapped a long yellow cashmere scarf around her slender neck. She hoisted a large tan bag in a repeating pattern of L's and V's over her shoulder as Hollister and I produced our cards.

Nicole didn't invite us inside her trailer. She didn't come across as rude—just in a hurry to get somewhere. She shifted her weight restlessly, answering each of our five questions before we'd finished asking them. Had I been concerned with capturing her replies with any degree of accuracy, I'd be at a total loss. Not only was Nicole's Parisian accent hard on my ear, but she spoke with a speed matching her flips on the trapeze. I barely understood a word she said. If Hollister was catching any of it, I couldn't tell. My crime-solving partner stood staring dreamily at the woman. When it came time for the grand finale of our performance, I had to give Hollister a sharp elbow to the ribs to regain her attention.

"Oh, right, Chet . . . you said it."

Instead of expressing surprise or curiosity when hearing our request for a final comment, Nicole looked at us as though we were unwelcome relatives who had come asking for free tickets to the show. She turned abruptly and walked away, leaving behind a whiff of what I wanted to believe was Chanel Nº5.

After a moment, Hollister said, "Her skin is perfection."

"Odd reaction, don't you think?"

"What can I say? I call them like I see 'em."

"Um. Yeah. I'm talking about Nicole's reaction to our news."

"She's French."

"I don't think that really explains it."

"Oh, really? And what do you make of her reaction/nonreaction?"

"If I were a cool, calculated killer, I would try hard to show no emotion. Give no indication to the frothing cauldron of worry and guilt below the surface."

Hollister hooted a laugh. "Yeah, you could be right, Chet. Or it could be that Nicole Armand simply doesn't give an eff."

Chapter
Forty-One
Funny Story

Although it seemed that most of the Mysterium cast and crew had been around when Hollister and I had arrived, most had now left. The grounds were eerily dark. And quiet. And rain-soaked. Thankfully, we had accomplished our mission. We could leave.

"Hayden?"

I jumped. The voice, although familiar, startled me.

"What are you doing here?"

Surprised by Vlad's sudden appearance, I managed only "Oh, I'm . . ." before my brain locked up. After too a long moment had passed, Hollister stepped forward.

"Hey there, Vlad." She thrust out a hand. "Great to see you again. I'm Hollister. I came with Hayden on opening night. We met briefly after the show. Thanks again for those tickets. That was super generous."

Vlad smiled politely but gave me a wide-eyed look, still awaiting my answer.

"Yes, why *are* we here?" I said. "Truth is—"

"It's all my doing." Hollister chuckled. "You don't know me, but I can be a real pain in the butt. I've been a terrible pest about pleading with Hayden to give me an insider's look at Mysterium. As you can see, I finally wore him down, and here we are." She spread her arms in a little voila gesture.

Giving me the stink eye, Vlad said, "You should have said something. How did you even get in?"

"Funny story . . ."

When it became clear to Hollister that again I had nothing, she took the wheel. "I know the guard. We go way back. Long story, but she owes me. Oh gosh. I hope this doesn't get her into any trouble. She was only doing me a favor. Hayden thought it would be fun to surprise you."

Not wanting to interrupt her impressive improv, I just nodded.

"I'm surprised all right," he said, seeming to buy it. He glanced toward the group's trailer. "The guys are about to leave, but since you came all this way, I suppose you can say hello. Quickly." He gave me another annoyed look. "You really should have said something, Hayden."

Unlike my first visit, when we stepped into the trailer, all three guys were fully clothed. The air in the small, cluttered space was heavy and damp, undoubtedly because of their recent showering. We exchanged greetings with Marku, Florin, and Stefan. The unexpected encounter with Vlad had begun awkwardly, but Hollister had smoothed out any rough edges. Now my thoughts shifted to the possibility that one—or more—of these guys could be a killer. I didn't sense a threat, but we were outnumbered two to one. Moreover, if anything could be said about these guys, they were supremely fit and worked brilliantly as a team.

For a moment, I considered dropping our lie about knowing the killer's identity, but thankfully caught myself. These guys still knew me as a friend of Vlad's and a hotel employee, not as Chet Blaze, cub reporter for the *Seattle Gazette*. As there was nothing to be gained by prolonging our visit, I signaled to Hollister that it was time to go and stepped toward the door. "Okay, well," I said, giving a casual wave, "you all have a good night."

The room's vibe changed abruptly. Stefan locked eyes with Marku, then with Florin and Vlad. They nodded, appearing to have just silently reached a decision. Marku moved behind me and slid the deadbolt, locking us inside. My stomach dropped. The saying *I nearly pooped my pants* became suddenly all too real. Hollister and I traded alarmed looks.

"Why are you really here?" Vlad said, his expression, like the three other guys, was hard and menacing.

I stared back at him, too terrified to speak.

"We . . ." I glanced again at Hollister. Her eyes were scanning the room. For an escape route? A weapon? A portal to another dimension? Seeing that she wasn't going to bail me out on this one, I tried for a breezy tone and croaked, "We just came by to say hello. To say how much we enjoyed the show. Is there a problem?"

Clearly, there was a problem.

"Yeah, you could say that," Marku sneered. "We look out for one another. You come at one of us, you better be prepared to take us all on. We deal with things our own way."

Stupid, stupid, stupid. I'd spent the past week focused on suspects other than Adrenalin! I'd allowed Vlad's charm and good looks to blind me from considering him—*them*—a threat. But now, much too late, it all fit. Adrenaline! refused to accept

Kennedy's proposed changes to their act. And the wig! One of them, wearing the blond wig Vlad had borrowed for drag, and stealing a pair of scissors from the costume shop, had killed her. I'd been a complete idiot in refusing to see what had been staring me in the face the entire time.

Finally, Hollister found her voice. "Listen, guys, you don't want to do anything you'll regret. You're already looking at one life sentence. There's no reason—"

"What?" Marku blurted, his eyes bugged..

Again, the four guys exchanged glances. This time: confusion.

Florin wagged his head, as if waking from a potent drug. "You can't be serious. You think *we* killed Kennedy?"

"Nice try," Stefan scoffed.

Marku said, "We all know who's guilty here."

Hollister raised a hand, her fingers spread wide. "Whoa, whoa, whoa. You think Hayden and I are the killers?"

The strength of Hollister's denial seemed to rattle the guys' certainty.

Stefan shook his head. "I saw you talking with Sasha."

"And I remember seeing you"—Florin pointed at Hollister—"a few days ago, entering the costume trailer. There's no mistaking that Mohawk."

Marku raised his voice. "You two show up out of the blue. Start lurking around. What are we supposed to think?"

My chin dropped to my chest, and I expelled a breath I hadn't realized I'd been holding.

"We've been lurking around," Hollister said, "because our friend was a friend of Kennedy's. A woman named Sarah Lee. They grew up around here and went to the same college. When Kennedy was a no-show at a fundraiser she'd promised to perform at, Sarah Lee went to her hotel room. She found Kennedy's body. Hayden and I have been searching for the killer so Sarah Lee isn't wrongly accused. And speaking of lurking around, we spotted two of you peeking into the costume trailer. As if that's not suspicious."

"Oh my god!" Marku protested. "That doesn't make us murderers. We're trying to get dirt on Sasha. Enough to get his ass fired."

"We detest him," added Florin.

Thinking of my school principal, whom I despised roughly twenty percent of the time, I said, "Bosses, am I right? They can be such a pain."

Stefan scoffed. "Pain doesn't begin to describe it. The Smilov family and us go way back. All the way to Bucharest. Boris is a criminal, a horrible human being, and the apple didn't fall far from the tree." He paused. "You have such an expression?" Registering my nod, he continued. "Anyway, he's not to be trusted besides being bad at his job. We thought maybe with Kennedy's arrival, with her being his equal on the artistic side, we might feel some relief. Sure, she had some nutty ideas about how upscale she could make a circus, but ever since her death, Sasha has been emboldened. Throwing his creative opinions around as if they were worth a leu." He added, "Sorry—Romanian currency. It's like a couple of dimes."

"So you suspect Sasha of killing Kennedy?" Hollister said.

Vlad shook his head. "Don't know. He did seem threatened by her confidence. We were all genuinely surprised by how aggressively she was moving to make changes."

"Why didn't he push for his sister to get the artistic director job, then?" I wondered aloud. "Or was he overruled by his father."

This time Florin explained. "Those two make sibling rivalry look like a bar fight. Yazminka is a star of the show, no doubt. But currently, she is one rung below Sasha. We suspect he prefers to keep it that way."

My memory replayed the argument Hollister and I had overheard while trapped in the magician's crate. Yazminka had said to her brother, "Please. Kennedy was an amateur. You thought you could control her but discovered you couldn't."

I now understood: Sasha hadn't supported his sister's bid for the artistic director job because he feared her power in that role. Instead, he had pushed for Kennedy. Had he gotten more than he'd bargained for? Had he murdered her because of that? The possibility was starting to take hold. But nothing so far explained "the other matter" Yazminka had mentioned. My eyes met Vlad's.

He fumed, "You've been lying to me this entire time. Do you even work at the hotel?"

If I'd ever been more embarrassed or ashamed, I couldn't think of when. "I wanted to clear that up. There was just never the right moment."

Vlad shook his head and muttered, "Unbelievable," before looking away.

Gratefully, Hollister did the mop-up on our conversation by explaining the real reason for us being there—laying our trap. The guys seemed at once impressed by our bold act and dubious about its success.

"You think the killer will go hunting for you?" Marku asked. "That he'll try to silence you for knowing his identity?"

"And what if he does?" Stefan added. "What then? You're dealing with someone who has proven they are capable of murder. This isn't a game. Shouldn't you be leaving this to the professionals?"

Everything the guys said was true. But they didn't know the details of our plan. I wasn't overly confident. And yet, it was just crazy enough that it might actually work.

As we turned to leave a second time, Stefan said, "Wait!" He removed a bottle of clear liquid with a hard-to-read label from a cabinet. Taking his cue, Marku sprang toward the counter and pulled six red plastic cups from a stack.

"If you're going to go through with it, you could use a drink for good luck." Stefan poured two fingers of vodka into each cup before passing them around the room. "Something tells me you might need it."

"To catching a killer!" Marku declared.

"To catching a killer!" we all said with cups raised.

On the way out the door, Vlad caught my arm. "I'm extremely pissed at you. And I'm pretty sure I'm going to stay pissed for a long time. I'm not sure I ever want to see you again, Hayden." He leaned in and kissed my cheek. "But please be safe. Don't do anything more stupid than you've already done or got planned. If I change my mind, I'd rather you were in one piece."

Chapter Forty-Two
Crazy Scheme

The *slap, slap, slap* of water against the dock muted the sound of Hollister's and my footsteps as we approached Jess's houseboat. The constant rain had made the walkway slippery, so we took extra time to keep our footing while balancing backpacks and bags of fast food that we'd picked up on the way.

Jess greeted us on the landing. We shook the rain from our coats and hurriedly sat down to eat. We couldn't know if or when the killer would take the bait, but we didn't want to be stuffing fries into our faces when he, she, or they arrived. Our plan was simple, in concept anyway. An hour earlier, at Mysterium, we had primed the rumor mill with news that two freelance reporters knew who had murdered Kennedy Osaka. We were banking on that information quickly reaching the ears of the killer—and with it, the particulars on our fake business cards, primarily Jess's address.

Hollister and I had decided on the houseboat because of its location, a long and wobbly walkway the only way to and from the house. Jess had agreed to host our "sideshow," as he called it, stipulating that we not tell him a single word about what we were up to. His exact words: "I prefer not to get disbarred over whatever crazy scheme you kids have cooked up, thank you very much."

I wiped my chin with a paper napkin and tossed the grease-stained bags and crumpled wrappers in the waste bin beneath the sink. Jess pulled a laptop from his bag as I slipped on my coat. "I'm going to catch up on paperwork. Does that work for whatever it is you have planned?"

"Perfect," Hollister said. "We need to look busy, as if we're working on the story."

"The story?" Before Hollister could reply, Jess pumped the brakes. "Never mind. I don't want to know."

"Just need to help Hayden get set up," Hollister said. "Be right back."

Outside on the porch, I knelt and emptied my pack. Once clad in a black rain slicker, black ski hat, and black running gloves, Hollister assisted me in arranging things. The first task was confirming the operation of the floodlights and security camera that Burley had borrowed from her brother, Roy. I still thought the man was a jerk of epic proportion, yet he'd agreed to help when his sister asked. So I guess he deserved credit for being a good brother.

Next to do was getting me situated in the kayak, where I would float about twenty feet off the dock between Jess's and the next-door neighbor's houseboat, acting as a sentry. Anyone approaching Jess's place would be visible to me, but they wouldn't see me bobbing in the dark. If the killer did show up, I would text Hollister the letter Q. She ruffled my hair and said, "Quest! I love it."

Registering my expression, she said, "Queer?" Paused. "Queen?"

I nodded, not revealing my far less inspiring actual reason: Q's location in the upper corner of the keyboard.

The moment Hollister received my text, she would flip on the floodlights, blinding the visitor, and start recording video. I would dial 911 and hope for the best.

From the porch, Hollister gave me a critical eye. "You ready? Still good with the plan?"

"Couldn't be better. I feel like a Navy SEAL."

"Navy GUPPY. Maybe."

"Say what you will. I'm feeling it."

"Yeah, well." She turned serious. "Don't go getting any ideas about being a hero, Hayden. No matter what happens, stick to the plan."

Hollister knew me too well to think "being a hero" figured high on my list of aspirations, but I appreciated the sentiment. Saying "don't do anything stupid," while more apt for the scheme, lacked positivity. We wished each other luck, and Hollister went back inside.

There was nothing to do now but wait.

I noted the time: 7:50 PM. Not only was it possible that no one would come, but my gut told me that was the most likely outcome. Much of our plan relied on a sequence of events, none of which we could be sure would happen. Still, one thing was certain: I was already cold and uncomfortable.

Thirty minutes into the wait, the first wrinkle in our plan came to light. I couldn't text while wearing gloves and holding the paddle. Texting was a crucial element of the plan. Hollister and I could hardly maintain an element of surprise if we were shouting across the water to each other. After balancing the paddle across the kayak's cockpit to prevent it from slipping into the lake, I gently coaxed off one glove. As I tapped out a message, one from Hollister appeared on my screen: *You missed check-in. Something wrong?*

I wrote back: *Gloves! All's well.*

She replied: *Do we need to switch?*

Me: *I got this.*

Hollister: *Hmm. Sure?*

Me: *YES, MOTHER!*

While I'd been texting with my crime-fighting partner, the kayak had floated a one-eighty, the bow pointing away from the houseboat. I twisted around on the seat. Face pressed to the glass, Hollister peered out the window for visual confirmation. Though I doubted she could see me in the dark, I flashed her a thumbs-up.

The hour passed with excruciating slowness. Hollister and I hadn't set an expiration time on our trap. Regardless of the stakes, I was ready to call it "game over" when my watch's short hand reached ten. I shifted my weight on the thinly cushioned seat for the umpteenth time, causing the kayak to rock. My left butt cheek had fallen asleep or was frozen. Either way, I wasn't looking forward to another sixty minutes in the kayak, lying in wait.

No sooner had I slipped my glove back on than a vehicle's headlights swept across the parking lot. Moments later, someone shut off the engine and lights. I listened for a door closing or voices but heard nothing. Whoever had just arrived was most likely a houseboat resident on the other dock. And yet, despite the long odds, I had a strange feeling. *This is it.*

I pinched the tip of my glove between my teeth, tugged it off, and texted Hollister.

Someone is hear.

Ignoring the typo, I focused on minimal motion while readying myself for action. I knew Hollister and Jess would be sitting at the kitchen table. To anyone halfway up the dock, they would appear to be cranking away on our blockbuster story. My eyes searched the shoreline for any movement. Several minutes passed. Whoever was out there had walked off in another direction, was still in their vehicle, or was standing on the shore. A frigid tingle shot up my spine. Call it Spidey sense, but I knew someone was staring down the dock and assessing the situation. I could envision their perspective: the long dark dock leading to an unfamiliar houseboat would cause wariness in just about anyone. Several more minutes passed. My phone vibrated in my pocket.

Hollister: *???*

I answered: *Not sure. Stand by.*

I squeezed my phone.

Clomp . . . clomp . . . clomp.

The shape of an adult-size body approached. Man? Woman? Given the distance and the dark, I couldn't tell yet. I gripped the phone tighter still. Waited.

The darkness, combined with the floating walkway, demanded deliberate steps, slowing one's natural pace. As the person neared, I identified the build as a man's and his stride—even considering the moving dock—as a strut. As he came into clearer focus, I could see he was bald and had a voluminous beard. And thanks to a westerly breeze, I could smell his cologne.

Chapter Forty-Three
Throw Down

Alexander Smilov.

My mind did loop de loops. Sasha? What did Sasha have to gain by killing Kennedy Osaka? The murder had jeopardized Mysterium's run. It was a damaging blow to the business Sasha's father had entrusted him to run. And yet, there was no mistaking it was him advancing on the houseboat.

Struggling to stay calm, I prepared to text Hollister our code letter when Sasha stopped about ten feet short of the houseboat's porch. I couldn't see his eyes, but he seemed to be looking at the house. From my position just above the water's surface, I was too low to see what he saw, and yet I knew he was watching the two reporters—Bernice and Chet—that he had spoken with only hours earlier. That *was* part of our plan. We intended to lull the killer into a false sense of control. He would wrongly think that the two people who knew his identity were within his sights, blithely tapping away at their keyboards. Sitting ducks, as it were.

Given the effect on my nerves, the lake's gentle swells might have been a tidal wave. Finally. The moment that Hollister and I had worked for.

Sasha took a step. Then another. Like a cartoon villain, he began to creep toward the porch with exaggerated loping steps. Another five, maybe six, feet, and he'd enter our trap. I started counting down. Four, three, two . . .

Sasha stopped abruptly. The dim porch light caught the shadow of movement.

Dammit, dammit, dammit!

Morris, the orange tabby, sauntered onto the porch and plopped down. He rolled onto his back, wriggled, and stretched. Stupid animal! If I sent the code now, Hollister would trigger the lights, and the video would start recording. But Sasha was just outside the camera's field of view.

The standoff between human and cat lasted only twenty seconds but felt like an eternity. With a loud thud, Sasha broke the stalemate by landing a big boot on the porch.

I hit "Send."

The floodlights triggered. Sasha stumbled forward. Suddenly, Morris was underfoot. The cat screeched and sprang. Sasha let out a muffled yelp and jumped back, trying to shake the animal from his pant leg. He fell hard onto his butt, crying out in Russian. Hollister burst out the door. She avoided stepping on Morris but lost her balance and crashed onto Sasha. Jess bolted from the house, tapping frantically on his phone. Sasha reached out and grabbed Jess's ankle. Jess dropped the phone, sending it skidding across the porch. It dropped into the lake with an emphatic *plop*.

I paddled madly toward the action. The kayak smacked against the dock. I scrambled out. Jess had joined the fight to subdue Sasha. He was the top of a three-person dogpile. I shoved my hand into my pocket. My phone? Where was my phone? I spun around, dropped to my knees, and reached into the dark cockpit, desperate to feel the familiar shape. It must have slid far forward next to the foot pedals. There was no time. I raced to the porch. By the time I got there, Jess and Hollister were panting hard, standing over a surrendered Sasha.

"You people are freaking crazy!" Sasha shouted up at them. "Why did you attack me?"

"Because you're a murderer!" Hollister shouted down at him.

The look on Sasha's face was extraordinary. He was, as the British might say, gobsmacked. "I didn't kill nobody. I came to find out who killed Kennedy."

"You can't expect us to believe that," Hollister growled.

The trouble was, I did believe Sasha. He didn't seem a good enough liar to fake his look of confusion. He had followed us to the houseboat to try and convince us, again, to reveal the identity of Kennedy's killer. He had come for a name.

"Hollister," Jess said, "I don't think this is our guy."

"You don't really believe him?" Hollister said, incensed.

"Jess is right," I weighed in. "Sasha wants to find the bastard as much as we do. We have different reasons, is all."

Conflicted emotions were fast becoming my natural state. The current iteration was disappointment that our trap had captured an innocent person, mixed with relief that we had been unable to call the cops. I shuddered to think how we would explain ourselves. Perhaps we were fortunate that Sasha didn't seem inclined to involve the police either. We all shuffled inside, where the unmistakable scent of Sasha's cologne reminded me of why I preferred a guy to smell of soap and nothing more.

As many questions as must be swarming in Sasha's head, he chose to ask Jess and me: "You two twins?"

"That, sir, is a story for another day." Jess handed Sasha a tumbler of Stolichnaya as a peace offering. Sasha threw back the drink in one swallow. Acknowledging my wide-eyed look, Jess said, "The brand is purely coincidental."

Sasha had scraped his chin, and a wicked bruise was forming on his right cheekbone. He downed a second glass of one-hundred-proof vodka as Jess rummaged in a freezer drawer for an ice pack. Meanwhile, Hollister and I tag-teamed telling Sasha our story, starting with Sarah Lee's fundraiser, at which Kennedy had been a no-show, and extending up to the present, where he had stumbled into our trap.

"You people are certifiable." Sasha reached for the bottle. "You want to help your friend? Sure, okay. I get that. But you're messing with a killer. Do you have even the slightest idea of what you're doing?"

It was a fair question. If forced to answer, I'd have done us no favor. Hollister and I were one thousand percent amateurs. We made it up as we went along. Despite our spectacular failure, my embarrassment was outweighed by pride: we were willing to throw down for a friend.

"Okay, so this is a bit of a cluster," Jess said, "but Hayden and Hollister did manage to lure you here, didn't they?" Jess handed Sasha a tube of antiseptic ointment and a box of Band-Aids. "You proved the ruse could have worked. It just duped the wrong person."

I appreciated Jess sticking up for us, though I suspected it was no actual endorsement of our methods.

"So if you didn't kill Kennedy"—I pointed at Sasha—"then who did? It wasn't Adrenalin! Which leaves as suspects"—I counted on my fingers—"Yazminka, Kit, Zell, the mysterious woman in the hotel . . ."

"No!" Panic flashed across Sasha's face. "Zell never went to the hotel."

I started to point out that he'd misunderstood what I'd said, but his remark skidded to a stop in my brain. What Sasha heard me say was ". . . Zell, the mysterious woman in the hotel." He'd conflated what I'd thought were two different persons.

Hollister picked up on it too. She said, "What do you mean that wasn't Zell at the hotel?"

Sasha's fumbled explanation reminded me of my students when coming up with impromptu reasons for submitting identical essays. "I'm just saying that it wasn't her. You've seen Zell. She's shorter and has green hair. That woman was blond."

And there it was.

Sasha hadn't argued that Zell was innocent of the murder. Instead, he'd focused his defense on Zell having not been the woman seen in the hotel lobby. There was a slight problem: he hadn't seen the video. He couldn't have known the woman was tall and blond.

I recalled something: during the telephone conversation between Kit and Sasha (aka Alexander) that I'd overheard while hiding in Kit's shower, she had admonished him to "do more than just handle the produce." She had threatened to go to his father: "If word gets back to the big man, that will be your barn to clean." Adding to that, the Adrenalin! guys had complained that Sasha's womanizing had embarrassed his family, namely, his father, one too many times. They believed Boris Smilov had nearly had it with his philandering son.

And there was more: the argument between brother and sister while Hollister and I were trapped in the magician's cabinet. I finally understood what Yazminka had meant by the "other matter." She had said, "You thought you'd get away with it? That no one would find out? How could you think that is remotely possible? You will be found out. And when that happens, I will not try to save you." Then, "Do it, or I'll have no choice but to tell—Father is extremely predictable." Yazminka hadn't been accusing her brother of murder. She'd been calling him out on his latest dalliance and warning him to end it.

My hand clapped my mouth. I gasped. "It was Zell at the hotel! But her visit in disguise had nothing to do with Kennedy's murder. Zell went there to see you."

Chapter
Forty-Four
Stumble and Fall

Dumbfounded, Jess, Hollister, and I stared at Sasha. The revelation that Zell was the blond woman in the video was a stunner, yet learning that her being at the hotel had nothing to do with Kennedy was its own shock.

Sasha stood abruptly, too agitated to sit still, and started pacing. "I was working late the night Kennedy was killed. I was in the tent the entire time—the security guards will vouch for me if you don't believe me. Earlier that day, someone had stolen my phone. Then, later that evening, pretending to be me, they used it to text Zell. They told her to come to my room at seven and to ensure no one recognized her.

"Zell didn't question the message. Why would she? We had talked about the necessity to keep our hookups a secret. She knew that no one could know. People would talk. Word would get to my father. I couldn't have that. Plus, Zell knows other performers are staying at the hotel. And so she disguised herself. It couldn't have been easier. Every day she is surrounded by costumes and wigs."

"But your phone? Surely it was password protected?" I said.

His look of embarrassment answered my question.

Hollister pinched the bridge of her nose. "Don't tell me. One, two, three, four, five, six?"

"Six ones," he mumbled.

"Zell was set up," I said. "You both were."

Sasha pressed a palm to his forehead, showing off a black spider tattoo on the back of his hand. Despite his bad boy affectations, behavior, and fragrance, I almost felt sorry for him. Almost.

"When Zell and I heard the news about Kennedy, we realized we were screwed. We understood how bad it looked."

"Okay," Hollister said. "So you couldn't risk anyone, especially your father, knowing about you and Zell. What would he do anyway? Fire you? Demand you return home to Romania? Assign you to another Smilov circus in Kazakhstan? That explains why you haven't gone to the police. But you had to know the hotel would have video of a sketchy-looking woman coming and going right around the time of the murder. The truth will come out, Sasha. The police will figure out it was Zell. It's only a matter of time. Honestly, what was your plan?"

"Plan?" Sasha barked. "I had no plan. I could only hope the police would find the real killer before someone figured out it was Zell in the wig and why she was there. But one thing's for sure. After that night, I broke it off. I can take no more chances."

Fascinating. I examined Sasha's face, searching for any indication, some tell, that he was lying. Because he was.

Sasha's calling card: his cologne. I had smelled it in the costume shop during my second visit just after I'd seen him come out. Zell had looked disheveled, and items that should have been on the large sewing table had been knocked to the floor. I started to call him out but stopped. Sasha was a liar. It seemed he'd say anything to cover his romantic tracks. But at that moment, it was beside the point. We needed him on our side. We had a shared enemy.

Jess shook his head, marveling. "It's a damning set of facts. Zell is recorded on video at the scene, entering and then fleeing in disguise. And let's not forget the scissors. Presuming they were indeed snatched from the costume trailer, they would surely have had her prints on them."

"But what about Sarah Lee's prints?" I asked. "Wouldn't her prints be on them now?"

"Yes. But that doesn't mean Zell's were wiped away," Jess said. "I bet they're still there."

Sasha whined, "This is all Kennedy's doing. Her and her foolish ideas. Now I'm the one paying the price."

I let the beginning and end of his idiotic remark slide and focused on the middle part: *her and her foolish ideas*. My thoughts did more somersaults than Adrenalin! on stage. I knew from firsthand experience at my school that not all workplace changes were universally welcomed by staff. When Mr. Keebler got the vice principal job over Ms. Holland, a more veteran teacher, she had made life miserable for the rest of us until her requested transfer came through. Near the end of the school year, the tension had reached a boiling point. I feared Ms. Holland's hostile posts to our staff Facebook group and her nasty notes pasted to the cupboards in the teachers' lounge would escalate to property damage or an all-out meltdown when Mr. K was announced to the students at assembly.

"Hear me out," I said to Hollister and Jess. "Kennedy was appointed Mysterium's new artistic director. She had ideas for a new direction for the show. 'Elevating the elegance' was how she'd described her vision." I directed my next words at Sasha. "When hiding in Kit's shower, I recall her telling you on the phone: 'Regrettable . . . but one thing's sorted. This girl won't be doing rope tricks at the concession stand.' I had dismissed the remark as some countrified metaphor. But I was wrong. Kit had been speaking literally. One of Kennedy's creative changes would have been to demote Kit from a solo performer to a lobby entertainer during intermission."

Hollister wagged a long-nailed finger. "Kit seems way too proud to put up with such an insult. And with her mother attending opening night? Mm-mm. I don't think so."

I added, "Can you imagine her humiliation in having to explain to her mother that she was no longer a star of the show and instead was competing with Sasha here, for attention, next to the popcorn stand?"

I turned to Sasha and recognized the look on his face—it was the same one a student wore when I caught him googling answers to exam questions. "You suspected Kit this whole time, didn't you?"

He reared back in defense. "I'm responsible for operations. It's my job to make sure the show runs smoothly. Kennedy told me about the changes she was planning. She had to. She needed my help to implement them. Some were okay, an improvement even. But I didn't agree with all of them—especially her intention for Kit. Not only would Kit have been furious, but so would everyone else in the cast and crew. Despite being a bit hokey, her act is an audience favorite. Stripping Kit of her solo act would have created a firestorm. As if I need more drama in my life. My father is always and already on my ass." He shrugged, lifting the shoulders of his leather jacket. "But what could I do? As the artistic director, it was Kennedy's decision. You've seen Kit's act. It was the least elegant of anything on stage."

I now had a solid guess at what had set the murder in motion. "So you tipped off Kit."

Sasha's face turned ashen. He nodded. "The bowie knife missed my head by three inches." He confirmed the measurement with his finger and thumb. "Had she meant for it to hit me, it would have. It was a warning. She wasn't going to stand for it. When I learned what happened to Kennedy, I suspected Kit had confronted her and—"

"And clearly, that conversation didn't go well," Hollister said. "You put a target on Kennedy."

"But the scream?" Jess said. "If Kit killed Kennedy, why would she phone the front desk and report hearing a scream? A scream that she had caused?"

Eager to share the unfolding of events as I now understood them, I said, "There was no scream. It happened only because Kit said it did. Here's what I think *did* happen. Kit killed Kennedy just before seven o'clock, then returned to her room to wait for Zell to arrive. From the peephole in her door, Kit had a direct line of sight to the room opposite hers: Sasha's. Kit would have seen Zell, disguised as a tall blond woman, knocking on her boyfriend's door. She would have waited there longer than normal because she wasn't dropping by on a whim—Sasha had invited her to come there at the precise time. The genius of it. That ensured enough time elapsed between the blond woman's recorded entrance and exit from the hotel for Kit to have murdered Kennedy."

Hollister said, "But if he didn't have his phone—"

In dramatic Hercule Poirot fashion, I thrust an accusing finger at Sasha. "That's why you searched Kit's trailer. You were looking for your stolen phone. You never received Zell's messages that night asking where you were. Kit did. When Zell eventually gave up and left, Kit immediately reported the scream that had never happened. And when she made that call, she tightened the noose of her plan. The timing of that call would have been registered somewhere in the hotel's telephone system, as was the time stamp on the video recording Zell in disguise run-walking through the lobby shortly after."

"And Sarah Lee?" Jess said. "How is it possible she never saw Zell?"

Signaling *"I got this,"* Hollister raised a hand. "Zell was outside Sasha's door when Sarah Lee stepped off the elevator onto the sixth floor. Then, as Sarah Lee entered Kennedy's room, Zell finally gave up on Sasha and left. They never saw each other."

Completing the story, I said, "As security was on their way up to the sixth floor, Zell was on her way down to the lobby. The scheme was perfectly planned and timed by Kit to make it appear as though Zell arrived at the hotel, went straight to Kennedy's suite on the sixth floor, murdered her, then fled."

Jess nodded his understanding. "Never imagining someone else would stumble into the crime scene."

"Where is Kit now?" I asked Sasha.

"When I left the grounds, she was still there. I noticed the light was on in her trailer. She planned to stay late to get in some extra target practice."

Hollister was already pulling on her jacket.

"There must be another way," Sasha said frantically. "When word of this gets back to my father—"

"Listen, Sasha." Hollister served a hand. "With a killer on the loose, your daddy issues figure low on our list of concerns."

Sasha stood. "I will go with you."

"Suit yourself." Hollister zipped her jacket.

Running down the dock, Hollister awkwardly tugged the keys from her jeans, and with a *bleep bleep*, unlocked Mo's doors. I squeezed myself against the center console so Jess could fit in the passenger seat next to me. Seconds later, Hollister had the Porsche flying down the dark street at sixty miles per hour, a half block ahead of Sasha in his muscle car.

"This isn't safe." Jess gripped the dashboard. "You need to slow down."

Jess had never ridden with Hollister, so I appreciated his concern. I shared it.

"Sorry. No can do, Jess." Hollister down-shifted, taking a corner at thirty-five. "We've got a cowgirl who's due her comeuppance."

"She's a murderer!" Jess exclaimed. "I'm calling the police."

"Good idea," I said. "Except your phone is at the bottom of Lake Washington."

"Then you do it." Jess braced himself against the door as Hollister turned hard to the left—might his fingertips leave permanent indentations on the dashboard?

"I'm pretty sure mine is somewhere in your kayak."

Hollister hadn't taken her eyes off the road but must have sensed us staring. "It's in my front pocket."

I reached across her lap. She batted me away. "I'll get it as soon as it's safe."

Jess knocked against my shoulder as Hollister made a hard right. It might have taken us thirty minutes to reach the staff entrance at legal speed, but given the night's late hour and pedal-to-the-metal pace, we arrived at Mysterium in less than half that time. Hollister slammed the brakes, bringing Mo to a skidding stop. We piled out of the car as Sasha pulled up beside us. Holding the phone to her ear as she ran, Hollister did her best to give a CliffsNotes summary of the situation and our location to the cops. The chain-link gate was padlocked. Sasha dug in his pocket for a key.

As the four of us raced onto the grounds, we heard the first gunshot.

Chapter Forty-Five
Wedgy From Hell

Sasha, Jess, Hollister, and I raced inside Mysterium's tent. Spotlights illuminated center stage. Zell was strapped to the ginormous wheel encircled by colorful balloons. Mounted on the bucking mechanical bull, Kit aimed a rifle at the wheel.

Sasha sprinted toward the stage. "Stop! You crazy—"

Pop!

An orange balloon exploded just inches below one of Zell's Doc Martens. As Kit readied another shot, Sasha was halfway down the dark aisle.

Like a team of seasoned soldiers, we fanned out. Hollister took the right aisle, Jess the middle, and I was on the left. We started our hurried descent toward the ring.

"Kit! Don't!" Sasha leaped onto the stage with a thud.

Kit swung the barrel of the gun around. "Well, well, well. Look what the cat dragged in. If it isn't our resident Russian

Romeo." She reached down and flipped a switch below the saddle. The machine began to slow.

Sasha shouted across the ring to Zell, "You all right, babe?"

"Do I look all right to you?" she hollered back as she spun on the wheel.

"I know the truth!" Sasha pointed a finger at Kit. "It was you. You killed Kennedy."

Sasha was either brave or incredibly stupid. Either way, he had created a standoff—finger versus rifle. His presence held Kit's attention, a helpful diversion from our rushed creep toward the stage.

Hollister and I had been inside the tent three times. First for the preview, a second time when Kit had mistaken us for stand-ins, and a third time for the full show. Jess never had. He didn't expect the disproportionate drop of the last step. He stumbled and fell.

Kit twisted in the saddle, looking around to where she heard him hit the floor. She saw Hollister and then Jess. I crouched low, hoping she wouldn't visually sweep the entire area.

"Well, lookee here," Kit said, swinging around the rifle's barrel to point at Hollister. "If it isn't the photographer"—she shifted her aim left—"and her partner, the cub reporter. Come on up here. Kit's got a bone to pick with you two."

Kit hadn't seen me. Mistaking Jess for me, she presumed both *Gazette* staffers were accounted for. As Hollister and Jess stepped up into the ring, I crept to the opposite side of the stage. Kit had the only weapon. And from her perch astride Thunderclap on the raised stage, she would easily see anyone approaching before they could get close enough to try and disarm her. I spun in a circle, looking for an idea. My eyes fell on the props Lady Valentina had juggled during her act. Lifting a torch from the table, its billiard ball-like heft surprised me. I shoved the prop into the back of my waistband. Before I thought through what I was doing, I placed a trusty Converse onto the first rung of the ladder to the trapeze platform and started to climb.

Kit said calmly, almost jovially, "You know, years ago when I was just startin' out in rodeo, another girl, her name was Penny— my, oh my, how I hated that Penny—stole my only pair of jeans from the dressing room. Penny had put on weight, you see, and couldn't fit into her own pants anymore. Having no other option, I squeezed myself into the pair Penny had left behind. In retrospect, I should have seen it coming. Those Wranglers were so tight I could barely walk. How I managed to get a leg over the horse, I still can't say. Knowing where you come from, Sasha, I don't reckon you've ever seen barrel racing, but you sit low in the saddle, and there's a good bit of friction down there between your legs. Those jeans continued a steady ride up north with every tight turn. And, Sasha, there's *a lot* of turns. Only one way to describe my agony that day. It was a wedgy from hell. I vowed right then and there, never again would anybody take from me what's rightfully mine."

While Kit gave her little Ted Talk, I reached the top of the platform.

From the wheel, Zell yelled, "Hello? Remember me? If someone doesn't stop this thing, I'm going to hurl!"

While climbing, I'd formed an idea. Kit would easily see anyone approaching at eye level. What she wouldn't see coming was an attack from above. This was not a time to consider the potential downside of what I had planned, which I estimated as a fatal forty-foot fall. I'd come too far to question whether this was the best possible plan or the worst ever.

Carefully, I unhooked the trapeze bar from the platform and held it in one hand. With my other, I pulled the heavy torch from my pants and pressed it between my thighs. I gripped the bar tightly with both hands. I had one missile. One chance for a direct hit. Though I figured my plan still might work if I got close enough; the sound of the torch slamming onto the stage would at least create a distraction that might upset the power dynamic below.

While I psyched myself up, Zell shouted a promise "to barf all over the balloons" unless someone got her off "this mother ##### piece of ####!"

Using her spicy words as inspiration, I started my countdown. Three . . . two . . . one. I took a deep breath, squeezed my legs together, and launched from the platform.

The abrupt tightening of the rope made a whipping sound that reverberated throughout the mostly empty tent. Hearing it, Jess's and Hollister's heads snapped upward. Kit, noticing their sudden shift in attention, followed their gaze.

I spread my legs.

Kit took a sharp intake of breath. With a frighting *thwack,* the torch—instead of hitting Kit as I'd hoped—struck the barrel of the gun. It fell to the stage and fired. A balloon above Zell's green hair exploded, releasing a burst of confetti as Kit slid ungracefully from the saddle and sprawled onto the stage. Hollister and Zell wasted no time. They grabbed one of Kit's lariats and tied it around her. Sasha ran to shut down the wheel.

Only then did I get some deserved appreciation. Jess yelled up at me, "Nice work!"

Hollister, however, read the situation with appropriate concern.

"A little help, please!" I shouted down at them.

Jess now caught up to Hollister's thinking. I needed a way off the trapeze.

Sasha helped Zell down from the wheel; she promptly made good on her promise to empty her dinner onto the stage. A frenzy of voices filled the tent as several cops raced down the aisles, guns drawn.

"Seriously! I can't hold on forever!"

"Sasha!" Hollister shouted. "The trampoline!"

I swung back and forth like a slowing pendulum and watched them all scrambling around below. There was much confusion and shouting as the cops clambered onto the stage. While Jess explained to the police what was going on and why a Mysterium star was hogtied and lying on the stage, Hollister and Sasha frantically worked to position the trampoline beneath me. Even from that height, I could hear the conversations below. One police officer was suggesting we wait for the fire department. I liked the idea of a ladder but doubted the truck would fit through the tent's entrance. Besides, there was no time. My hands were starting to slip.

Sasha nodded to Hollister. She replied, "Are you sure? Like absolutely sure?"

"Yes, yes. Sure."

She shouted up. "Okay, little dude. Jump!"

Sasha added, "Try not to land on your head!"

The Adrenalin! guys were right. Sasha was terrible at his job.

"You can do this, Hayden!" Hollister cheered. "It could be worse."

Appreciating the first part, the second infuriated me. "Really! And how is that exactly?"

"There's no ring of fire!"

I shouted, "Incoming!" and let go of the bar.

The speed of a body falling to earth is 9.8 meters per second or one hundred and eighteen miles per hour. You pick up such fun facts by subbing for other middle school teachers. I hit the trampoline in less than two seconds. The height of the bounce was unexpected. It sent me fifteen feet back into the air. On the fourth bounce, I buckled my knees, bringing my never-to-be-repeated solo act at Mysterium to an end.

The cops, now numbering at least a dozen, applauded.

"You all right?" Jess asked from the side of the trampoline.

Too worked up to speak, I flashed a thumbs-up.

Hollister climbed up and slapped my back. "Hayden is *not* okay." She fired two finger pistols into the air. "Little dude is eff-ing amazing!"

Chapter Forty-Six

Hot Air

The Decemberists woke me at 5:50 AM. I had set my alarm ten minutes later than usual to give myself an extra bit of shut-eye, fully aware the benefit was mostly psychological. Rounding up, I'd gotten two hours of sleep. After stumbling in at three that morning, it had taken me ninety minutes to wind down from the night's and early morning's events. Already pushing the limit, I figured I could enjoy sixty more seconds nestled in the warmth before prying myself out of bed. Skipping work would require that I call in sick. But I wasn't sick. And today of all days was "Diorama Extravaganza." My kids would present a small-scale model and short story on a person of American historical significance. I couldn't disappoint them by not showing up. And truthfully, along with the days before holidays, seasonal breaks, and "Herstory Heroes"—another of my curriculum innovations—it was among my favorite days of the year. And so I wriggled out from beneath the toasty covers and padded across the chilly floor to the bathroom.

Thirty minutes later, I was blowing heat into my hands as my gutless compact car spit cold air from its measly heater. I was long overdue for my next vehicle, preferably something with a working radio and door locks, and I realized that once I moved in with Jerry, I could finally turn that modest dream into a reality. For now, the next thirty-seven minutes would give me time to think. And shiver.

Seventeen. If I had counted correctly, that was the number of days, from Kennedy's murder to last night, it had taken for Hollister and me to identify the killer and clear Sarah Lee of suspicion. Ultimately, the motive hadn't been jealousy at being passed over for a promotion to artistic director, as Jerry and I had first hypothesized. Instead, the reason had been the prospect of a humiliating reassignment to the lobby half-time show.

Ten minutes into my commute, the heater decided to produce lukewarm air. My thoughts returned to Kit and why she'd gone off the deep end. I tried to wrap my head around it. For some people, their work defines their identity. What I knew of Kit's backstory—raised by a single mother in humble circumstances— she had excelled beyond all expectations. If there was a greater height for a cowgirl sharpshooter to achieve, I couldn't imagine what that might be. When Kit learned that her new boss planned to demote her from a featured solo act to an embarrassing side-show, her outrage was understandable. But she'd been unable to manage her fury. And because of that, a woman was dead, and Kit was sure to spend her days remembering life in a spotlight that would fade with each passing year of a life sentence.

Earlier that morning, Hollister, Jess, and I had talked briefly in the parking lot. When I'd wondered aloud if Zell's stagger-ing had been caused by drinking or drugs, Jess conjectured that she'd been wearing high heels. "Trust me," he'd said. "If you're not used to them, heels can be rough. Let alone trying to run in a pair." Hollister had shrugged. "I'll have to take your word for it." Recalling Zell's scuffed Doc Martens, I suspected Jess was right.

The sun had only just come up, and I was one thousand percent exhausted. Still, there was no way I would not be heading straight to Burley's house after work. Although Hollister and I hadn't discussed a celebration, I knew we would spend the evening at Burley's place. We had the entire day to exchange texts and make arrangements. I could pick up our usual Thai takeout but worried it might not be special enough for the occasion. Champagne was suitable, but Burley didn't drink alcohol—though she loved to uncork the bottle. Balloons? She never tired of inhaling helium and singing the best of Bruce Springsteen.

Today, I would try not to fret about the next three days, during which I had to complete my apartment packing, finalize moving arrangements, pick up Alice, and settle into the upstairs floor of Jerry's townhome.

Of course, I wouldn't be me if boys didn't elbow their way into my thoughts. First up, as always, Camilo. As we ran in the same circle, I'd have to see him at some point and find a way to peaceably coexist, hard as that would be for a while. But I was moving on. It was long overdue. Then there was Vlad. Although I wasn't sure about my feelings for him—or confident that he'd forgiven me for not telling the truth about who I was and what I'd been up to—perhaps that was best. Fresh off the Camilo experience, I could use a break.

I pulled into the school's parking lot. My principal, Ms. Koelsch, had already parked her new monstrosity of an SUV (did she get the irony of having a Sierra Club sticker on her back window?) in her reserved spot, along with taking two feet of our vice principal's space. I shook my head at her cluelessness. Knowing Mr. Keebler as I did, he wouldn't say anything and would just park elsewhere. Would I complain? The old Hayden, the pre-Hollister-era Hayden, would have grumbled and fussed, but only silently. But the new-and-improved Hayden, I was proud to say, would say something.

Reluctantly, I shut off the engine. Not only did the act mark the official start of the school day, but the heater was finally turning out hot air.

Chapter
Forty-Seven
Moving On

After mummifying my television with a moving blanket and packing tape, I realized too late that the big screen would be inaccessible for the evening. Hollister and I were scheduled to pick up the rental van at eight the next morning. She'd give me grief if I wasn't ready to roll, so if anything, I had overdone my preparation. By way of example, the fridge was completely bare—no milk for my morning coffee—and all my clean underwear and socks were at the bottom of a suitcase I had already stowed in the trunk of my car.

I looked around my boxed-up apartment. I really would miss the place. Feeling a funk coming on, I argued the positives. I would finally be in a position to save money each month. Having a dog would be fun. And despite sharing a home with Jerry, I would have nearly twice as much space to myself. Still, it was a big change. And dealing with change wasn't my strong suit.

I flipped open my laptop, intent on finding something mind-less to stream. Instead, a different thought struck as I hit the power button: time for a Mates on Dates post. I knew exactly what I wanted to say.

MATES ON DATES: Post No. 27

Today is the last night I'll ever spend in my apartment at Orca Arms. Those of you who have visited me here know how sad I'll be to close the door behind me for a final time. And yet, to be honest, the apartment has its issues. For years, I have battled mold in the bathroom. The walls have no insulation. And there's no dishwasher or in-unit washer and dryer. I could go on. So what gives? Why am I so down in the dumps? I think it's because as imperfect as this place is, it's what I'm used to.

Expanding on this theme, I realize that I've prioritized my comfort with what's familiar over the uncertainty of making a change—even if that change promises something better.

This theme has relevance to dating. Watch and learn ☺. I've been stuck on a guy for far too long. Although it has taken me six months to come around to reality, I am ready to acknowledge that it's never going to happen between this guy and me. I need to move on.

Why has it taken me so long to see what others saw imme-diately? Surprisingly, saying adios to my apartment has given me the insight to answer that question. My relationship with this guy was never great. We were never even a couple. I settled for the occasional moments when I received attention, buoyed by the possibility that despite all observable evidence, we might someday be together. The truth? Settling sucks.

I settled for the emotional crumbs I got by chasing after him. As much as he made me crazy, living with the downside had become my routine. How many times had I reassured myself with the old chestnut *"It could be worse."* Think about those words for a moment. How has such drivel stayed around? Hold me to this, but I swear I will never again utter such an empty platitude. Instead, I'm instituting a replacement: *It should be better.*

Starting tomorrow morning, as I lug my worldly possessions up the stairs to my new digs, I'm going to strive for better—on the home front, romantic front, and all-around Hayden front. The more I focus on improving each aspect of my life, the better my entire life will become. Okay, I admit that sounds a bit grandiose. After all, I'm not training to be an astronaut or starring on Broadway or playing in the Wimbledon final. Instead, I am breaking up with my not-boyfriend, adopting a hyperactive squirrel chaser, and moving in with my ninety-one-year-old friend. But that's my life. And I'm betting that on the excitement scale, it's not that much different from your own. So appreciate the good you've got. Hug a friend, pat a dog, and don't try to convince yourself that bargain tea is ever acceptable. And remember, when things are not great, don't settle. If you're not willing to put in the work to make them better, who will?

Till next time, I'm Hayden
And remember, if you can't be good, be safe!

Chapter
Forty-Eight
It's in the Stars

"Upstairs?" Hollister rested the last box from the moving van on her hip.

"Garage, please." In addition to using one space for my rolling wreck, Jerry and I had agreed to share the other half for storage. Never having a reason to peruse the garage before, I learned that his past activities included golf, fishing, and—curiously—fencing. Fencing was one of those sports I thought about only once every four years during snippets of Olympics coverage. The masks, the swords, the arcane and incomprehensible rules made for a mesmerizing show. Might his gear fit me? I made a mental note to try it on as soon as I got the chance.

From where I stood on the sidewalk, I could hear Jerry calling to Alice as they played fetch in the side yard. There were studies on animal companions' positive effects on people; had I ever doubted those claims, I had only to peer around the corner to be convinced. Alice's arrival had shaved a decade—or two!—off

Jerry's age. He giggled and hooted and, as best he could, threw a saliva-soaked tennis ball to the opposite end of the yard with the intensity of a major league pitcher.

My phone vibrated, alerting me to a text. Vlad confirmed our coffee date the following morning. The Adrenalin! guys had made rumblings about making Seattle their home base after the show's scheduled run. I didn't want to get my hopes up, so I stored the information alongside other future events of low probability: my tennis serve winning me easy points, Hollister letting me drive, and me getting used to Jess Gemalto's nearly identical appearance. I had planned to introduce Jerry to Jess, but that would have to wait. Jess's latest surprise was that he was studying for his pilot's license, and a crucial exam was looming, demanding that he dedicate every spare moment to study.

Burley poked her head outside the front door. "Vittles are getting cold, kids! Mama's not waiting much longer. Hurry it up. The rest of us are about to dig in. With or without you."

Sarah Lee had kindly offered to transport a few breakable items in her Beetle. Camilo had arrived with Burley to help empty out the van. We hadn't spoken since the awkward moment at Hunters. It was cool that he'd come. And I appreciated his acting as if nothing had happened between us. He was his usual happy self, smiling and joking. It was all I could do to suppress my longing and focus on the fact that we were just friends, and that was the best thing, really.

Camilo had set the table and arranged the three large pizza boxes on the counter next to the sink. The Margherita pizza with triple tomato, basil, mushrooms, and artichokes was reserved exclusively for Burley, the lone vegetarian among us. Salad filled a large bowl at the center of the table. Jerry claimed to have made the wooden bowl himself decades ago. I wondered if its creation predated his fencing days. There was more to my new roomie than I'd imagined. I gave him a grin, which he returned with a Groucho Marx–like bouncing of his bushy eyebrows.

Hollister pulled a six-pack of beer, a large bottle of hard cider, a demi bottle of rosé, and a quart of apricot nectar from a paper bag. The booze brought to mind my now-next-door neighbor, Aunt Sally. I was grateful she was in Tacoma for a weekend Bible study retreat. My friends wouldn't have minded if she'd joined us, but I'd have been constantly distracted with concern for how she was dealing with the boisterous and sure-to-be-irreverent party atmosphere.

"Beer?" Hollister asked Jerry. He replied with a slight separation between his thumb and index finger as he lowered himself onto his usual chair. Camilo sat next to Jerry, Burley between Sarah Lee, and Hollister next to Burley. I took the remaining spot between Jerry and Hollister.

"A toast to my compadres," Burley said, lifting her jug of nectar. "There's no way to sugar-glaze it. The last few weeks have been a doozie. But despite all the unpleasantness, three things happened along the way to put a spring in this old mare's Crocs. First, I was reminded that my friends are better than huckleberry crullers. Second, Helen's eggs hatched, reminding me that I'm remiss in sending Brother Roy a thank-you note for camping out in the barn. And so, my friends . . ." Burley hoisted her jug high, accidentally clanking it against the ceiling light.

"Hold up," Hollister said. "Aren't you forgetting something?"

Burley frowned, perplexed.

Seeing that she needed an assist, I said, "You said *three* things happened along—"

"Oh! Right!" Whatever it was, she positively beamed at the thought. "I was reminded that life is too short to keep putting off that tattoo you've always wanted."

Moments like these were why I loved my eccentric friend more than words could express. There was always a surprise, and when it dropped, it was guaranteed to be entertaining.

"No freakin' way," Camilo said. "Tell me you didn't."

"I got Minnie Mouse on my derriere." Jerry said. "One of my first wife's many bad ideas."

That we let Jerry's statement pass without any follow-up spoke to the overwhelming fascination we all had for Burley's announcement.

"Well?" Hollister said. "You going to show us or what?"

Burley set down her jug and rolled up her sleeve. We jumped from our chairs and huddled around her as if released by a starting gun.

"Treasure map?" Camilo leaned closer.

"It's a constellation," I said. Burley wasn't just an astrology enthusiast; she was a fanatic. Though, like everything that entered her orbit, she gave it her own unique spin.

Hollister reached out and traced the five gently curved lines, each one connecting two small stars. Together, the lines created the shape of a larger five-pointed star. Having based my expectation of Burley's new ink on her usual aesthetic, I was startled by its simple elegance.

"It's lovely," I said.

"Don't suppose we could work a trade?" Jerry chuckled.

"Tell us about it." Hollister grasped Burley's hand.

"There's a Buddhist saying, 'Friends are stars.' I've always thought those words got it right. Most answers are found in the stars. But there's another place I find answers. And they're sitting around this table. No matter the question, you always point me in the right direction. So you see what I did? I put the two together."

Burley pointed to the highest star on her shoulder. "This one here is Sarah Lee." She drew a fingertip down to a second star. "This one is Hayden." Up and across. "Here's Hollister." Straight across. "Milo man." Down and across. "Helen."

I laughed. "You put me at emu-level!"

Burley looked slighted. "Oh, Helen only manifests as an emu, now, Hayden. She's actually lived many fascinating lives."

"I was just joking," I said. "I'm honored, Burley. Truly I am."

"We all are," Camilo said.

"And see here?" Burley tapped the large star formed by the five smaller ones. "This one is me." She added a wink. "I'm bigger than most."

"They broke the mold," Hollister said, cracking open a beer.

We retook our seats and began filling our plates. I reached for my drink and realized something. "Hey, Burley never finished her toast. It's bad luck if you don't do the clinking glasses part." I nodded across the table at Burley. "The floor is yours, milady."

Burley raised her jug but shook her head. "No, sir. I've had my moment. We're here to celebrate your next chapter, Hayden. This one is all you. Sure as the stars will come out tomorrow, you'll know just what to say."

I raised my cider and looked around the table. Burley was right. I got this.

Awards, aka Acknowledgments

The Wise Counselor Award goes to my agent, Stephany Evans.

The I Couldn't Do This Without You in Oh So Many Ways Award goes to my partner, Brian Custer.

The Generous Support Accepted with Deep Gratitude Award is shared by Catriona McPherson, Kristopher Zgorski, Raquel V. Reyes, John Copenhaver, Greg Herren, Gigi Pandian, Ellen Byron, Nikki Knight, Kellye Garrett, Dru Ann Love, D. M. Rowell, C. J. Connor, Michael Craft, Leslie Karst, Queer Writers of Crime, Mystery Writers of America (special shout-out to Nor-Cal and SoCal chapters), and Sisters in Crime.

The Make It Real Award goes to the team at Crooked Lane Books.

The Razzle Dazzle Award is shared by Jennifer Bartlett for all things promo, photo, and design related; Stephanie Krimmel for her web-tech wizardry; and Brett Goldston for a keen, insightful eye.

Saving the most important for last . . .

The Best Reader Ever! Award goes to *you*! With countless books vying for your dollars and attention, I'm enormously honored and thankful that you chose to read this Hayden & Friends

Acknowledgments

Mystery. Representation—and relatability—matter. While not all of us will solve a murder with accidental cunning or swing from the rafters on a trapeze, we can relate to the thrill of adventure and the immeasurable joy of true friendships—both old and new. On behalf of Hayden, Hollister, Burley, Jerry, Jess, and Sarah Lee, thank you for joining this latest romp. It wouldn't be the same (or possible!) without you.